CHANEL CLEETON

FRENCH KISSED

CANARY STREET PRESS

**CANARY
STREET
PRESS™**

Recycling programs
for this product may
not exist in your area.

ISBN-13: 978-1-335-14728-8

French Kissed

First published in 2024. This edition published in 2024.

For questions and comments about the quality of this book, please contact us
at CustomerService@Harlequin.com.

TM is a trademark of Harlequin Enterprises ULC.

Canary Street Press
22 Adelaide St. West, 41st Floor
Toronto, Ontario M5H 4E3, Canada
CanaryStPress.com

Printed in U.S.A.

FRENCH KISSED

1

Fleur

I'd never spent much time thinking about men's backs. Clothes, watches, cars? Sure. Backs? Not so much. But then again, to be fair, no one's back looked like his.

I shifted in my seat, hoping the movement would keep me awake. Bad enough it was 9 a.m. but it was also my Project Finance class, which was a giant pain. So really, my back-ogling kept me alert. At least that was what I told myself as he stretched again, and I felt things. Lots of things.

Max Tucker sat in front of me, wearing a light gray T-shirt that vaguely translated to, *I don't care what I look like.* Your clothes could say things like that when your body screamed warrior sex god. Not that I was listening or anything.

He moved forward an inch, and I sucked in a deep breath, watching, fascinated by the muscles rippling under the soft fabric.

Compared to the rest of the guys here at the International School in London, there was something about him…something that didn't fit here.

It wasn't just that he was American or that he didn't have

money, although that was a big part of it. We went to a school where labels, wealth and appearances mattered, but more than anything, what counted most was swagger. You had to walk around like you owned the place, and at a school filled with the sons and daughters of world leaders and moguls, that was no easy feat. But even without the swagger, you noticed Max. He might have been more peasant than king, but his body was all god.

He was tall. The kind of tall that made me feel small, which at five-eleven was a challenge. His shoulders were so broad, he nearly blocked out the class. Reason number one why I sat behind him. If they couldn't see you, they couldn't call on you. And fuck if I knew *anything* about project finance. I was here because it was required for my fashion marketing major, and even though it was only the first week of classes, I was already over it.

The other reason, the one that had me squirming in my seat as I drank in Max's body, was that I *liked* looking at him. He was beautiful in a rugged way that really shouldn't have been beautiful at all. Costa had been elegance and sophistication, with eyes that hinted at wicked pleasures and dark sex.

Max didn't look like that at all. He was too open, his eyes too expressive, his face too easy to read. He didn't look like he had secrets, like he'd ever had secrets. He looked solid. And while I'd once thought solid was the most boring thing in the world, it now taunted me, sitting inches away. It said, *Taste, touch, see.* It wanted me to reach out and curl my fingers around his gray T-shirt, slip my hand under the fabric and stroke the golden skin and hard abs his shirt hinted at.

Merde.

It hit me again, like a punch to the head. I wanted—no, after over a year of celibacy, *needed* was a better word—to get laid.

I knew I was hard up when I was lusting after someone like Max. Someone I hated. Someone who hated me.

Max

Fleur Marceaux's eyes bored into me like two lasers shooting at my back. Half the time I expected that when I turned around, I'd find a dagger there. The other half I thought of long, straight, light brown hair and deep brown eyes, ballerina-like legs, tanned skin and more attitude than one man could ever handle…or want.

I wasn't sure if it was a French thing or a Fleur thing, but either way, she took high-maintenance to new levels.

I turned in my seat slightly, just able to make out the curve of her jaw and her soft pink lips. Because I was weak, I allowed my gaze to dip down to take in the rest of perfection.

Even at a school like the International School, where most of the student body bathed themselves in designer labels and over-the-top outfits, Fleur took the cake.

I'd been around her enough last year when she'd dated my best friend, George—before she put his heart in a blender and hit "Liquefy"—to know that the only way to manage Fleur was to not let her mind-fuck you into submission. She always had the upper hand, so I made a point of taking it from her—because I liked it, and even more, because I liked the way it teased out a little line between her brows. The girl who glided through life looked annoyed now, and as much as I shouldn't have cared, her reaction did things to me. So I looked. A lot.

She was wearing a dress today. I had no idea what the color was—something between red and orange that clung to every inch of her body. The neckline dipped low framing mouthwatering cleavage. She wasn't curvy, and her breasts were smaller than average, her ass the same, but when her hips moved as she strutted down the halls, I'd always found myself unable to tear my gaze away.

I'd hated her for three years; been in lust with her since the first day I bumped into her in the hall freshman year. Total mind-fuck.

She glared back at me, her lips slanting into a hard line, and I met her gaze with a smug satisfaction I didn't completely feel. I never felt *satisfied* around Fleur—just needy, and edgy and wanting more. It made the game of chicken we constantly played with each other that much more difficult to win. Impossible, really.

I turned in my seat, adjusting my jeans, struggling to concentrate on the professor at the front of the room and not the girl behind me.

It was my senior year of college, just weeks before I started the long process of going through rounds of interviews for my dream job. Some companies began hiring in the fall of your senior year. I'd been waiting for this moment forever, and now it was here, and it was terrifying.

I heard my father's voice in my head:

What do you need with that fancy education? You think you're too good for home now? You just wait. You'll come home and end up working with your brothers at the bar.

I tried to block it out. Block out the doubt and the fear that he was right, that I couldn't do this. I was applying to some of the best investment banks in London, one of the most competitive cities in the world. My academic record had to be perfect.

"Eighty percent of your grade in this class will be a team project you'll work on for the entire semester," our professor announced from the front of the room. "The project will involve you financing a business venture. I'll give you the parameters, and you'll have to work within those guidelines to create a successful business. You'll be graded on a variety of factors, including how well you work together, the overall quality of your project, a written paper and a presentation before the International Business faculty at the end of the semester. You can see how the individual components will be weighed on page four of the syllabus."

I thumbed through the pages, unable to ignore the feeling that Fleur was watching me again. Didn't she care about her grades at all? Rumor had it that her father was filthy rich, but what the hell was she going to do after graduation? Live off Daddy? Did she even care about her education, or was college just a series of parties for her?

The International School was a good school, but it also attracted a certain type of student. Some like me were on scholarship and had taken out student loans. Taking your education seriously had an entirely different meaning when you knew you'd be spending the next ten years of your life paying it back. If I got lucky, got the kind of job I'd been working for all along, I could turn ten years into two.

"Part of being successful is meeting the challenges thrown your way," the professor continued. "You may not always like your coworkers, and there's no 'fair' in business. You may be paired with a weaker group, and you can only work harder to overcome your shortfalls. So in the spirit of creating an authentic business environment, you won't be allowed to choose your partners as was done in previous years."

Groans erupted throughout the classroom. I understood his point, but the odds of me getting a good partner were just drastically reduced. Maybe a quarter of the class took their major seriously and cared about learning. The rest of the class was like Fleur; their degrees were pieces of paper to hang on walls at family companies where they had secure positions waiting for them after graduation, and an impressive title like "vice president" they would add after their name before they turned twenty-five.

I had over one hundred thousand dollars in student loans, and the offer that I could sleep on the saggy couch in my parents' living room for a couple weeks after graduation—if I paid rent.

"If you're sitting in an odd-numbered row, turn behind you. Congratulations, you've just met your new business partner."

Wait, what?

I counted the rows, dread filling me when I came to mine. *Fuck.*

There was a moment when I thought about saying something to the professor, a stupid wistful moment that vanished as soon as it came. I turned slowly, as if my body could prolong the inevitable. But it couldn't, and it didn't, and the next thing I knew, I was face-to-face with my nemesis-slash-crush.

Fleur's lips curved, and her eyes filled with a knowing glint as if she recognized my discomfort and loved it. Her voice came next, that hint of a French accent some masochistic part of me gravitated toward like a sailor caught by a siren's song.

"Hi, partner."

Fleur

We faced off at a little French café around the corner from school. Professor Schrader had released us early so we could go over the project with our partners. Normally, I would've been thrilled—thirty minutes less of class was always a win—but at the same time it meant thirty minutes of my life spent with Max.

He scowled at me across the table, and I got a little preview of what the next three months would hold. Fabulous.

I plastered on a saccharine smile completely at odds with my tone. "Are you always like this, or is it just me?"

Max jerked his head up from the notebook he'd been scribbling in—he had freakishly small handwriting—and stared at me blankly as if he'd almost forgotten I was there.

My eyes narrowed. "Believe me, I'm no happier about us working together than you are."

Okay, that was an outrageous lie. My GPA hovered dangerously around a 2.0, and I needed to pass this class to graduate. Max was allegedly a genius. I had the better end of the deal here. Unfortunately, he was just *so* Max.

I leaned in closer, trying to sneak a peek at the notebook in front of him. "What are you doing?"

He looked back down at the page, his face hidden, his voice barely over a mumble. "Coming up with a plan for the project."

"Aren't we supposed to talk about it?" I asked, torn between annoyed and hurt that he didn't even ask what I wanted. He probably figured I wasn't smart enough to contribute. "Shouldn't we come up with a project together?"

No way was I going to end up with something boring. If I was going to have to stare at numbers all day, then at least give me something pretty to look at—besides Max. A fashion label, something I could handle.

"Hello?" I waved my hand in his face and was met with silence. He wasn't particularly talkative on an average day, but this was ridiculous.

Max let out a little huff of air as he leaned back in his chair, his palms behind his head. I was treated to the view of big, tanned biceps, and long, corded arms. His shirt rose with the motion, displaying an inch of his abs before it snapped back into place as he slouched forward in his seat.

"Fine. What kind of project do you want to choose?" He stared at me expectantly as I struggled to transition from that hint of ab to finance. "Well?" There was a challenge in his voice we both knew I couldn't rise to, and a gleam in his eyes that said what I already knew. He'd written me off as an airhead a long time ago.

This was what I hated most about Max. He always made me feel like I was an idiot. To be fair, compared to him, I probably was. I didn't like school, found most of it to be a giant waste of time. And I didn't love my major. The fashion part was great, but the rest of it? Business was my father's thing, not mine.

It would have been easy to blame the language barrier— English, after all, was my second language—but it wasn't that. Boarding school in Switzerland had been in English and French, and my grades had still been dismal. I'd spent more time hooking up with Costa than studying.

And now, at twenty-two, with less than a year between me and graduation, I regretted it. Regretted all the times I'd blown off studying to go clubbing; all the time I'd wasted on things that didn't really matter, and on the one person who didn't.

I didn't like the way people like Max looked down on me, but it was all so far beyond me. It felt like I was constantly playing catch-up, starting a story in the middle when everyone else had begun at the beginning. I got Cs and Ds occasionally and skipped class when I could get away with it, because sitting in classrooms listening to subjects everyone else so easily understood was sheer torture.

I had no clue what I wanted to do with my life. No clue who I was supposed to be.

It hadn't really bothered me until now.

I blamed Samir. Half-French, half-Lebanese, he was my best friend, and thanks to our French mothers who were sisters, my cousin. But most of all, he was my partner in crime. When I'd been slinging back Cristal at clubs, he'd been right there next to me. It was what everyone around us did. It was normal. And there was safety in numbers; it was how you knew you were doing what you were supposed to, that your life was going according to plan. Eventually, we had to grow up, but I'd always thought I'd have more time. But then Samir had graduated and enrolled to get his master's, and he'd given everything up for his girlfriend, my other best friend, Maggie.

He was more serious, more driven, just *more*. So was Maggie. They were talking about getting a flat together next semester and making all these plans, and I was happy for them, really I was. I just wasn't sure where that left me.

I didn't have a future to get excited about. Didn't have someone to make plans with. I had a past I wished I could forget and a blackmailer obsessed with making me remember.

2

Max

I took my frustration out at the gym, hitting the weight machines until my muscles were screaming. It didn't help.

Today's meeting with Fleur had been a disaster. We'd spent thirty minutes alternating between arguing and ignoring each other. I'd kept my head buried in my notebook while she froze me out. At this rate it was going to take us three years to do the project, and I'd be paying off my student loans working at my father's run-down bar.

I had to get it together. I had seventy thousand reasons I needed to play nice with Fleur…somehow.

I keyed in the code to our room, greeted by the sight of my roommate George playing Xbox.

He was one of the few British students at the International School, and I always wondered if that sense of being different was what had made us such fast friends. He wasn't a scholarship kid like me. In a country where university education was a hell of a lot cheaper than it was in the United States, it was a little unusual that he attended an international university and paid the school's high tuition fees. But his dad was on the board of trustees so I figured that played a role.

Despite his family's money, George didn't have the same easy confidence and attitude that flowed here. He was a little nerdy like me, more comfortable staying in on weekends and playing video games than dropping thousands of pounds at a nightclub.

For a school that boasted one of the most culturally diverse student bodies you could imagine, it was ironic how many common threads you found. And money was the ultimate unifying factor.

"How was class?" he asked, not taking his gaze off the game.

I dropped into the seat next to him, grabbing the spare controller while he finished up his space exploration mission and switched over to multiplayer.

"Horrible."

"Project Finance, right? I thought you were excited for that one."

"Yeah, I was. He assigned us partners for our group project."

I took the remainder of my pent-up frustration out on the tiny avatar on screen.

"By the way you just killed that robot on our team, I'm assuming you aren't pleased with your assignment?" George asked, his tone dry.

I hesitated for a beat. We'd never had a big discussion about his breakup with Fleur. I knew he'd been really into her—although in all fairness, what guy wasn't?—and she'd broken things off after five months of dating. It had been almost six months since they'd broken up, but what if I was poking at something by mentioning her name?

"Who is it?" he asked.

I sighed. The school was too small for him to not find out anyway. "Fleur."

I expected tense silence and got laughter instead.

"You and Fleur are going to work together?"

I ran a hand through my hair. "Apparently."

George snorted. "Dude, she's going to eat you alive. She hates you."

I grimaced. "Yeah, I figured that out."

"No, I don't think you get it. I mean, she *really* hates you."

I glared at him. "Got it, thanks." Fleur could be difficult most days, but she did seem to have a special crevice of loathing in her heart with my name on it. "I don't get why," I complained.

George gaped at me, setting his controller down for a minute. "Seriously? You don't remember?"

I was fairly certain I remembered every single one of my interactions with Fleur in vivid detail, and still, nothing came to mind.

"No, I don't." I gestured for him to keep playing, needing the distraction.

"How do you know why she hates me?"

"She told me when we were dating. I asked her why she had such a problem with you. I don't think it's a big secret or anything; she was up-front about it. You haven't ever asked her?"

Impatience filled me, and for the millionth time, I tried to pretend I didn't care that she looked at me like I was something stuck to the bottom of her shoe. "Yes, because we spend so much time talking about our feelings."

I watched in annoyance as my avatar got taken out. Not my day.

"You walked into that one," George commented.

I grunted in response, waiting to respawn.

Finally, he put me out of my misery. "She's pissed about the nickname."

"What nickname?" I asked.

"You seriously don't remember?"

"I seriously have no clue what you're talking about."

"She's angry because you gave her the Ice Queen nickname. Hates-you-with-the-fire-of-a-thousand-suns angry."

He had to be joking. "Everyone calls her the Ice Queen."

"According to her, everyone started calling her that after you did."

I struggled to remember, tried to think of anyone who would have heard me use it. I was pretty much at the bottom rung of the International School social world, a complete and total non-entity. I'd never considered that anyone knew, or cared, what I thought. Least of all someone in Fleur's circle.

Fuck.

"Who the hell does she think I shared it with? I can count the number of friends I have at this school on one hand, and you're among them. Did you spread the nickname?"

"Like I had a death wish."

"Besides, what was that, freshman year?" It had to have been. I'd spent sophomore year doing a study abroad in China, and Fleur already hated me last year when she started dating George. This was unreal. Only at a school as small and cliquey as the International School would something like that stick. I'd say it was high school all over again, but my high school hadn't been this bad.

"Who carries a grudge like that for three years? And over a nickname? Besides, why the hell does she care what I think anyway?"

George shrugged. "Beats me. We didn't exactly have an in-depth conversation on the topic. I asked her, and she told me and that was pretty much it. But if you're going to have to work with her, you're probably going to want to apologize or something. I don't know. She's big on grand gestures. Maybe lie down in traffic for her," he joked.

I winced. This was going nowhere good. Knowing Fleur, she'd probably let me get run over a few times.

Fleur

My next meeting with Max didn't go much better.

"You're late," he grunted, not bothering to look up from his desk in the library.

Rude.

I'd meant to be on time, I really had. But then I'd taken a nap after class and had forgotten to set an alarm. I didn't wear a watch—it took up unnecessary accessory space—but at most, I was a few minutes late.

I sank down into the seat across from Max, waiting for him to look up and acknowledge me. If we couldn't get through a thirty-minute meeting without biting each other's head off, then I wasn't sure how we were supposed to do this for a full semester.

I struggled with my temper, trying not to let him get under my skin. I wasn't sure what I was more annoyed about: him snapping at me or him ignoring me.

Okay, that was a lie. This was our typical banter; we ruffled each other's feathers. Last year we'd fought constantly while I'd been dating George, and it had become our natural rhythm. Max ignoring me wasn't even kind of okay.

"What do you want to do today?" I asked, determined to overcome his mood and get him to notice me. I leaned in closer, inches between us, my voice friendly, bordering on flirty. "Should we divide up duties or something?"

I may have also flipped my hair. Whatever.

His head jerked up and caught me midflip, and I was pinned by the weight of his gaze as I realized I'd outplayed my hand. Flirting was my go-to. I could turn it on and off with ease, and I'd learned early on that a smile and a hair flip could go a long way. It worked when I needed an extension on my paper, when

I wanted a guy to notice me, when I didn't want to wait in a queue at a club. It always worked.

Not with Max.

Apparently, he was impervious to both, and even worse, he looked at me like he'd figured out the giant secret I'd always known: I was definitely more trouble than I was worth. On one hand, his assessment elevated him in my estimation. It was hard to respect guys who fell for it all. I wanted to scream, *It's a freaking push-up bra, bronzer and lash-enhancing mascara! Control yourself!* On the other hand, I had limited tools in my arsenal, and he'd just rebuffed my best one.

This wasn't how it was supposed to go down.

Max's eyes narrowed, and then he shook his head, his lips tightening in a harsh line that should have made him ugly, but only made me want to put my mouth on his and tease the line away.

The look he gave me was nothing short of icy. "You're thirty minutes late."

Inwardly, I winced. Apparently, I'd napped longer than I'd thought.

"Maybe you don't take this seriously, but I do," he continued. "So no, I don't want to divide up duties. Not when you're clearly blowing this off. I'm going to go to Schrader if you don't pull your weight. Coasting on your looks while I do the work isn't going to happen."

My cheeks reddened as his words hit their mark. He'd just cut through layers of pretense to get to the heart of everything. I'd been judged and found wanting, and *that* made me angry. He was right, and somehow, that only made things worse.

I glared at him, not sure if I was angrier with him for calling me out or myself for how small he made me feel.

"Fuck you."

He rolled his eyes, clearly bored. "Do you have anything cleverer to throw at me?"

No, that was the problem. I really didn't. Pretty, yes. Clever, no.

In my mind I hurled insults at him in French and English. Outwardly, I struggled to keep my temper in check. I think he liked getting a rise out of me, liked seeing that I had a reaction to him poking me. Maybe I wasn't a genius like he was, but if I had anything, I had my pride, and I clung to it now like a life raft.

The old me would have given in to the explosion. Not anymore. I was trying to be someone else...someone better.

I took a deep breath instead, then pasted a fake smile on my face. "So sorry I was late."

My tone made it clear I didn't mean a word, but at least I'd beaten down the pain and awkward temper swirling inside me.

Max scowled, and a glimmer of satisfaction flitted through me. It was totally childish, but he brought out the absolute worst in me, and it was impossible to resist the urge to mess with him. At least now I felt in control. Somewhat.

"What's on the agenda, fearless leader?" I asked.

Annoyance flooded his voice. "How old are you? Five?"

"We can't all be as serious as you are, *Max*." I barely resisted the urge to reach out and rumple his hair. Maybe flirting wasn't working, but teasing seemed to be getting under his skin.

He closed his eyes for a moment, as if uttering a quick prayer. When he opened them again, his gaze pinned me.

"Can you please just cooperate for the next thirty minutes? I can't afford to fail this class, and believe me, I get how much you don't like working together. I feel the same way. But we don't have a choice, so I need this to go quickly and painlessly. Can you do that?"

I bristled at the bossiness in his tone, but I couldn't ignore his point. I doubted this grade was as important to him as it was to me. I wouldn't graduate if I failed this class. And if we couldn't work together, or if Max told Professor Schrader I wasn't doing my part, I didn't doubt that I would fail. I told myself this wasn't surrender, only a stalemate. One I desperately needed.

I nodded. "Fine. Thirty-minute break on hating each other."

His eyes closed again. "Thank you."

Max

We worked in silence, dividing up the packet Professor Schrader had given us, taking notes we could compare later.

Luckily, I'd gotten most of my work done before she arrived, because once she did, I alternated between wanting to kiss her and strangle her.

That this somehow turned me on was seriously fucked up, and beyond distracting. *Everything* about Fleur was distracting.

She couldn't sit still while she worked. Her pen was constantly in motion—between her lips, twirling around her fingers. She must have crossed and recrossed her legs ten times in thirty minutes. And the hair flipping was killing me. Every single time she did it, I wondered if her hair was as silky soft as it looked, and then the scent of her shampoo would hit me, and I'd think about fisting my hands in her hair, pulling her toward me...

"Max!"

My head jerked up, and then I was staring into Fleur's big brown eyes.

"What?"

She shot me a strange look. "I wanted to know when you wanted to meet up again."

It took me a few seconds to answer her. "Well, he wants to see a proposal soon, so maybe in a couple of days."

Fleur nodded, her expression intent, and I wondered if she

really was going to start taking this seriously. I'd been surprised when she'd started working and the fight in her disappeared. Even more surprised when she'd offered to read a large section of the packet.

"I can email you my notes," she offered, a hesitant expression on her face. "They're probably not great, but I tried to get what I thought were the important points on the assignment."

I studied her for a moment, unable to resist the temptation to look my fill while she sat in front of me. It seemed like all my interactions with her had been furtive glances and stolen moments. Maybe that was why I was greedy now. I didn't want to look at her, and yet I couldn't look away.

"Or if you would rather not rely on my notes, I understand," Fleur added.

I focused on the words coming out of her mouth, realizing I'd never answered her. I waited for the snide remark or angry flash of brown eyes, but I was met with uncertainty instead, and a pang of guilt hit me. I only teased because that was what we did. I'd never imagined she would care, but strangely enough, it looked like she did.

"No, your notes should be fine." I hoped I was right. "Thanks for doing that."

Fleur nodded, her gaze hooded, and I wondered if I'd imagined the vulnerability I'd seen a minute ago.

She confused the hell out of me. I never knew what I'd get with her, and today was no exception. She'd started off prickly and difficult, but once she'd settled in, she'd loosened up, softened. The girl who sat in front of me now actually seemed interested in the project, and I didn't know what had precipitated the change.

I wasn't sure which one was the act, either: this girl who

looked like she cared or the girl who had stomped in here full of attitude that kept the world at bay.

They were both dangerous. And in a weird way, they both made me want more.

3

Fleur

"I'm having a crisis."

My friend Mya rolled her eyes. "Let me guess. Someone showed up wearing the same outfit."

I flipped her off. "This dress is Cavalli, and there was a wait list, so no. But nice try."

Maggie sighed from her spot at the table. "Is it effed up that I've actually missed this?"

I had, too. The three of us sat in the cafeteria for family dinner. My family had never been big on eating meals together. Hell, half the time my parents weren't even in the same country, and my mother barely liked to eat. So this was kind of a big deal for me. People came and went, but Maggie, Mya and I were the heart of family dinner. They weren't just my roommates; they were my best friends. And honestly, after everything we'd been through the past two years, more than anything, they were my family.

Mya and I had known each other for years but hadn't really become close until my sophomore year at the International

School. Mya had a rough time with her parents' divorce last year, but she seemed to be doing better now. Her father worked at the Nigerian Embassy in London, and Mya split her time between her mother's home in Lagos and her father's flat in London.

Maggie and I had been roommates my sophomore year, but we didn't become friends until Mya brought her into our social circle. At first, I hadn't been a fan of Maggie's. She'd been an outsider, and I wasn't big on letting new people in. I'd had enough people I'd cared about stab me in the back without having to voluntarily add to that list. But little by little, we'd learned to trust each other, and while the trust had been shaken a bit when I found out she'd been fooling around with Samir in secret, she was there for me when it counted, and I made a point of doing the same for her.

Right now I needed advice, and as much as I hated it, I knew it was good for me, like carrots or spinach—maybe even some tough love.

"Can we focus on me for a second?"

Maggie grinned. "Dude, don't we always?"

Mya snorted.

"What's the problem?" Maggie asked.

I looked around the cafeteria for a minute, checking to see if anyone was paying attention. Gossip spread around this place like wildfire, and I'd had enough rumors about me to last a lifetime. I'd locked everything down tight lately.

I used the voice I saved for my juiciest gossip. After all, presentation and delivery were everything.

"Schrader paired me with Max for our semester project in Project Finance."

That got their attention.

"Like George's Max?" Maggie asked.

Like George, my rebound after Costa annihilated my heart and the ex-boyfriend-whose-heart-I'd-broken's-best-friend Max.

"The one and the same."

Maggie winced. "Well, on the bright side, he's really smart. George told me Max spent his sophomore year in China studying finance. He's supposed to be a genius."

I made a face at that, remembering the rest of our first meeting in the café. "He asked me if I knew how to read."

Mya let out a shout of laughter. "Excuse me?"

"At our first meeting, he asked me if I knew how to read. And then he gave me some shit about how I needed to pull my own weight and he wasn't going to carry me through the project. That was after ignoring me for twenty-eight minutes of our thirty-minute group meeting." I was still pissed about it, and yesterday's meeting hadn't been much better. No one talked to me the way he did. Period.

"What did you say?" Maggie asked, a mix of fascination and horror covering her face.

It was kind of cute how expressive the American students were. They wore their emotions on their faces and in their eyes. Max was no exception. Whenever I caught him looking at me, I saw scorn, disapproval and disdain. I had a reason to dislike him, but what the hell was his problem?

I could chalk it up to the fact that I'd broken up with his best friend, except it had started way before that. He'd mocked me relentlessly when George and I had dated, and before that, thanks to Max, the "Ice Queen" nickname he'd given me freshman year had been impossible to shake.

I didn't normally care what people thought about me, but with Max it was different. He had a way of hitting where it hurt. His words weren't just careless barbs he threw out as a passing insult. No, he clearly saw through me, past the pretty outside to the parts inside me that I feared were ugly beyond repair. I could hate him for that alone. Everything else was just icing on the cake. So when he hit, I hit back. Harder.

Maggie spoke first, her tone cautious. "Don't you need to pass this class to graduate?"

I groaned.

Why were the things that were the best for you always a giant pain in the ass? It made it hard to want to be good.

Maggie shrugged. "Fine. If you want to be a fifth-year senior, I'll keep my mouth shut. I'm not saying I wouldn't appreciate having another friend at school next year…"

Of all of us, Maggie was the youngest, a junior this year.

"I get your point. If it were anyone else—"

"But it's not anyone else," Maggie interrupted. "It's Max. And you can't fight with him and expect to pass. I've heard about Schrader. He failed Omar in one of his classes."

"Everyone fails Omar." Samir's sidekick was in even more danger of becoming a fifth-year senior than I was.

"I'm just saying. Don't screw around in his class, Fleur. You hating Max isn't worth you not graduating." She paused. "I've talked to him about school before. He has a ton of student-loan debt, and he's trying to get a big banking job. He needs this. Make up with him. Be nice."

"I hate playing nice."

Mya grinned. "So that's why you're so horrible at it."

They pretty much had this down. Maggie worried and clucked over me like a mother hen, and Mya kicked my ass into gear when I needed it. It mostly worked. I'd known Mya the longest, back to our boarding school days in Switzerland, and she was one of the few people who got away with giving me a hard time.

"In my defense, he doesn't make any effort, either," I continued, ignoring her last statement.

Maggie made a face. "That's really mature. Take the higher road. Show him you're better than him. That's right up your alley," she teased.

"True. It is hard being this perfect," I responded, completely deadpan, trying to laugh at the irony of how far off my words really were.

You couldn't show weakness in a school like this. Especially not when you teetered precariously on a pedestal made of smoke and mirrors.

Mya rolled her eyes. "God, you're obnoxious."

I grinned, settling back into our routine. "You love it."

"Well, Max doesn't, so maybe play nice," Mya suggested with a smirk. "Or else you'll be sitting here next year eating this crap." She poked at the orange-colored glob on her plate. "And your new roommate might not be as amazing as I am," she replied, matching my tone and expression exactly. She shook her head. "You're so rubbing off on me."

"You should be so lucky."

Maggie jerked her head, interrupting our banter. "Fleur, you want to make nice with Max? Here's your chance. He's sitting at dinner by himself. Trust me. You have better odds of success if George isn't around."

I turned and spied Max sitting alone at the table, his back to us. He wore a navy blue T-shirt. His hair was damp at the ends as if he'd just taken a shower.

Do not think of water dripping down…

"Go," Maggie urged. "And when he annoys you, just think of the phrase *fifth-year senior* before responding."

The weird thing about all of this, the thing I would never admit to anyone—especially not Maggie and Mya, who would give me shit about it forever—was that Max made me…uncomfortable. I wasn't sure if it was all the hard knocks I'd had lately, but he always took me down a peg or two. And given everything else, I wasn't sure I had many pegs left before I'd fall.

I hesitated, weighing the odds of following their advice, envisioning myself sitting at this same table, another year older, while my friends were out in the world doing exciting things and having adventures. Sure, Maggie would still be here, but she was a year younger. She was supposed to be here. I was supposed to be a grown-up, and yet I felt anything but. At least Maggie had her life together. I was the hot mess.

"Fine. I'll play nice with Max."

Maggie grinned. "Good." She shooed me off. "I'll see you later."

I pushed back my chair and stood, brushing my palms against my Cavalli. I could do this. Maybe.

Max

I noticed her perfume before I saw her. It smelled of flowers, and money and seduction in a scent I'd never smelled on anyone else. Likely never would. It figured she'd have a signature perfume or something like that. And then I saw her, and like always, it took a moment to adjust to her beauty.

She was almost too beautiful. Maybe that sounded stupid, but there wasn't another way to describe it. It was like that moment when you first turned on a light, and it was so bright that it was nearly blinding—and not in a good way. Fleur wore her beauty like a weapon, slicing through mere mortals with a careless arc, leaving destruction in its wake.

She could do with some imperfections—her nose a bit bigger, her lips less full, her hair less shiny. Something, *anything*, to make her look like a real person. Anything to make wanting her ache less, to ease the thrust of it that left me completely skewered.

I would have understood my attraction to her if I'd been one of those guys who got off on being with a hot girl. I mean, sure, I could appreciate it as much as the next guy, but looks had never been my primary motivating factor. Was it nice to have something pretty to look at? Absolutely. Did that get boring after a couple minutes? Yeah, it did.

If all my past girlfriends had one common denominator, it was that they were all smart—a little nerdy, like me. I fit with the kind of girls who liked sci-fi movies and video games. Chill girls who didn't spend an hour doing their hair and makeup or own more pairs of shoes than there were days in the month. And yet, as Fleur slid into the seat across from mine, apple in hand, my pulse picked up and everything else stood at attention.

"I've come to make peace."

I blinked as the sentence rolled off her tongue and into the air surrounding us, her eyes dancing with amusement. Maybe it was the accent. It was hard to resist an accent, especially one that called to mind silk, lacy lingerie and heat.

"Peace?" It seemed like a foreign concept around Fleur.

She nodded, taking a bite out of the apple, her full, pink lips sliding across the cherry red. I stared at her mouth, mesmerized. It should be a sin to eat fruit like that.

She continued, wholly oblivious to my reaction. "Look, I need to pass this class. You need to pass this class. And we could do the whole, 'I hate you, you hate me,' thing for the rest of the year, but really, what's the point?" Her lips curved. "I think we should hate other people."

I was silent for a beat. "Are you hate breaking up with me?"

Her mouth spread into the kind of wide smile I'd seen her give her friends, but had never been lucky enough to have flashed my way. "I think I am. Look, it's not you. It's me. Hating you is nice and all, but it's just not fulfilling me the way I need it to. I need more than you're able to give me." She flashed me a playful, pitying smile, leaning closer, too close, her tone dropping as if she was sharing a secret meant only for me. "Don't take it personally. You did your best. It's not easy to keep up with me. Many men have tried."

"Maybe if we shook things up a bit?" I teased, struggling to keep a straight face. I'd never seen this side of Fleur before. Playful suited her even as it surprised me. It had always felt like she was laughing at me, never with me. Now I was on the other side of the velvet rope, and I liked it more than I should have. "Maybe if we kept the mystery alive. Things have been a little flat lately. We haven't even explored the possibilities of pranking each other. I could pour Jell-O in your shoes—"

"And I could kill you."

I laughed, unable to resist pushing her further. "But we haven't even had hate-sex yet."

God, she sparkled back at me. Her eyes lit up with a sort of wicked pleasure that told me she enjoyed screwing with me as much as I liked returning the favor.

"Do you want to have hate-sex with me?" she teased, her voice coming out with a purr that bathed me in heat. Her voice lowered in a tone that was distinctively her bedroom voice, something my body had never heard from her lips, yet recognized instantly. "Have you been dreaming about it, fantasizing about it? Do you wake up in the middle of the night wanting it?"

Desire slammed into me. Her words lingered between us, filling the air like the perfume that teased my nostrils, beckoning me closer, like the accent that wound its way through my body with promise. At some point in our exchange, we'd both started moving toward each other, until now we leaned over the table, less than a foot between us, her lips taunting me, tempting me, seducing me.

Had I dreamed of her, fantasized about her, woken up in the middle of the night hard, wanting her, even when she'd been with my best friend? *Yes.*

Other guys might have fantasized about porn stars or lingerie models. I fantasized about Fleur Marceaux.

And wasn't it my luck that in this case, reality far outstripped the fantasy.

Fleur

I shouldn't have said it. As soon as I did, I wished I could take it back, wished I could return to my table and my friends and put much needed space between Max and me.

I hadn't been thinking. I'd treated him as if he were any other guy, as if I could fling flirtations and sex at him without any intention of following through, forgetting that he was Max, that there was always an awkward tension between us that lingered like a bad smell on the Metro.

It was a joke, a stupid, flirty joke. One most guys would have met with innuendo or an invitation. But Max just looked at me like he'd been burned.

"That was a joke."

"Ha ha," he replied in a dry tone, an uncomfortable expression on his face. He looked as though he was in pain, and I wondered if I'd sunk to new lows. I was literally driving men away.

Oh, how the mighty have fallen.

I took another bite from my apple, struggling to think of some way to salvage the conversation. I blamed him for the awkwardness and myself for getting into this position in the first place. I'd never been cautious, always been the type of person to remember to put the brakes on *after* I was already going over the cliff.

"We should probably set up some time to meet," I offered, backpedaling the shit out of my Manolos. Things had ended at our last meeting, and we hadn't set an official time or decided on much of anything really. We were such an odd pairing— like plaid and polka dots—that it was hard to imagine us ever coming to an agreement. "For the project and all," I added.

He nodded, thankfully not giving me a hard time about my obvious discomfort. "Are you free tomorrow?"

"I'm done with classes at two. Want to meet after that?"

"Yeah. We can meet in the library and come up with a topic," he suggested.

"Sounds good to me."

I hovered there, not sure if I should stay or go. He was still eating, and he was by himself, but my whole purpose for coming over had been to set things up for our project and to make some semblance of peace. Mission accomplished, but I still couldn't bring myself to get up from the table. It was like when you accidentally attached yourself to something magnetic—I didn't want to be there, and yet the pull held me in place. And somewhere in all that tension was the flash of ego that said I wasn't the type to tuck my tail between my legs and run.

The corners of Max's mouth quirked up. "You can go."

Did he just dismiss me? My eyes narrowed. How did this keep happening?

"Excuse me?"

He gestured to the room at large with a wave of his big hand. "I know you're worried about your reputation. What will people think if they see you sitting here alone with me?" His voice dropped to a mock whisper. "The horror. Not a designer label in sight."

"I don't care about my reputation," I snapped, unsettled by the way he was trying to handle me, by my inability to regain my footing. My words somehow straddled the truth and the lie. I did care, but not in the way he thought.

Did I care if people thought it was weird that I was sitting at dinner alone with Max? People could deal. But the rest? The secrets my blackmailer threatened to expose? Yeah, I cared. Even when I shouldn't have.

We stared at each other for a moment, and I knew we both thought of the same thing, of the picture of my naked body that half the school had seen last year—*Did he see it?*—and the tatters of my reputation that were left behind afterward. You had to have a reputation to care about it, and I had a series of scandals, instead.

It had all started last year with an anonymous email asking for money to keep from exposing my secrets. Or if I was really being honest, maybe it started earlier with my drug overdose at the end of sophomore year. Or the boyfriend who'd cheated on me and left me for my former friend. Or even earlier when I'd lost my baby just weeks into the pregnancy freshman year.

Last year my friends had begun hearing whispers about Costa and the unnamed girl he'd allegedly gotten pregnant. No one knew it was me, but it was only a matter of time.

Then had come the naked photo plastered around the school— the one I'd let Costa take with his phone a million years ago when we were dating. I hadn't paid a dime, and yet the emails kept coming, and I couldn't help but think that none of this was about money at all.

Someone liked messing with me, and while I had no shortage of people who didn't like me, my ex-boyfriend's girlfriend dominated my short list. Costa might have left the International School in a cloud of disgrace after his parents learned he'd been screwing around, but his girlfriend Natasha—the girl he'd left me for—was still here, and she wanted to take me down.

"Maybe I care about my reputation," Max joked, pulling me out of my past and back into the present. "Can't have people thinking I sold out and became one of the cool kids."

I rolled my eyes, trying to push all the ugliness out of me so I could breathe again. "Don't get your boxers in a twist. I'll leave you to your dinner—" I peered at the magazine sitting next to his food tray "—and the fascinating read on European bond markets." I flashed him my most blinding smile, more to screw with him than anything else. *"Au revoir."*

I felt his gaze on me as I walked away, a stare that left a flash of heat in its wake. And I told myself that if I did "the walk"— the one where I lengthened my stride, hips swaying, hair flipping, the one that said, *Watch me, want me, wish you had me*—it would've been out of habit and not because of the boy whose eyes were currently glued to my ass.

4

Fleur

It took me three outfit changes before I was satisfied. An hour was spent trying out different hairstyles, perfecting my makeup, discarding clothes as if it was Fashion Week, not a study session in the library. But that was the problem. I knew how to dress for Fashion Week, for dates, for dancing on tables at nightclubs. I didn't know how to dress for this. Didn't know what to wear with Max.

If yesterday was any indication, today would be awkward. I needed the added support of a killer outfit and, at the same time, needed to look good without trying. It was a delicate balance I hoped I'd achieved.

I settled on a pair of black leggings. They hugged every inch of my lower body, making my already long legs look even longer. I threw on a low-cut white top that sort of screamed boobs and added a pair of black leather booties that laced up in a look that roughly translated to bondage on my feet. I wore my hair down, curling the ends. It was my bedhead look, and while nothing about my outfit said studying in the library, it gave me the confidence I needed to face Max. The slightly dazed expression on a pair of freshman eyes as I walked by helped.

But then I walked into the library and headed to the back, and when I saw him, the swagger in my stride disappeared like a deflating balloon.

Max sat at a small table surrounded by books. He stared at me as I approached, his lips pursed together, his eyes full of something I couldn't read but that looked nothing like lust. Where the freshman boys had looked at me like I was a piece of cake they wanted to eat, Max looked at me like I was something he didn't order and wanted to send back.

He started at my feet of all places, at my shoes, his gaze traveling up one article of clothing at a time. He didn't look hungry, didn't look interested, he just looked as if I were a puzzle he was trying to figure out, and I stood there as if presenting myself for his approval. And I wasn't. I totally wasn't. I didn't want him to like me, didn't want him to want me, certainly didn't want *him*, and yet, even as I repeated the words to myself over and over again in my head like a song on repeat, my body heard a different tune.

So while I stood there telling myself I didn't care, that it didn't matter that I'd spent an hour trying for perfect, for sexy, for irresistible, and he was looking at me like he'd already passed, my nipples were tightening, a familiar heat settling low in my stomach. The pull of arousal at the sight of him shocked my system to the core. It felt like my body had been stuck in freaking winter for years and, suddenly, spring was coming.

Max's shoulders were overwhelming today, barely constrained by a green shirt with sleeves pushed up to expose tanned forearms and a sprinkling of hair. The color only made his eyes more noticeable, and for a moment I just stared, getting a little bit lost, until something flickered in those eyes, something that pushed me out and back into my own body. I stayed there until my gaze drifted down to his hands and the pen he held. I watched, fascinated, as he threaded the pen through his fingers, playing with it idly, stroking it, until I was so mesmerized by his motions that I couldn't look away, and I was jealous of a freaking pen.

His hands were big like his body, and I wanted them on me, in me, wanted him to take me back into the library stacks and push me up against one of the shelves. Heat rose in my cheeks as I blushed for the second time in as many days. I imagined what it would feel like with his strength against me, his touch holding me in place. I wondered how he would be in bed—if he was a virgin or if he knew what he was doing. I *wondered*.

And then I realized I'd been standing there, staring at him, for at least a minute. Did he know he had this effect on me? Did he care?

Was that it? Had I become so screwed up that I now only wanted men who didn't want me back? Or was it just him?

Max

I forgot my words. All of them. Or I swallowed my tongue. Or maybe both.

I couldn't work with her. It wasn't even that I didn't like her, or that she didn't like me, or that I had a strong suspicion that she was lazy, or even that I was pretty sure she knew nothing about project finance. I literally couldn't function around her. I turned into a complete idiot in her presence, incapable of stringing together a sentence. It was embarrassing and pathetic, and I didn't know how I was supposed to concentrate or do anything but stare at her and wish I could look away.

I might not have gotten a ton of action, but I was far from a virgin, and yet, something about her made me feel like one.

We faced off for a minute, and then she slid into the seat

across from me and her knee brushed against mine. We both jumped. Pain shot through my leg as my knee hit the table.

Fuck.

"Are you okay?" she asked, that French purr sliding over me, the look of concern in her eyes a surprise.

"I'm fine."

My American accent sounded so gruff around her. There was no lilting, no easy sway to my voice. It reminded me just how different we really were, beyond even the obvious, surface differences. She was so out of my league it wasn't even funny.

I looked over at her, trying not to imagine those heels of hers teasing my leg. Those sexy straps were imprinted in my brain. If she was mine... If she was mine, I'd have her naked in nothing but those heels.

For the five months she'd dated George, I'd been plagued with guilt over the things I'd fantasized about doing with my best friend's girlfriend. I still felt a little guilty now, but more than anything, I was worried I was being an idiot. I'd seen the way she'd discarded George, and she'd liked him in the beginning, even though I'd never anticipated that pairing. It was impossible to not feel like a masochist, especially considering how much she'd already made her disdain for me clear. And then I remembered what George had said...and our "hate truce"...

"I'm sorry about the Ice Queen thing."

Like a Band-Aid, it seemed best to just rip it off.

Fleur's eyes widened, and for a moment her entire body stilled. She wasn't a calm person by nature; her body was never at rest. She gestured with her hands when she spoke, her eyelashes fluttering, her fingers toying with her hair, flipping the ends over her tanned shoulders as if she knew that the motion guaranteed all eyes would be on her.

And then her gaze narrowed, and something clenched in my gut as I wondered if she was going to flay me alive or forgive me. "Why?"

I struggled to come up with the right answer, because suddenly it mattered.

"It was a careless thing to say, and I definitely would never have said it if I'd known it would take off the way it did." I'd had the nerd thing thrown my way enough to not want to humiliate anyone else, even Fleur. "Honestly, I didn't even know I was responsible for its popularity until George told me. I'm sorry. Really sorry. If I could take it back, I would."

"Why did you say it?" Her eyes fixed on mine, emotion lingering beneath the surface. It hit me then that she *cared*, that my answer *mattered*, and while it didn't mean much, it was *something*.

And because I'd had a thing for her for forever, I suddenly wanted to give her everything, all the answers she sought, anything to make her see me. And not just as George's annoying friend or the asshole who gave her a nickname that had plagued her, but as someone who mattered, someone who mattered to her.

"Because I was an idiot." The words tumbled from my mouth, too much and not enough at the same time.

"Was?" she asked, a hint of teasing in her voice.

She *would* make me work for it. Then again, she was the kind of girl you didn't entirely mind working for.

"Was. Am. Whatever."

Her lips curved. "So that's your apology?"

Yeah, I guessed it was. Was it enough? Who knew with her. I'd liked girls for years, been friends with them, had several girlfriends, and yet, none of them were like her. She was a mystery shrouded in a puzzle, hidden in a challenge that seemed impossible to win. She was the ultimate gamble, and it was difficult to not feel like the deck was stacked against me.

"What else do you want?"

There was exasperation in my voice but also a hidden plea. I wanted to give her what she wanted, if only she would tell me what it was.

"Do you really think I'm an ice queen?"

The question caught me off guard because the take-no-prisoners Fleur I'd thought I'd figured out wouldn't have cared about my answer. For the first time I looked at her, really looked at her, and realized that she might not be the Fleur I remembered from freshman year. That maybe she'd changed, and if she had, I wanted to see if we could be more than just two people who couldn't stand each other. After all, wasn't that what the hate truce was about?

Did I think she was an ice queen?

No.

How could I think she was cold when all it took was me sitting across from her for my body to feel like it was on fire?

"I think you're a little terrifying and you know it. I think you like it. You wield your beauty like a weapon and wear your swagger like a crown that makes everyone else bow down." I paused for a beat. "But no, I don't think you're an ice queen."

Silence filled the space between us, and then she spoke.

"You think I'm beautiful?"

Trust Fleur to focus on that one.

"You know you're beautiful," I answered wryly, refusing to elaborate and feed her ego. I was as close to humiliating myself as I was willing to get. I couldn't make it too easy for her. I'd seen how George had let her walk all over him, and I didn't want to just be another guy she managed.

Her lips curved again, and this time she flashed a genuine smile. "I do," she teased. "But somehow I didn't think you'd noticed."

Didn't think I'd noticed? I'd spent most of the past year terrified that she'd see the way I looked at her and say something to George.

"I noticed."

I wasn't sure who was more surprised by my candor. Maybe it was the fact that we were in the library, my home turf and a place out of her comfort zone, but I felt more confident, slightly less awkward. And Fleur looked at me differently. And suddenly the hope I'd had freshman year, the first time I'd seen her, came rushing back to me.

The hope that she'd see me, smile at me. The hope that I had a chance.

I waited for the joke or the cutting remark, waited for her to dismiss me the way I'd watched her dismiss others. But she didn't. Instead, she nodded, like I'd told her something particularly important that she'd file for future use. I waited to see if she would say anything, to see where this was going, but it didn't go anywhere. We sat in silence for a minute, and then she gestured toward the paper in front of us.

"So, project finance."

Right. It was the topic we should discuss, and the one I was least interested in.

"I had some ideas for the project. Maybe a tech company," I suggested. "We could finance an app."

Fleur made a face. "No."

"It's easy," I argued.

"And boring."

"Then what kind of project do you want to do?"

She looked unsure of herself again, much like she had during our first library study session, and it was so unexpected, so human, it made me want to listen, whereas before I might have made a dig.

"I was thinking we could do a fashion app."

I struggled to keep from groaning. I should have known getting her to agree to something wouldn't be easy.

She held up a hand, and like magic, my protest died in my throat.

"Just hear me out. It's a billion-dollar industry. There's a huge market for it, and with your business skills and my fashion sense, we could come up with something fun *and* profitable. And it wouldn't make me die of boredom."

She flashed me another blinding smile that I was pretty sure was intended to make sure she got her way. She was way too good at it. But of course, she knew that and likely had known it her entire life.

I grinned, unable to resist Fleur trying to charm me. "How would this fashion app work?"

"Well…"

For the next hour I somehow managed to focus on the project. It was hard, especially with the way her teeth would sink into her lower lip when she was pensive and how, when she leaned forward, I was treated to the slightest hint of her lacy bra. But somehow my willpower lasted long enough to hold a conversation with her without getting distracted by sex—too much.

And by the end of it, we'd come up with an idea that wasn't half-bad. Fleur had some interesting ideas about using designers as sponsors to help raise revenue. A fashion app wasn't something I would have ever considered doing on my own, but it was unique and a chance for both of us to play up our strengths.

"When should we meet next?" Fleur asked, gathering up her books.

"In a couple weeks?" The first piece of the project was due in mid-October.

She nodded. "Sounds good to me."

Finally, I couldn't take it anymore, and curiosity got the best of me. "Are you going out later?"

"No. Why?"

"Your outfit."

She almost looked embarrassed...and then she looked intrigued.

"You think I look like I should be going out?"

Sort of. I mean, what did I know about fashion? Every time George had dragged me to one of Fleur's parties last year I'd stuck out like a sore thumb. I'd learned the hard way that sneakers should not be worn to London nightclubs and that my wardrobe was seriously lacking.

"Yeah, I guess. You look nice," I mumbled, wondering if I sounded as dumb as I felt.

Fleur smiled, flashing me a cat-that-ate-the-canary expression.

"Nice, huh?" she teased. "Care to elaborate?"

I groaned. I should have known better. "I'm not doing this." I grabbed my books and stood up. "You don't need me inflating your ego."

Her smile deepened as her eyes danced, and my heart lurched. "Maybe I like it."

I froze as if her words were a hand that had reached out and held me in place.

What the fuck?

We'd never done this before. Yesterday she'd been flirty in the cafeteria but I'd sort of figured that was an accidental thing. Like she'd just been her natural self and I'd accidentally gotten caught in the crossfire. But now that this had happened twice?

Part of me wanted to stay and talk with her, wanted to flirt with her. But another part of me, the sensible part, told me to get out now while I had a chance.

Better to walk away first than be left behind.

But she didn't just let me walk away. That wasn't her style. So as I tried to put some distance between us, tried to convince myself that the flirtatiousness I'd heard in her words had been in my imagination, she called me back.

"I'm not going out later." There was a pause that had me stopping in my tracks, and an invitation in her voice that had me falling. "I dressed this way for studying."

And even though she didn't say it out loud, the words lingered between us anyway—the possibility of them, at least.

I dressed this way for you.

5

Fleur

It came an hour before I was supposed to go out on Friday night.
One line that both infuriated me, and made me want to
throw up:

Did you really think you could stay on top forever? Can't wait
to watch your fall...

I hated the chill that spread down my limbs, loathed the
dread I had to push out. A torrent of blistering French escaped.

I'd had the emails traced last year, only to discover they each
came from a different internet café in London, the kind of place
that catered to travelers and ensured anonymity. Nothing about
the information had really been news to me. I knew this was
coming from the International School, albeit indirectly.

They weren't blatant threats, so I doubted the London po-
lice would care. They had their hands full with much bigger
problems than someone with a grudge. I'd played around with
the idea of telling the school, but so far there was no actual evi-

dence that this was coming from a student. I knew, but I didn't
have proof. And the more attention I gave my blackmailer, the
more I let the bastard destroy my life.

Whoever was behind this liked the uncertainty of it. It was
unpredictable, designed to keep me on my toes. Sometimes I'd
go weeks without an email. I fought the feeling of constant para-
noia with everything I had. And the emails demanding money
had changed into messages like this one when I hadn't paid.

I saved the email to the folder I'd created to keep a record of all
the correspondence I'd received in case I needed it in the future.
I shut my laptop and went back to doing my hair and makeup.

I wasn't going to give them the satisfaction of seeing me fall.

"You're not having fun."

I turned to face my cousin Samir, ready to raise my voice
to be heard over the beat of the music. I switched from French
to English out of habit, even though the rest of the group was
several feet away.

"I am."

He pointed to where Maggie and Mya danced on one of the
raised platforms in the center of the nightclub. "Since when do
you pass up an opportunity to dance?"

I shrugged. "It's been a weird week. I have some stuff on my
mind. I'm stressed about graduation."

And someone who wants to take me down.

Samir drank from his whiskey and Coke. "It's only the first
week back. How are you already worried about May?"

"I'm worried I won't graduate if I don't get my GPA up," I
admitted.

I shouldn't have agreed to go out in the first place, should
have spent the night catching up on reading. There was so

much of it I wasn't exactly sure where to start. I'd spent years blowing off assignments, so the workload was kind of a shock.

"Do you need help in some of your classes?" he asked, concern in his voice.

I laughed, taking a sip of champagne. This was the embarrassing part. "Try all of them."

We might have both been partiers, but Samir at least managed to get good grades.

"I'm fine. Really. You don't need to worry about me or fix me."

"I'm not trying to fix you, but I am worried." He was quiet, his gaze flickering to the dance floor before returning to me. "You don't seem like yourself. I can tell you have a lot on your mind, and I want you to know that you can talk to me." Another beat passed. "Maggie's worried about you, too."

Maggie and Mya were the only friends I'd told about the blackmail emails, about the baby I'd lost, about all of it. Samir knew what had happened with the photo last year, and of course, my overdose, but that was it. I didn't know what it was, but for some reason it was both easier and harder to tell him things. Maybe because we'd known each other for so long, or because we were family, or maybe I didn't want to worry him when he had enough worries of his own to deal with. Whatever it was, I didn't feel like I could tell him everything, and more than anything, I hoped Maggie would keep my secrets.

"I'm fine." I fixed a smile on my face, trying to look like I wanted to be here, as if my mind wasn't racing and I wasn't completely and utterly lost in this mess that had become my life. I'd thought the alcohol, the music and the bodies would be enough to distract me. Apparently, I'd been wrong.

It had become a tradition—going out clubbing to celebrate the start of school. We came back to Babel because it was the place where we always celebrated our milestones. It was Samir's favorite club in London, probably because it was where he'd first kissed Maggie. My player cousin had turned into someone sentimental and surprisingly sweet. Even though he'd been with Maggie for a while now, it was still an adjustment—a happy adjustment—after a lifetime of knowing the other Samir.

"I thought you were supposed to be taking a break from all this clubbing stuff," I commented. "Turning over a new leaf and all that."

Samir's family had expected him to marry the daughter of a family friend and one of his father's political allies in Lebanon when he'd graduated last year. Instead, he'd broken things off with her for Maggie and, ultimately, had chosen to walk away from his expected role in his father's political campaign in favor of a graduate degree in Middle Eastern politics.

He flashed me a grin that still had enough of his bad-boy charm to make me shake my head. Thank God Maggie could handle him; I wasn't sure who else could. He was a handful, and I meant that in the best possible way. After all, we were pretty much cut from the same cloth.

"Come on, I fell in love. I didn't change my personality. I can still enjoy a night out." His tone softened, and his eyes lit up the way they always did when he talked about her. "And it's Maggie's junior year. I don't want her to miss out on having a traditional university experience just because she's dating someone older."

"I don't think Maggie cares." She wasn't exactly what I would call a party girl.

He shrugged. "Still, I want to make her happy. Give her as much as I can. These nights aren't as frequent now that there's less money, but I can at least make special occasions happen."

I felt so many emotions at once. A burst of pride and love. Samir wasn't just family. He had been my best friend since we were kids, and I loved getting to see this side of him—especially since Maggie and I were so close. And yet, at the same time, his words were a knife twisting in my heart that I hated myself for feeling.

What would it be like to have someone love me like that? What would it be like to have a guy give me romance?

I'd thought I'd had that with Costa. Thought that all the drama and passion, make-ups and breakups meant we loved each other. I'd thought that the intensity counted for something, but in the end, it hadn't meant a thing.

"You guys are disgustingly cute," I teased, my smile lessening the sting in my words.

He shrugged, his expression sobering into an emotion most girls would give their right arm to have directed at them. "I love her. And I wouldn't go back to the way things were before her for anything."

"I know. And it's great. But I'm going to leave if you keep talking like that," I warned with a grin.

He laughed. "Please. Just wait until you find the right guy. You'll be watching romantic movies and calling him *sweetie* and *honey*."

I flipped him off. "I would die."

And still…

I wanted a guy to look at me the way Samir looked at Maggie. I wanted a guy to care enough about me to try, and buying something expensive because he *could* didn't count. I wanted to matter to someone who loved me enough to give me more.

"We're going to find you a guy," Samir vowed, his jaw set in determination.

"Who, Omar?" I scoffed as my gaze trailed over to where Samir's sidekick sat charming a group of girls. And I used the word *charm* loosely. Throwing money at them was probably far more appropriate. What Omar lacked in personality he made up for with the size of his bank account. "No offense, but every guy you know is kind of an asshole."

"True," Samir conceded. "Maybe just a one-night stand, then," he teased.

I rolled my eyes, not bothering to respond. Since the miscarriage, I'd only had sex a few times, all of them with Costa. All of them while he had a girlfriend, Natasha, the girl he'd cheated on me with and left me for. The girl he'd sworn to me repeatedly that he was going to leave to come back to me. It hadn't been a great experience, although to be fair, maybe that had been the universe paying me back for hooking up with a guy with a girlfriend, even if she had taken him from me first.

I'd thought that he, more than anyone, would have understood how hard it had been for me to have sex with him after the baby we'd lost, but he hadn't. And I hadn't been able to deal. The sex had been awkward as hell, and each time left me feeling sad and orgasmless. I couldn't wrap my head around having sex with someone. Not after losing something I'd loved so much, gone in a pool of blood in the middle of the night.

I was such a mess.

"What about that guy?" Samir asked, pointing to a suit-clad Brit standing against the wall, staring at me like he was interested. I flashed the guy a smile out of reflex, with no real heat or interest behind it. I needed someone who challenged me, someone who made me feel. Now that I'd seen what it looked like up close with Maggie and Samir, I wanted more.

It was the ultimate irony that Max's face pushed its way into my mind.

"Not my type," I answered, turning away from the Brit.

"You're too picky."

My eyebrow rose. "Really? I seem to remember you having impossible standards."

He groaned. "I was an ass then."

"Maybe I'm an ass now."

And if that means I'm selective about who I have sex with, I'm to-
tally fine with it.

"I don't want you to mope after Costa for the next five years of
your life," Samir said, his tone sobering. "He's not worth it. He
never was. You just never wanted to see it. You're worth more."

"You think I'm moping after Costa?"

"Isn't that what you were doing last year?" The unspoken,
after your overdose, lingered between us. "You barely dated, and
when you did it was that guy George, and we both know that
was never going to happen. Were you ever even into him?"

"I wanted to be," I answered honestly.

Samir made a small sound of disgust. "You shouldn't have to
convince yourself to like someone. It either happens or it doesn't."

That was the problem. I'd lost the ability to feel the moment
I'd lost my baby and my world had been torn away from me.
The problem with feeling was that it was all or nothing—and
all meant too much. It meant giving something or someone the
power to leave you in shreds, and it wasn't something that was
easy to walk away from.

I'd learned that lesson all too well.

"It's easy to give advice when you're in the perfect relationship with the girl you love and have this big future ahead of
you."

Samir winced. "I'm not trying to lecture you."

The ridiculousness of those words leaving Samir Khouri's
lips was enough to give me momentary pause and put things in
perspective a bit. A couple years ago he would have been right
by my side.

Time to grow up.

"Well, you kind of are. You all are. Do you think I don't know
I'm the group fuckup?" I tried to keep my voice even, tried to
not let my temper shine through, but of course, I failed miser-
ably. "You have Maggie and she has you, and Michael sort of

does his own thing, and it always works out for him. And Mya doesn't let much get to her. Don't you think I want things to be easy? Don't you think I want to be happy?"

My voice rose with each word. It was every thought that had been plaguing me for months and I'd been too afraid to say. And really, Samir didn't deserve to deal with all my bullshit, but I'd always sucked at impulse control. Hence the overdose, and the partying, and the bad sex…

"I'm sorry. I'm tired, and cranky, and stressed and I shouldn't take it out on you."

He shook his head. "After everything you've done for me, flying to Saint-Tropez to drag me back and convincing me I was screwing up my life by letting Maggie walk away? After you encouraged Maggie to give us a shot? I'm pretty sure I owe you everything."

I leaned forward to give him an air-kiss, struggling to get my feelings under control. I was numb; I had been for a while, but below the layers of ice, emotions swirled inside me, threatening to burst to the surface. I was terrified of what would happen when they finally did.

"Well, I do have a personal shopper at Gucci, and she can help you out should you feel inclined," I joked, knowing Samir didn't buy it for a second. I pulled back, feeling like the walls and ceiling were closing in on me, the alcohol too strong, the beat of the music too loud, the people too overwhelming, my shoes pinching too tight, everything somehow wrong. "I'm tired. I'm going to go home."

"It's your senior year."

I grinned ruefully, wrapping my arms around him for a quick hug. I didn't like being fussed over; it wasn't my style. I liked attention, sure, but never when people worried about me; never when the cracks showed. Samir knew that, and because he loved me, I knew he'd understand that I needed space.

"It is. And maybe it's time for me to spend my nights at the library and not at the nightclub."

Samir's gaze ran over me with a mock-horrified expression. "If you went to the library dressed like that you would cause a riot."

I laughed and meant it for the first time all night, because the second he said the words, something new entered me, a spark that probably spelled trouble.

"Now, how can I resist an opportunity like that?"

If I was really turning over a new leaf, I would have gone up to my room, changed into jeans and a sweater, grabbed some books and headed to the library to study. That would have been the sensible thing to do.

There was still enough of the old me, though, to head to the library dressed exactly as I was, because if I was honest with myself, I'd admit I wasn't going to the library to study.

If I'd learned anything in the five months I'd dated George, it was that Max religiously spent Friday nights studying in the back of the library. And if I'd learned anything in the past week, it was that being around Max made me feel things that lit me up inside. After the restlessness and sadness that had hit me in the club, I needed that spark.

I caught a cab outside Babel, headed back to school and walked into the library like I was walking back into the nightclub.

Because I could.

I ignored the looks that were shot my way and the whispers that weren't really whispers at all. The thing about being notorious was that people were going to talk about you whether you liked it or not. When over half the school had seen your naked body, your options became limited. I could have slunk into the shadows and prayed for obscurity, but I was pretty sure that was exactly what my blackmailer wanted. So fuck him—

or more likely, *her*. If someone was going to make a spectacle of me then I was going to do it on *my* terms…and show everyone I didn't care what they thought about me in the process.

And then I saw her.

Of all the gross things about the Natasha situation, one of the biggest ones was how similar we looked. Costa clearly had a type, and it was impossible to not feel like we were both just interchangeable brunettes with long legs and dark eyes. Once upon a time, Natasha and I had been close. At least I'd thought so.

Our gazes locked across the library, hate flowing between us. She gave me a once-over, and then her lips curved into a smirk. I had to resist the urge to flip her off.

Let her think what she wanted to. I wasn't here for her.

I kept walking and found Max in the back of the library, huddled at a table in front of some dusty bookshelves, not another soul in sight. He had headphones on, his attention completely absorbed in the book he was reading and music he was listening to.

As usual, he was dressed in a black hoodie, a mossy-green T-shirt and a pair of jeans that weren't anything remotely fashionable.

And then his head jerked up and our gazes met. I watched as I saw myself reflected in his eyes while he pulled off his headphones.

The look there staggered me.

Max

Fuck me.

She was going to kill me, no question about it. I was going to die in the library of a heart attack at the ripe old age of twenty-two. If the sight of her yesterday had been mind-blowing, this was something else entirely.

I'd seen her dressed to kill before—on the rare occasions George had dragged me out to a club or party, on the nights I'd had to watch them go out on dates. Those had been the nights I'd dreamed of her, of her body moving against mine, of my mouth on hers, my hands exploring all the places I'd imagined. Those had been the nights when I'd gone to bed hard and wanting, and woken up filled with ache and need, my body covered in sweat.

I'd dream of her tonight.

She wore a dress. Well, sort of. There wasn't much to it, and while I knew nothing about fashion, I thanked whatever fashion gods had created it with everything I had. It was black and clung to every curve of her shape like a second skin. The fabric had a bit of sheen to it, beginning just over the curve of her breasts and ending just below her ass. She wore spike heels that flaunted her long legs, and called to mind fantasies of me between her thighs, her heels digging into my back, adding pain to pleasure.

But wasn't that the thing about her...everything about her was so much it hurt?

Her hair hung down her shoulders, perfectly straight, her lips full and lush and bathed in some pinky color. Her eyes held a kind of trouble that I wanted more than I'd ever wanted anything in my life.

"Hi."

Her voice was smoky, low, and it was impossible to feel like this wasn't some secret meeting. I'd seen her dressed like this before, and yet, everything about this time felt different. This was the *library*, not a nightclub, and girls didn't wear fuck-me heels and dresses like that in the *library*. It made the whole thing sexier, took the forbidden element up a notch, and I wanted her here, now, against the stacks, my hand under her dress, my mouth covering her moans.

It was different this time because now I knew that she'd dressed for me when we'd studied, and I couldn't help but wonder why she was here. She wasn't even holding a book, and the optimistic part of me, the hopeful, longing part of me, wondered if it was possible...

Was she here for me?

6

Fleur

"Hi."

Max echoed my greeting, the same dazed expression still on his face.

My legs shook slightly as I crossed the distance between us, as I held his gaze, wondering how it would be possible to live up to the awe I saw in his eyes and if he'd always looked at me like this and I'd just never noticed.

I gestured to his books, not bothering to sit. Standing gave me an advantage, and considering the emotions ripping through me, I'd take every one I could get.

"Studying?"

He nodded.

"It's Friday night," I teased, hoping I didn't seem as nervous as I felt. "Don't you ever take a break?"

"I have job interviews coming up," he answered, his expression still slightly dazed. "No clue what they're going to ask me. Must be prepared."

I took another step forward. I didn't really know what I was doing anymore. My thought process was, as usual, a jumbled mix that, when dissected, ultimately came down to the fact that some part of me wanted Max, even though I wasn't even sure I liked him. And I was terrible at denying myself the things I wanted. So here I was, playing with fire.

"What are you doing in the library?" he asked. "I would have thought you'd be out at a club or something."

"I was. I went to Babel for a beginning-of-semester party with Mya, Maggie, Samir and Omar."

Max made a face. "The A-team."

I shot him a quizzical look, and his lips curved into a heart-breaking smile.

"It's an American thing. Sorry. I forget sometimes. So why are you here?" he asked, his voice casual...too casual.

I gave the safe lie rather than the dangerous truth. "I realized it's my senior year and I need to try to take school more seriously. Less nightclub, more library."

He blinked. "You don't have any books with you." He drew the words out like each one told him something about me, which I supposed they did.

Anticipation filled me, buzzing through my senses, lighting me up more than the champagne, the music and the glitzy club. There was bewilderment in his tone, but also a spark, one I hadn't felt in years.

I took another step closer, loving the flare of awareness reflected in his eyes. I didn't know where I was headed, or what I'd do when I got there, but I had to move.

I stopped when I was so close that our legs touched, mine bare against the scratchy denim of his pants. Max sucked in a breath, and the air seemed to grow heavy between us. My throat tightened as I longed to reach out.

"I figured you'd be here," I confessed, my voice a whisper pushing for release.

It was late, most of the International School was sleeping, and we were here in this nearly deserted corner of the library, two people who couldn't have been further from a natural fit. It was a night for the impossible to become possible.

"You came here looking for me?"

There was that voice again, and that accent that was cute on Maggie and something else entirely on Max—gravelly, deep, rough, undeniably male.

Max swallowed, and the disbelief in his voice, and in his eyes, pulled at me in a way nothing had before. There was a vulnerability to him I'd never seen. It spoke to the side of me that hadn't been okay in a long time.

I shrugged, struggling for nonchalance, trying to pretend my heart wasn't beating a million beats a minute. And then he rose from the chair, slowly, surprisingly graceful for his size, and any hope I had of control completely disappeared.

Max

I had to be dreaming. That was what I told myself as I stood, moving toward her like she was where I belonged.

My brain had abandoned me somewhere between seeing Fleur in that dress and hearing the interest in her voice. I didn't really understand, didn't know what she wanted, but I knew this: if I only had this moment with her, and tomorrow we would go back to the way we were before, when she was out of my reach, then I was going to take it. I'd rather regret kissing Fleur Marceaux and possibly embarrassing myself, than miss the chance I'd been dreaming about for years.

I reached out and grabbed Fleur's hand, lacing my fingers

with hers until our palms connected. I waited for a beat, for the snarky remark, for embarrassment to flood me, for sanity to kick in. For something, anything, to tell me I was making a huge mistake, until all I felt was the heat of her palm against mine and the shudder that rippled through her fingers.

I tugged her forward, moving with a confidence I'd never felt before and an urgency that had been building inside me since the first time I saw her freshman year. I felt reckless, like someone I'd never been, but I'd been fantasizing about her for three years, and now she was here, and suddenly, years of want and need came to the surface, refusing to be contained.

I maneuvered her over to one of the bookcases in the quietest corner of the library, a few feet away from where I'd been studying. There was no one around, and it was late, and nothing mattered beyond the way her body moved in sync with mine. Some part of her wanted this, and the part of me that craved it was more than happy to give her what she wanted, even if it was just this moment.

I settled my palms on her hips, her hip bones pressing against me as I stared down at our touching bodies, my hands spanning her slim frame. She sighed, the sound lost somewhere between us.

You weren't supposed to have a chance with the girl you fantasized about. There was something safe in the unattainable, something that didn't involve having to put yourself out there, risking rejection. But right now, with the scent of her perfume swirling around and the feel of her body against me, I didn't want the fantasy. I wanted the girl in front of me who looked as nervous as I felt. And even as the urge to chicken out flickered through me, I beat it back because this was *Fleur*.

I leaned in closer, moving my hands from her hips and placing them on either side of her head, palming the bookshelf, struggling to concentrate on the leather spines against my skin rather than losing myself to the feel of the girl against my body.

Don't fuck this up.

The words ran through my mind on a never-ending loop, gaining momentum like a freight train.

I rocked my hips forward just an inch, pushing her back against the bookshelf, too turned on to care that she could now feel every inch of how badly I wanted her.

Fleur's eyes widened, but she didn't speak, as if she somehow knew words would ruin this moment, whatever it was. And it hit me that this was real, and it was happening, and I'd somehow stunned the girl who knocked me on my ass.

I reached down, capturing a lock of her hair, wrapping the brown silk around my fingers, tugging her toward me. I'd always wondered if her hair felt as soft as it looked.

It felt better.

She arched her back, pressing her hips against my body, a sound escaping her lips that was somewhere between a moan and a purr.

Fuck me. I was done.

Fleur

With one touch of his lips against mine, everything I'd thought I'd known about men was flipped on its head.

Despite the rumors, I hadn't kissed a lot of guys. Costa had been my first and he'd been unbelievable, probably because I'd been far from his first. Then there had been a few random guys in clubs, kisses that were tinged with too much champagne and the beat of loud music. Those hadn't been great kisses; they'd been ruled by my need to obliterate all that had happened. Kisses weren't so good when there was someone else in your head.

And then there'd been George. Nice George. George, whose kisses were okay, nothing spectacular. Not bad, not good, just nice. He'd kissed like I figured a nice boy should—no roving hands, no demanding mouth—easy, gentle, sweet.

Surprisingly, Max kissed like a bad boy, and considering I was a far cry from a good girl, that was just fine with me.

His hands came down from their resting place above my head to curve around my back and waist, yanking me against him. I would have guessed he'd be a hesitant kisser, and I would have been so wrong.

He kissed like I was everything, like all he wanted was to kiss me. Costa had kissed like he could; George had kissed like he wanted to, but never could quite take charge. Max kissed like he *had* to kiss me, and that made all the difference.

His lips were firm, his tongue and mouth bold, his hands bolder still, his body hungry. He arched me forward, bringing my body in line with his. If we'd been anywhere else, if we'd been in private, I would have used his strength holding me in place to wrap my leg around his waist, rocking against every inch of him, reveling in how badly he wanted me.

But we weren't in private, we were in the library, and I'd totally lost control.

He released my mouth with a harsh breath, moving down, his lips and teeth grazing the sensitive curve of my neck. My moan filled the silence around us.

He ignored the sound, his mouth continuing down the same trail, teasing a shiver out of me. All he had to do was touch me and I was ready to combust. It had been an embarrassingly long time.

His hands moved up from my waist, fisting in my hair again,

tugging lightly in a move that had me tilting my head back, giving him more of my neck, more of me.

"Soft," Max mumbled against my skin, the rumble from his mouth vibrating against my throat. "Silk."

Words tumbled out in French in a strangled gasp.

Max froze, my body trapped under his. He pulled back slightly, inches separating my body and his, his hands still tangled in my hair, holding me in place.

I blinked, focusing on the boy in front of me, as if that would change the image staring back at me. He was hot, but he wasn't my usual hot, not by a long shot. And by the look in his eyes, I wasn't what he expected to find looking back at him. But here we were, so hell, I looked at his raw beauty, and I wasn't shy about it.

His brown eyes widened; his cheeks flushed. A lock of his hair fell forward across his forehead, and at that moment I realized that while he'd had his hands on me, I hadn't been able to return the favor. I'd been too surprised, too caught off guard, by the kiss. I'd let him kiss me without exploring the parts of him that had been pulling at my stomach for the past few months, sneaking up on me so that I couldn't even pinpoint the moment when I'd stopped looking at Max as someone I loathed and started looking at him as someone I wanted.

And just like that, parts of me that had been sleeping, walking through a haze, woke up.

The rest of my body might have been shy, but my hand turned greedy. I reached out without thinking, only wanting, and placed my palm on his chest, feeling his sharp intake of breath at my touch. His shirt was between us, but it wasn't enough of a barrier to dull the beat in his chest that had me closing my eyes.

Thump. Thump. Thump.

His heart beat against my palm, strong and fierce. My eyes flickered open, and I stared at the point where I touched him, where I felt him, and wondered if anything would make me let go.

"You spoke French."

I looked up, even in heels, up higher still, until our gazes collided. My mouth parted, but no words came out. I was afraid to speak, afraid that whatever spell had descended on this little corner of the library would simply disappear. I didn't know what I wanted when the veil lifted, didn't know what he wanted, but I knew I wasn't ready yet.

"I'm French," I mumbled, the words fumbling out of my mouth with uncharacteristic clumsiness.

The corner of his mouth curved, his smile lopsided. "I noticed."

Neither of us spoke, that crooked smile still on his face.

I tilted my head to the side, trying to figure out what it was about Max that made me this way. I couldn't tell if it was how long it had been since anyone made me feel things, or his eyes, or the way he held me like I mattered, or the way he kissed me like he couldn't stop.

He returned the favor, staring at me until I couldn't take it anymore. I worried that if he looked too closely, he'd see too much. I needed the veneer; without it, I wasn't sure I could face the world.

"What?" I asked, my voice shaky.

His head shook, and the other corner of his mouth turned up. "I don't know."

I pulled my hand away from him slowly, his eyes on me, until it dropped to my side, my fingers curling into a ball. My heart pounded a bit faster.

I bit my lip, watching as his throat bobbed, his eyes riveted to my mouth. I couldn't resist; I let my tongue dart out, doing a quick swipe across my bottom lip, tasting my peppermint gloss and the remnants of his mouth on mine. And then he moved forward again and I lost my mind.

Max

She tasted even better than I'd imagined, felt better than any fantasy. Now at night when I closed my eyes and my head hit the pillow, it would be her scent, the feel of her curves against my body, that got me hard, the silk of her hair between my fingers and her kiss that made me pant for more.

And then she did that thing with her lip and I had to take her mouth. So I did.

She opened for me instantly, her lips accommodating mine. The first kiss had been an introduction; this was an exploration.

Her body molded itself against me. There were no soft curves with her, no handfuls to grab. Her body was all harsh angles, unforgiving planes that made you work for it.

So *Fleur.*

She didn't just let me kiss her. Our mouths battled, our tongues tangled, existing in a constant sway of give-and-take.

Her teeth sank down on my bottom lip, sucked it into her mouth, and I groaned, my hips pushing against hers.

"Touch me," I whispered, not sure if I was asking, or begging, or telling. I didn't even care. In this case, the ends justified the means.

Her hands came around my neck, her fingers linking, pulling my head down even closer to hers. In her heels, she was tall enough that I didn't have to bend down to kiss her; even out of her heels, she was tall in a way I liked. When you were a few inches over six feet, tall was nice. The legs for days were a bonus on a girl who didn't need any extra points, not when she hit every single ball out of the fucking park.

Her fingers unlinked, her hands moving up, threading through my hair, gripping a handful, tugging on the ends.

Jesus.

A thud sounded somewhere, breaking into the pounding noise in my head. I didn't want to let her go, having her in my arms was the best feeling in the world, but we were in the library, and it was past midnight, and most importantly, it was Fleur, and everything she did was front-page news. And the last thing I needed was George finding out I'd kissed his ex-girlfriend from the International School gossip chain. So I released her when all I wanted was more of her. More of this side of her, at least. It was easier when we were using our mouths for something other than fighting.

I let her go slowly, feeling like she was slipping through my fingers like sand.

Her head arched back, hitting the book spines behind her, looking up at me, a slightly dazed look on her face. I loved that look, wanted to memorize this moment, wanted to revel in the fact that I'd put it there.

I shoved my hands into my pockets, struggling to think of what to say after the most mind-blowing kiss of my life.

Nothing came to mind. Luckily, Fleur was anything but shy.

"That was…" Her lips curved into a smile. "Interesting."

I bit back a laugh, loving the way her brown eyes lit up. "That's one word for it."

"Would you choose a different word?" she teased.

"Confusing. Complicated. Fucking amazing."

Her smile deepened. "That's two words."

This time I did laugh. "So it is."

"I should go before I cause an even bigger scene than normal," Fleur announced.

I nodded.

She didn't speak. Instead, she leaned forward, her lips brushing softly against my cheek, her perfume filling my head, her body grazing mine. My eyes closed.

"Good night, Max," she whispered.

When I opened them again, she was gone.

7

Fleur

"Are we going to talk about why you left last night?"

I shrugged. "I was bored."

Maggie's eyes narrowed with concern. "You've never been bored at Babel before."

My lips curved. "Actually, I have been. You're just normally too into Samir to notice."

"Burn."

I laughed. "You and your little American sayings."

I shifted in bed, pulling my knees up to my chest, burrowing farther under the covers. It was early, way too early considering how late I'd gone to bed. Maggie didn't look much better than me. When I'd gotten back from the library she'd still been at Babel. I had no clue where Mya was.

Maggie's expression changed. "I'm worried about you."

I groaned. "It's too early for this."

"You won't talk about it."

"Because I don't want to talk about it."

"You need to deal with it."

"I am dealing with it," I protested.

Maggie shook her head. "Then why don't you look happy? You used to love going out, and last night you looked like you'd rather be at the dentist. You're not yourself."

"Is that a bad thing?"

"It is when you're surrounded by people who love you and just want to see you happy."

My eyebrow rose. "Like Samir?"

She flushed. "I didn't tell him everything. Really, I didn't even tell him anything. Just that I was worried about you. He is, too."

I sighed. I knew they were, but in a way that only made things harder. It was impossible not to feel like I was letting them down.

"I love you guys, but I need a bit of space. I'm dealing with things in my own way. Costa messed me up." I pushed out the words despite the razor scraping at my throat. "Losing the baby about killed me." Maggie whitened. "And let's be honest here. George was a nice guy, but deep down, I knew he wasn't the guy for me. And I hurt him in the process because I needed something he couldn't give me. I don't want to do that again. Maybe I just want to be more cautious this year." I thought of last night. "Well, more cautious than normal," I amended.

My tone softened because, honestly, if I owed anyone an apology, it was Maggie. She was the one who'd called an ambulance the night I'd overdosed sophomore year; she'd saved my life. As overprotective as she could be, I knew it was because she loved me, even if it could be stifling sometimes. I wasn't used to this kind of love or concern, though. I'd pretty much been on my own for as long as I could remember, so it was welcome. Just a little hard to handle at times.

"I promise I'm not going to go off the rails again. I'm not that girl anymore. I need you to trust me."

"I do." Maggie got out of her bed and crossed the room to me, wrapping her arms around my waist. I wasn't much of a hugger, but she'd changed that. I hadn't been kidding when I said my friends were my family.

"This year's going to be different. I can feel it," Maggie said.

I couldn't disagree with her. After last night's kiss, everything felt different.

Whereas kissing Costa had always meant sex was soon to follow, this hadn't been like that at all. It had been a kiss that was content just to be a kiss. As if my lips on his were more than Max had ever expected. Costa would have pushed for more, and I would have given it.

It hit me that the thread that had run through my relationship with Costa—that nervous, edgy, keep-me-on-my-toes thread—hadn't been about love, or passion, or want. It had been fear. The fear that he'd toss me aside for another girl because he was bored or because he never cared enough to hold on to me like I mattered in the first place.

With Max I felt safe, and that was better than I ever could have imagined.

Max

I woke up starving.

I blamed my hunger on last night's lack of sleep. After Fleur had left me in the library, after that kiss, I'd been too keyed up to go to bed. I went for a run this morning to clear my head, but that hadn't helped much. She was still in there, impossible to ignore. And as much as it was driving me wild, part of me didn't want to ignore her. I liked her under my skin like this, in a way that was real. I liked being able to remember the taste and feel of her.

I showered and then made my way down to the cafeteria, hoping to catch the tail end of brunch and alternating between looking for Fleur and wanting to avoid her.

Part of me needed to know if she was as confused about this as I was, if that kiss had lodged itself in her brain, too, refusing to be pushed out. And part of me was afraid that she wasn't, and it hadn't, and all it would take was one look to slice me in two.

Who would I get this morning—the Ice Queen or the girl who had been burning up in my arms?

And then I walked into the cafeteria and I heard the sound of her laughter, and my whole body stilled.

Fleur stood by the drink fountain with Maggie, her head thrown back, long brown hair raining down. It was a mass of tumbles and waves that made my heart clench.

Sometimes she wore her hair perfectly straight, each strand gleaming. But other times, during exams, or early mornings, or when I caught her at the gym, her hair was messy in a sexy, just-got-out-of-bed look that took hot to a whole other level.

She wasn't wearing makeup, and she'd dressed casually in tight black workout pants that fit perfectly across her ass, and a hot-pink workout tank that showed off her tanned skin and cleavage.

Her head turned to the side, and our gazes locked across the room. This was the moment. It was a moment that felt like an eternity, and then those lips that I'd kissed curved into a smile that hit me in the gut. Her eyes sparkled with something that looked like amusement. No, better than that. Like we had a secret no one else knew about. I couldn't keep my lips from spreading as the answering smile took over my face. Her chin jerked in acknowledgment before ducking back down.

I looked away, walking toward an empty table, my heart hammering. I didn't know how to play this one. Part of me wanted to go over and say hi. At the same time, it would look weird considering our hate truce had only been a few days ago. And I hadn't talked to George about any of this, and worse, I had no clue how to tell him I'd kissed his ex-girlfriend.

I ate my breakfast, focused less on the food than the girl in front of me. I wished Maggie would go away. I mean, I liked her, but I wanted a chance to say something to Fleur in private. I wanted to see where we stood after last night.

Fleur

"What do you have planned for the rest of the weekend?"

I turned my attention away from Max's table to focus on Maggie.

I shrugged. "Studying, I guess."

She looked at me like I had three heads. Fair enough, weekends used to be reserved for partying. But this was the new me. Sort of.

"You're really taking this whole getting good grades thing seriously, aren't you?"

There was surprise in her tone, and while I knew she didn't mean to make me feel bad, it stung just the same.

"I'm worried about not graduating." I should have worried about it all along. Unfortunately, leaving things to the last minute was also classically me.

"How are things going in your Project Finance class?" she asked. "Are you and Max getting along better?"

"You could say that."

"Could say what?"

My head jerked up as our friend Michael slid into the seat across from me. Michael was one of the few other exceptions to my not being friends with Americans. It wasn't that I made a point of not liking the American kids; we just typically didn't have a lot in common. Except for Maggie. And Michael, whom I'd basically inherited from Mya. And now, apparently, Max.

I was surrounded by Americans.

Maggie answered for me. "Fleur was just telling me that she's getting along with Max."

Michael grinned and wiggled his eyebrows suggestively. "Getting along or *getting along*?"

I rolled my eyes.

"I'm just saying. If I weren't in a relationship, I'd be interested. That boy is hot," Michael teased.

Tell me about it.

Maggie burst into laughter at the exact moment that Max turned his head and looked over at our table. Our gazes collided. God, I hoped with every fiber in my being that he didn't know we were talking about how *hot* he was.

I felt my cheeks burning up.

The corner of his mouth curved, transforming his whole face. *Merde.*

It was one thing to kiss Max at night when I was feeling reckless, another entirely to feel this fluttering in my stomach at the sight of his smile. I'd learned the hard way that flutters spelled trouble.

"Fleur!" Maggie waved her hand in the air. "Are you okay?"

I forced myself to look away from Max. "I was just distracted. What?"

She nodded toward Michael. "We're going to head to Chelsea to do some shopping. Do you want to come?"

I shook my head. "Go ahead without me. I think I'm going to sit here a bit longer." I hesitated, racking my brain for a plausible excuse that would have me saying no to shopping. "Mya said she might swing by for brunch," I lied. "We haven't really had a chance to catch up since school started."

I waited while they finished eating, my heart pounding. It felt like it took them a year to get up from the table, but when they finally did, I sat, trying to figure out what I was going to say to him. I sat there until I couldn't sit anymore, until the weight of his stare was enough to have me pushing my chair away from the table and standing, my limbs full of nerves.

I didn't do nervous, but somehow Max seemed to disprove everything I knew about myself. So apparently, I did nervous, and he brought it out in me.

I crossed the distance between us, the tables and chairs separating us nothing compared to the invisible barrier created by the International School social hierarchy. This was the second time in two days I'd sought him out. Discretion was going out the window, and I didn't care. I felt different around him; he took the gaping hole inside me and filled it with something as simple as stomach flutters. And as much as I was a little terrified of the flutters, I recognized what they meant. I didn't feel dead inside anymore.

I *felt*.

Max

Her walk was like a dance you couldn't help but watch. When I walked, I put one foot in front of the other, not caring about anything other than getting where I needed to go. Fleur made the act of walking look like the getting there was more important than the destination.

She didn't hesitate this time as she slid into the chair across from mine, a smile teasing her mouth.

"Hi."

Her *hi* whispered its way through my body.

"Hi," I echoed like an idiot. Again.

Her smile deepened. "I saw you sitting here by yourself and thought I'd stop by. Hate truce and all that."

I swallowed and grinned. "Right."

For a moment neither of us spoke, and then Fleur sighed.

"Let's not make this awkward, okay?"

"Make what awkward?"

Her eyes narrowed, and her voice lowered as she leaned in closer to me. "The kiss."

"*Kiss* might be a tame word for it."

"We're both adults, and it happened." She was quiet for a beat. "I don't want to make it difficult for us to work together on the project."

"Are you having a hard time concentrating?" I teased, unable to resist the urge to screw with her a bit. She looked so cute like this, trying for her usual swagger but a little off her game. I'd never seen Fleur be *cute* before.

She fluttered her eyelashes at me in a move that was clearly practiced. "Please. You're the one who couldn't keep your eyes off me all brunch. You've been eye-fucking me for the past twenty minutes."

Very few women could deliver a line like that. Fleur rocked it.

"Try longer than that." I grinned. "So you noticed me noticing you…"

Her eyes widened, and her lips curved. "You wish." Her words might have been designed to shoot me down, but her tone was all flirt and all Fleur. She was way too good at this, and she knew it.

"Maybe I do," I teased, struggling to keep my tone light under the truth in my words. One kiss—well, one night of kissing—and she'd already sucked me in deep.

She leaned forward another inch, and I allowed my eyes to dip, taking in her cleavage. I wanted her again. Bad. Wanted

her even as I realized this had the potential to be a spectacularly disastrous idea.

When she and George had first started dating, I hadn't really gotten it. I mean, yeah, I got why he was into her, but I
couldn't understand why he would get involved with a girl he
had to have known would eventually break his heart. But now
I understood...

She made the ride so good you didn't care.

"What are we doing here?" I asked, my voice low. It took
effort to ask the question like it was a casual one, even more to
keep myself from caring too much about her answer.

And then she said something that somehow seemed like both
a promise and a challenge.

"Want to find out?"

8

Max

I had to tell him.

I sat next to George on the couch in our room, playing our favorite video game. He was kicking my ass, mainly because I'd stopped paying attention somewhere along the way and, instead, spent most of my time going through all the ways to tell him I'd kissed his ex-girlfriend.

We weren't a couple, it had only been one kiss, but there was a code. He'd been my best friend since I'd started at the International School and my roommate for two years. I owed him the truth, even if I wasn't sure what the truth was exactly. All I had was *I kissed Fleur*, and nothing beyond that.

"I need to tell you something," I blurted out, throwing the controller on our coffee table as a drone took out my avatar.

George set his controller down.

I sucked in a deep breath and let it all out.

"I kissed Fleur."

He just stared at me, not speaking, and I wondered if he'd

heard me. Nerves mixed with guilt as each second passed, and the tension inside me grew. And then he spoke.

"Fleur?"

That one word contained a lot—mainly six different variations of shock.

"Yeah." I stared at my hands, not sure I was ready to look at him, afraid of what I'd see there.

He swallowed. "Shit."

Shit.

"When?" he asked, his voice strained.

"Last night. It wasn't planned. It just happened." Which wasn't an excuse at all.

It was hard; we were in a gray area. They hadn't been together for a long time now, and they'd never had sex, and still, I felt guilty. But when it came down to it, I didn't feel guilty enough to not kiss her again.

George cut through all the bullshit and got to the question that mattered most. "Are you going to keep doing it?"

"If she lets me, probably," I answered honestly. "I don't know what to say, man. I know she fucked you over—"

"She didn't fuck me over," George interrupted, his voice quiet.

I looked over at him now, unable to read the expression on his face. Something twisted in my gut.

"She broke up with you."

"She did, but it wasn't working. I knew it. She knew it. I'd hoped that things would change, that eventually she'd be as into me as I was with her. I'd hoped for that since the beginning. It's a bad way to start a new relationship."

"I'm sorry. About all of it."

George's tone was wry, and this time he did look at me. "Sorry you kissed her?"

I sighed. "I'm not sorry I kissed her. I know that makes me a dick. I'm sorry because you're my best friend, and I don't want to ruin our friendship. Or hurt you." I couldn't lie. We all deserved better than that. "But if I had to do it all over again, I'd still kiss her."

There it was.

"Because she's Fleur." He said it like her name was explanation enough, which it totally was.

"Yeah."

I knew he got me on some level, but that didn't make this any easier.

George sighed.

"You okay with all of this? I can give you space if you want."

My question hung between us.

He shook his head. "It's cool." He hesitated for a beat, and something that might have been guilt flashed in his eyes. "I knew when I started dating Fleur... I knew how you felt about her."

Jesus.

"How?"

"You noticed her. A lot. She's hard to ignore, but it was different with you. I knew it, and I dated her anyway." He shrugged. "It's Fleur."

There really wasn't anything left to say.

"Are you dating now?" he asked, his voice stumbling over the words a bit, clearly still coming to terms with this change.

"No. It was just a kiss." An amazing kiss. "I don't know where her head is."

He nodded, his expression hooded again. "But if she wanted to date, you would."

The knot in my stomach grew. "Yeah."

George picked up the controllers from the coffee table, handing one to me while he queued up the next game. His gaze didn't meet mine as the next words left his mouth.

"Be careful, man."

I nodded, and even though I could tell he wasn't completely over it, I gave him the space he needed.

We spent the next hour blowing up planets on our game.

Fleur

I stared at my inbox, heart pounding, anger spiking at the email in front of me.

I saw you.

Three words from an anonymous email address. The same email address that had sent me the blackmail letter before and the email a few nights ago. Three words that could have meant anything, and yet I knew… My blackmailer had seen me kissing Max.

I didn't care, not in the embarrassed sense, but it made me angry that someone thought they could screw with me like this. It wasn't anyone's business who I kissed.

I was just so tired. Tired of the game, the parties, of always having to look a certain way and say certain things. I was sick of everyone watching me, of living my life on a pedestal and under a microscope.

It had been cool three years ago. I'd loved London, loved the parties and the fashion. I'd spent my nights getting drunk on champagne and then falling into Costa's bed. Until I woke up and realized how bad he really was for me.

The thing about having everything on the surface was that you had everything *on the surface*. I'd never been accused of being particularly deep, but even I got tired of shallow and superficial. I'd wanted more from Costa. I'd wanted the family I'd never had, the promise that he'd be there for me no matter what. I'd wanted the fairy tale. But I'd failed to realize that while I'd wanted deep, he'd wanted easy, and in the end he'd won, leaving me with nothing.

Now I was somewhere stuck between the girl I'd been and the girl I wanted to be.

I closed my laptop, grabbing a pair of trainers from my closet. I had one of those metabolisms that could handle pretty much anything, so despite what everyone thought, I didn't work out for vanity. I did it because it was one of the few ways I could clear my head, and it had the added benefit of not giving me a hangover like my other head-clearing activities. Working out kept me sane when the walls started closing in, and now after another email and last night with Max, I needed to breathe. I needed the peace and quiet to sort my head out.

I needed to run.

I ran in Hyde Park before heading to my gym on Kensington High Street. I didn't really have a preference between running on the treadmill or in the park; each had their benefits. The treadmill made me feel like I was fighting, the pounding of my feet on the belt its own form of release. The park made me feel full inside. There was something about all that green. I was a city girl through and through, but even I craved something else occasionally.

Today was one of those truly perfect London days. It was late September, that time when London hovered between summer and fall. It was warm enough that I was comfortable running in my tank top, but there was enough of a breeze in the air to hint at the changing season. The leaves were on the cusp of turning, the colors reminding me of one of my favorite Prada dresses. It was a beautiful day.

I jogged over to the gym, blood pumping, a thin layer of sweat on my body, my mind already clearer. After the overdose sophomore year, my parents had sent me to a "wellness spa" to "solve my problems," as my father had put it. I hadn't been big on sitting in a circle and talking about my feelings, but I had discovered exercise as my own brand of therapy. Yoga centered me, kickboxing let me kick some ass and running allowed me to escape.

I bounded up the stairs, heading for the weight room. My gym in Paris was one of the fanciest and most exclusive gyms in the world—the kind of place where you would find yourself on a treadmill next to a movie star. This place was the total opposite. It wasn't crappy, but it was nondescript. The school had worked out a deal for students to use the gym since the International School didn't have its own facilities.

I started off on the leg machines first, working through a circuit that had my muscles screaming. I was just finishing up my last set of reps when I saw him.

Max was on the other side of the room lifting weights while a burly guy spotted him.

I'd seen him at the gym before, and I'd be lying if I didn't admit that I always had this reaction to him. I was pretty sure all the women felt the same way about the sight of Max's body lifting weights, his muscles exposed, sweat dripping...

My type might have been Gucci loafers and Rolexes, but that didn't mean I couldn't appreciate what was right in front of me.

I appreciated it a lot. For at least a minute. Maybe two.

He wore a gray T-shirt with the sleeves cut off and a pair of black shorts that hit him at the knee. His biceps were big and sculpted, his legs muscular. His dark hair fell forward over his brow as he lifted the weight again, and I watched in fascination as his body braced to support itself. Sweat dripped down his face, and his eyes blazed with determination. He completed the rep and set the weight down. I froze as his head turned and he caught sight of me.

A smile spread across his lips and a familiar ache settled low in my belly.

The smile grew, his eyes on me as he said something to the guy who had been spotting him, exchanging a complicated handshake.

I waited to see if he'd come over and speak to me, trying to string together a coherent sentence, when suddenly he moved over to a black gym bag against the wall. He grabbed a towel from his bag, wiping his face and grabbing a fresh shirt, this one white. He rose, lifting his shirt up over his head and throwing it into the gym bag, and all hope of coherent fled.

Abs. Abs everywhere. Work-of-fucking-art abs.

Max walked toward me, tugging the fresh white T-shirt over his head, the fabric a curtain coming down on the best show I'd ever seen.

He stopped a couple feet away.

"Hi."

I forced my gaze up until our eyes met. "Hi."

He grinned. "Good workout?"

Way better now.

"Yes."

His lips twitched. "Are you okay?"

I froze. "What?"

"Are you okay?" he repeated. "You're flushed. Hard workout?"

He totally knew. "Something like that."

His grin deepened, and a dimple popped out. *Hello.*

Max shifted back and forth, rocking on his heels, studying

me the whole time. I struggled for inscrutable as I stared back at him, even if it was hard to keep my lips from mirroring his in the face of that dimple.

Who knew a dent in your face could be so lethal?

"What are you doing the rest of the weekend?" he asked, his voice distracting me from his smile.

"Probably just studying."

"No hot parties?" he teased.

"No. You?"

"Definitely no hot parties."

I rolled my eyes. "You know what I mean. Any plans for the weekend?"

"I'm going shopping."

"Excuse me?" I didn't know a lot about Max, but it was clear that he didn't care about fashion at all. The few times George had brought him out with us last year he'd made little to no effort.

"I have the first round of job interviews next week," he explained. "I need a nice suit."

"You have job interviews next week and you waited until now to get a suit?"

"Yeah. Why?"

I gaped at him. "Because a suit must be tailored. You can't just buy a suit. It needs to fit perfectly. You're cutting it close. What day are your job interviews?"

I may have procrastinated with things like studying, but I did not mess around when it came to fashion.

He laughed. "Why do I feel like I just committed a crime? I'm just going to go to the high street to get a suit. It's not like I'm going to Armani."

Some part of me died a bit when he strung together the words *high street* and *suit*.

"Where are your interviews?"

He rattled off a list of investment banks that were so impressive even I'd heard of them. Every place where he was interviewing catered to a wealthy and exclusive clientele. There were expectations.

"You can't wear a suit from the high street."

His gaze darkened, and I knew I'd struck a nerve. "Fleur—"

"You can't." I hesitated, reaching for tact, which had never really been a strength of mine. "I get the money thing, but trust me. You're entering my world now. I know the type of guy who works at one of these banks. They're going to judge everything about you. Not just the finance stuff but also how you look. They want someone who is going to fit their brand. They'll want flashy."

The rest—*and you aren't flashy*—might have hung unspoken between us, but we both knew it was there.

"I can't afford a suit from fucking Armani."

I stilled. I'd always assumed Max thought he was above us—the clothes, the money, the clubs. I'd figured he didn't care and thought it was frivolous—thought *I* was frivolous—but now, hearing the frustration in his voice, I knew I was wrong.

He did care.

And it hit me then that it must be hard to be at a school like the International School, where guys were peacocks who flaunted their money and their families' power like brightly colored feathers designed to draw females in.

And it worked. Constantly.

For Max, it was all a game for which he didn't have the tools, and he had no hope of getting them. No wonder he sat out.

"It doesn't have to be Armani," I responded, my tone softer.

"Don't feel sorry for me," he warned.

"I don't." I flashed him a killer smile. "I'm the Ice Queen, remember?" I whispered playfully. "I don't feel normal human emotion."

He shook his head, the smile returning to his lips, some of the tension easing from his brow. I liked that I could do that.

"You're a handful, aren't you?"

"Are you just now figuring that out?" I teased.

This time he gifted me with another flash of his dimple. "No, I've been paying attention for a while."

Something warm wound its way through me.

I could play the whole "Ohmigod, he likes me, he really likes me" game, but that wasn't my style.

I'd modeled, even done that stupid music video—which, while it had seemed like a fabulous idea at the time and had succeeded in irritating my parents, wasn't something I was super proud of—so I got it. I was hot. Guys liked hot. Whatever. But right now, with the look in his eyes and the words coming out of his mouth, there seemed to be more. And that was new.

"I'll go shopping with you." The words escaped my mouth before I even realized it.

Max was quiet for a beat. "Why?"

"Because it sounds like you need help, and believe it or not, if there's one thing I'm excellent at it's shopping."

He laughed. "True."

"And you need me."

"Really?" he drawled.

"Absolutely."

He sighed. "I'm going to warn you… I hate shopping."

I grinned. "Somehow I already knew that."

"And I hate trying on clothes."

It was too much to resist. Something sparked inside me, and I let it flame.

"I'm sure I can help with that," I teased.

His eyes widened, and his voice turned husky. "Could be fun."

The spark turned into a full-on blaze.

"Oh, it will be," I promised.

9

Max

"This is not fun. You lied."

Fleur glared at me. "It would be if you weren't so grumpy."

"You've dragged me to six stores, we still haven't found anything and you promised me food two hours ago and haven't delivered. I ran five miles and strength-trained for an hour today. I'm hungry."

"After you find a suit," she sniped.

"I've found lots of suits. This one's nice." I held up a gray one, my eyes pleading with her to just decide so we could be done.

She shook her head. "It doesn't send the right message."

"What message is it supposed to send? It's a suit. Newsflash, it can't talk."

She smirked at me. "You're wrong about that. If you think clothes don't speak, then you're missing the whole point of fashion."

My head throbbed, my stomach growled and I swore my calf was cramping. I considered myself to be in pretty good shape, but shopping with Fleur was something else entirely. She was like an invading general, marching from shop to shop, drag-

ging me along with her. I wanted a beer, I wanted food and I
wanted to sit down.

"What does my outfit say?" she asked.

"Have you been listening at all? No idea."

"What does my outfit say?" she repeated, hand on her hip,
foot tapping against the ground.

Cute and annoying at the same time.

"That you always get your way? That you're hot?"

Her eyes narrowed. "What part of my outfit says that?"

She was right. I wasn't describing her outfit; I was describing her.

I sank down onto one of the sofas in the store, something the
shop had graciously provided for men luckier than me.

"Take pity on me. I haven't eaten in hours. Haven't had water.
I don't know what a pinstripe is, have no preference on double-
breasted versus single-breasted. I've never worn a suit in my life.
Where I'm from, you wear a suit when you go to court, get married, or go to a funeral, and that's about it. I'm trying here, but
I lost my will to live like two hours ago, and I'm sorry, I have
no clue what your outfit says other than that it makes every guy
who sees you—" *including me* "—want to take it off."

She laughed, not one of the laughs she employed like another piece of her armor, but a real laugh, one that had her
shoulders shaking.

"Fine. No more shopping. I have a feeling this will be our
lucky stop anyway."

I closed my eyes and offered a silent prayer to the heavens.
"Thank you."

She laughed and the sound skipped through me, leaving a
trail of want in its wake. It was a feeling I'd been fighting all
day. I'd never really hung out with Fleur one-on-one without
distractions, but she had a quick sense of humor and she was
fun to be around.

"What about this one?" she asked, holding up a gray jacket. I shrugged. "That one's nice."

Her eyes narrowed as she looked at the jacket again and back at me. "I think you might need something with a little more presence. A classic black suit gives a more powerful image. You want to walk into the interview like you own it."

She put the jacket back on the rack.

"Since you don't care about single-breasted versus double-breasted, I'm just going to go with single-breasted." She flashed me a blinding smile. "I want you to look like this suit was made for you."

I shook my head, fascinated by the intensity with which she approached shopping.

"Why do you care so much?" I asked, my tone more curious than anything else.

"Because it's important. You said you need this job, right?" I nodded.

"So I'm helping. It's not a big deal. Shopping isn't exactly a hardship."

Maybe she didn't mind the shopping, but it was a big deal. It was nice of her to help me out. Maggie had always said Fleur was loyal, but I hadn't believed her until now. I got it. Fleur was loyal, and the fact that she somehow counted me in her list of people to take care of was surprising.

"I'll take you to dinner after to make up for the torture," she promised. "You can even pick the restaurant."

I shook my head. "Only if you'll let me pay. Seriously. You're doing me a huge favor here, and even though I'm giving you a hard time, I really appreciate it."

"It's a deal. Are you ready?"

I forced myself to smile. "Let's try on some suits."

Fleur

I shifted the suits to my other arm, the heavy fabric weighing me down, the long trouser legs dragging on the floor slightly. If we were in a fancier store, a normal store, there would be someone to do this for me. I knew I was being a snob, and I wasn't trying to be, it was just hard when we had such different views of normal. We came from totally different worlds, and while I'd grown somewhat used to that with Maggie, it was different when it was a guy. There was ego involved, and male pride and a whole lot of things that made it a tricky situation to navigate. I'd compromised by going to the high street to save his budget, with the caveat that I chose the stores. So far the selection hadn't been bad.

I'd promised Max this was the last stop, but I hadn't put a limit on the number of suits I wanted him to try on. He was in the dressing room with number six now.

Part of the problem was his budget, the other his size. Most of the stores we'd gone to carried suits cut for European builds, not bulk. With his short time frame, custom-made wasn't really an option, especially when he couldn't afford it. And off-the-rack was turning into a challenge.

Luckily, I'd never found a fashion challenge I couldn't overcome.

I headed back toward the dressing room, three more suits in hand. He'd found a nice dress shirt that worked, so that was one problem down. Shoes and suit remained. Somehow, I was guessing he had big feet.

I rapped on the door. "I found a few more."

Muffled sounds and thumps came from the other side.

"We've been here an hour," he grumbled.

I bit back a smile. He was back to being surly. It was kind of cute on him. Most guys would be complaining a hell of a lot more than he was after being dragged all over London shopping. And his complaining was funny, although I'd never admit it.

"Just a few more," I cajoled. "Can I come in?"

I didn't wait for a response. I turned the knob, opening the dressing room door, and I froze.

Holy fuck.

Max stood in front of me in one of the suit trousers I'd picked, white dress shirt unbuttoned, trousers open enough to see a hint of the top of his black boxer briefs, giving me one hell of a show.

Gah.

Neither of us spoke.

I stared at that exposed patch of skin—tan, smooth, muscular—and warmth began to seep into me. I didn't think, I just moved. I walked the rest of the way into the dressing room and closed the door behind me, locking it with a click.

I dumped the suits on the chair in the corner of the room and then my arms were around his neck, my lips on his, and his hands cupped my ass as he pulled me up against him—hard—and I lost myself to pleasure.

Max

She kissed me like she had to kiss me, like she was made to kiss me. She kissed me like she wanted to take, and I gave her everything.

French spilled from her lips in a rapid tumble I couldn't even begin to decipher, and my heart turned over in my chest.

Her mouth pressed against mine, her tongue grazing me before I opened and tasted her heady and sweet flavor, our tongues tangling, bodies plastered against each other. She wrapped her arms around my neck, pulling me closer, her body fitting perfectly against mine. Her breasts rubbed against my chest, her hands traveling to the front of my shirt. She pushed aside the fabric, her palms flat against my skin. I was so hard already, but the second her hands touched my abs, just above my hips, my cock jerked.

She stroked my skin, exploring my chest until her hands drifted lower and lower, pushing the shirt off my shoulders with an impatience I easily matched.

My hands came up from the curve of her ass to the small of her back, reaching under her top to stroke at the smooth skin hidden under her clothes. I didn't care that we were in a dressing room, didn't care that she was Fleur, that she would likely crush my heart under the heel of one of her thirty pairs of shoes.

I wanted her. Fuck the rest of it.

Her hands moved up from my abs, tracing the planes of my naked chest, reaching higher to stroke the muscles on my shoulders and back. Someone moaned, the sound lost between our mouths. I wasn't sure who it was, wasn't sure where she ended and I began. My hands roamed higher, teasing her back, my fingertips grazing the lace around the strap of her bra, higher still until I held the back of her neck, stroking and teasing a shiver out of her.

She responded by pulling me even closer. Her legs threaded with mine, her lower body pushing against me in an unspoken demand for what she wanted and what I was determined to have.

Fleur

Best kiss ever.

I wanted Max. Bad. I had to have Max.

Done.

Max maneuvered me up against the dressing room wall, his hands reaching down to grip my hips. He lifted me up, cupping my ass, squeezing, stroking. I wrapped my legs around his waist, rocking against his body, his hard length bringing a shiver out.

Some infrequently used, rational part of my brain knew this was taking things a little too far—we were in public, in a dressing room—but a bigger part of me didn't really care.

He held me up with one arm, my body levered between his and the wall, the other gliding up, over my clothes, until he palmed my breast, his fingers stroking my nipple through the thin fabric.

Mon dieu.

My head lolled back, hitting the wall with a thud that sent a crack of pain through me.

Max froze. "Are you okay?"

"Fine," I mumbled, desperate for his lips on me again.

He fumbled with the hem of my top, his hands moving to my front, his fingers teasing my body, searching for skin. They slid under the fabric, palming my stomach, up, up, until his hands reached my cleavage. He pulled back, and all I could do was stare into his beautiful green eyes, stunned by the look reflected at me.

Heat flooded me, and without thinking, I moved closer to his body, craving it.

This was what had been missing before, this look, this feeling blazing through my body. I'd once told Maggie I wanted a spark; Max gave me a forest fire.

The sound of a salesperson talking to a customer filled the space around us, and then footsteps tapped against the wood dressing room floor, getting closer, closer…

Max groaned. "We gotta stop."

He was right, and yet it was the last thing I wanted.

He closed his eyes, a sigh escaping his lips. He moved forward, his forehead coming to rest against mine.

"As much as having sex with you right here, right now would be hotter than any fantasy I've ever had…" His lips quirked as his eyes fluttered open. "Well, besides that dream last night. We gotta stop."

I nodded, breathless as he released me, gently setting me down on my feet. I tilted my head up to meet his gaze. I liked that he was taller than me. Liked that he was so strong that I felt delicate in his arms.

I didn't get to feel delicate or sweet very often. It wasn't something I wanted to take on permanently, but it did feel good to try it on occasionally. It felt good to be delicate with Max.

"You okay?"

I nodded again.

He reached out between us, capturing my hand and lacing his fingers with mine. Something thudded in my heart. There was something so innocent about holding hands after that kiss, and *fuck me*, I liked that, too.

"Rain check?" he whispered, that dimple flashing back at me.

I beamed back at him. "Absolutely."

10

Max

I took her to a gourmet burger restaurant off Kensington High Street. It wasn't fancy, but I figured it was nice enough for Fleur. And I hadn't been kidding earlier. Thanks to the shopping and working out, I was starving.

As we walked down the street, I grabbed her hand, linking her fingers with mine. She didn't pull away. And the entire time, our kiss ran through my mind on a never-ending loop.

We sat down and ordered.

"This place seems nice," she commented.

"I wasn't sure you'd like it." I didn't want to admit to how nervous I'd been that she wouldn't like it. I figured her dinners were spent at restaurants I couldn't afford.

"Why?"

"It's not fancy. Typically, high-maintenance means high-maintenance in all areas," I teased.

She shrugged in a classically French way that somehow managed to be both sexy and adorable. "I'm selectively high-maintenance."

I laughed. "Now that's *not* surprising."

Her eyes narrowed playfully. "Are you really going to give me a hard time after I spent all day helping you shop for a suit?"

"Maybe I'm not saying that being high-maintenance is always a bad thing," I countered. "At least the way you do it."

She gaped at me. "You must be joking. After everything, you're now telling me that you like my attitude?"

I had a feeling we were venturing into stronger territory than *liked*, but I figured I'd save that bombshell for another day.

I matched her shrug. At least I tried to.

"I can admit that I was wrong. You can be high-maintenance. But if that were all you were, then you wouldn't have helped me out today. And you did help me—a lot. Let's be honest. Without you, we both know I'd be interviewing in a suit that made me look like a used-car salesman compared to everyone else. So yeah. I owe you. And I was wrong."

She blinked, her brown eyes getting bigger, staring at me like she was just now seeing me for the first time, and I was some rare brand of species she'd never encountered. Maybe I was. I didn't come from her world, didn't screw around like the guys she knew.

"I messed up. I messed up with you. I was wrong about the Ice Queen thing. I was wrong about a lot. I'm not afraid to admit it."

I took a breath to steady myself as I put it all on the line.

"I make mistakes. Plenty. But if you were mine, I wouldn't be the kind of guy who would screw around on you."

She paled.

"I know you know it, but Costa was an asshole. You didn't deserve how he treated you. No one deserves something like that." I took a sip of my drink. "And there's no contest between you and that Natasha girl. Not even close. He's an asshole, and he's an idiot."

She didn't speak. She just stared at me, her eyes becoming impossibly wider with each word that left my lips. I'd somehow stunned her into silence.

After that kiss in the dressing room, I wasn't playing around. I figured she was a hell of a lot more experienced than I was, but she wanted me. And while making out in a dressing room wasn't the strongest foundation, it was something. I'd be a fool to not try to leverage that to more.

"What is this?" she asked, confusion filling her voice.

I didn't know what it was, but something in her uncertainty gave me the confidence to push on, despite the mad pounding in my chest and the white noise in my ears.

"I like you. A lot."

There, I'd said it. The ball was in her court now.

Her lips parted and then closed. And then opened again. Her lashes fluttered, and my heart clenched.

"Have you told George that we're hanging out? That we kissed?"

Of all the responses I'd expected, I hadn't anticipated George's name falling from her lips.

"Yeah, I did. I couldn't lie to him. We've been friends since freshman year, and he would have found out. I owed it to him to hear it from me."

She winced. "Was he upset?"

The concern in her voice surprised me again. Like everyone, I'd assumed she'd dumped George without a second thought. But the guilt in her eyes suggested something else entirely.

Once again, I revised my opinion of her. I seemed to be doing that a lot lately. At some point I probably just needed to start from scratch, considering everything I thought I knew seemed to be wrong.

"I don't think so. He needed a minute. I mean, it wasn't something he was expecting, but he was cool about it. I don't know that he's going to feel comfortable hanging around us, but I don't blame him. I think he understands." I read the expression on her face. "You're surprised by that."

"I am." She swallowed, her voice tight. "I hurt him."

I hesitated, asking myself if I was really going to go there. On one hand, I wanted to understand; on the other, I didn't know how much I could handle hearing. And George was my best friend. But somehow, I figured her explanation would explain more about her than her and George.

"What happened with you guys?"

She sighed. "Are we really going to do this? Talk about our pasts?"

My eyebrow rose. "I hate to break it to you, but my past is boring. I'm happy to tell you anything you want to know."

The look she gave me made her seem years older. "You know mine is more complicated than that."

I did know. I knew a bit, at least. I knew she'd dated Costa, possibly the biggest asshole I'd ever met. I knew he'd cheated on her and left her for Natasha. I knew Fleur had been so upset that she'd left school for a while freshman year. And even though I'd been in China at the time, I'd heard about her drug overdose at the end of sophomore year, only to be shocked to find out that the Fleur who came back junior year had a thing for George.

"What have you heard about me and George?" she asked.

"Not much. George and I didn't exactly talk about it."

It would have been a knife in my chest if I'd had to hear

about them. I would have listened because he was my friend, but it would have hurt like hell.

"He was upset?"

"Yeah. Like I said, we didn't talk about it, but as a guy who's into you, I can safely say he was upset."

Fleur sighed, and I was once again surprised by the remorse in her eyes and voice. There were layers to this girl, and I was beginning to realize I'd only scratched the surface.

"I never should have dated him."

"Why did you?"

She groaned. "Just so you know, I hate talking about this stuff. I especially hate talking about Costa. This is a one-time thing. I don't want to spend all our time together focused on the past."

That was fine with me. I had even less of a desire to talk about her and Costa than I did about her and George.

The waiter came to the table with our burgers, setting them both down on the place mats in front of us. When he left, I waited for Fleur to continue.

She stared down at her plate, no longer meeting my gaze. "The breakup with Costa was bad. I've put it behind me, and he's the last person I want to think of anymore."

I remembered the naked picture of Fleur that had made its way around the school last year, and because of that alone, I couldn't blame her.

"Okay."

She took a bite out of her burger, and her eyes closed, and I was distracted by the look of pleasure on her face. When she'd finished chewing, she continued talking.

"You weren't around sophomore year, but I'm sure you heard about my overdose." Her voice tightened, and the next thing

I knew, I'd reached out and taken hold of her free hand and laced her fingers with mine. I squeezed.

"Yeah."

"I was a mess last year. I knew I couldn't stay on the same path I'd been on. I needed to change my life. Get my shit together. George brought me flowers in the hospital. He was friends with Maggie, and he seemed like a nice guy."

"He is."

"And Maggie said he'd had a really big crush on me for a while."

He wasn't the only one.

"So I went for it. I wanted to like him. I really did. But from the beginning it just… Something was missing. We didn't spark. Do you know what I mean?"

Yeah, I did. I felt it every time I was with her. I nodded, afraid that if I spoke, I'd say too much.

"Maybe I should have said something sooner, let him off easy," she continued. "But the longer we were together, the worse I felt about the whole thing, and then finally it just seemed easier to pretend."

She looked down at her plate again.

"I knew he wanted things to go further with us, and I just couldn't. We had nothing in common. He didn't even really know me, and I'm pretty sure that if he had gotten to know me, he wouldn't have liked me anymore. He's just so nice, and I'm so…not," she finished as she looked up, her gaze locking on to mine.

"Nice guys don't like girls like me. At least they shouldn't."

I didn't know what it was about those words, but something clenched around my heart as soon as they left her mouth.

She was like a beautiful vase that had broken and been glued back together—technically she was whole, still stunning, but no matter where you looked, the cracks were impossible to miss. And even more, it was hard to ignore that they would always be there, always a part of her. And then I realized I hadn't been paying attention all along.

I'd been so wrong about her.

George had treated Fleur like she was untouchable, perfect. Like she'd been the girl we'd fantasized about since freshman year. Even when I'd given her a hard time, I'd always had this idea of her in my head. We'd thought she was immune to the insecurities the rest of us dealt with.

It was stupid, of course, but that was the thing with crushes.

They were more about you than the object of your affection.

The girl sitting across from me at the table wasn't the same girl who'd walked around the International School like she owned it. The confidence was still there, the arrogance as natural to her as breathing. But there were cracks, scars and chinks in her armor that had changed her. They were faint, but they were just as much a part of her as the glossy, shiny, magazine-like image.

They made her more interesting, and as much as it shouldn't have been possible, even more beautiful. She was real, and she was a survivor.

I'd never admired her before.

Now I did.

She wasn't the girl she had been, and whoever this girl was, I wanted to get to know her better.

I leaned back in my chair, studying her across the table. Away from the International School and everyone else, now that it was just the two of us, she seemed different. More down-to-earth, more normal. Like she'd stripped the armor away, and now I got to see the real Fleur.

She blew the fantasy out of the water.

"Let's try something," I suggested. "Let's try getting to know each other. I know what people say about you, what I thought and had wrong, but I don't really know you. Give me a chance to know you. Give me a chance for you to know me."

"What do you want to know?"

Anything. Everything.

I started off easy. "Where's home for you? Paris?"

"Basically. I haven't lived there full-time in years. I was at boarding school in Switzerland before I came to the International School."

"When did you go to boarding school?"

"When I was ten."

She'd been on her own for twelve years. It explained a lot. Compared to most people at the International School, there was something about Fleur that made her seem older. It wasn't just the fact that she'd clearly seen the world; it was the way she didn't really lean on anyone. She was close with Maggie, Mya and Samir, but there seemed to be a barrier that kept Fleur apart from her friends. She wasn't the type to ask for help or advice; she was fiercely independent.

"That's young."

She shrugged. "It was fine."

Normally, when people said they were *fine* it meant they were anything but. Fleur, on the other hand, really seemed over it.

"My parents weren't around a lot when I was younger, and my nannies pretty much hated me." A grin tugged at her mouth. "Justifiably so."

"You've always been a handful," I teased.

She laughed. "Pretty much." She took a sip of her drink, and then those brown eyes focused on me. "How about you?"

"I'm from Chicago. It's okay. I like to go back and visit my friends. I'm not super-close with my family."

"Why aren't you close to your family?"

Trust Fleur to be blunt.

"Let's just say we want very different things. They didn't understand why I wanted to leave Chicago or come to the International School." The old hurt was there, but she'd trusted me, so I did the same. "When I told my father I wanted to work in finance, he laughed and said I was dreaming."

Her eyes narrowed. "That's ridiculous. Everyone knows you're the smartest guy in our class. Of course you're going to get a job in finance."

The anger in her voice surprised me, and the fact that she defended me meant everything.

So many layers to this girl.

"So obviously your dad's a dick."

I laughed at the way she'd dispatched years of family drama with one word. She got to the heart of things.

"Now I get why you left Chicago. But why London?"

"I wanted something different," I admitted. "I had good grades and test scores, and I applied to a bunch of schools. The International School offered me an amazing scholarship package, and I liked their job stats for grads. For finance, London and New York are two major players. A degree from the International School will give me a foot in the door with a lot of banks here and will probably mean more than it would in New York." I just had to survive the interview gauntlet. "How about you?"

"I followed Samir here." Her eyes shuttered. "And my ex."

I waited for her to continue, feeling like I was getting a little more of her history.

"They used to be friends—Samir and Costa. All three of us used to be close."

I could see that. On the surface, Samir and Costa seemed similar—flashy watches, VIP tables and attitude.

"What happened?"

She shrugged again. "Samir didn't like the way Costa was treating me, and they had a big fight."

Samir rose a few notches in my estimation.

A bitter laugh escaped her lips. "He tried to tell me I should dump Costa, but I was stupid and proud, and I didn't listen."

Her face puckered like she'd swallowed something sour. "Do we have to do this thing where we unload our sad stories on each other? Mainly, my sad story. Can we just figure it out as we go along?"

I was pretty sure I'd say yes to anything she suggested. I wanted to get to know her better, wanted to know all of her, and the promise of her was there, dangling in front of me. I'd take it any way I could get it. Take her any way I could get her.

"I want to date you." The words flew out of my mouth before I could rein them in.

She blinked.

"I think we should take things slowly," I continued. "Get to know each other. No pressure."

It seemed optimistic to suggest taking things slowly when the second I touched her I seemed to lose my mind, but it also felt too important to rush things with her. Whatever she said about not wanting to talk about her past, it was obvious that it still weighed on her. I'd rather give her time to sort things out, time to decide what she felt about me, than take things too far too fast and ruin whatever real shot I had in the process.

I could do slow. It just might kill me first.

"We're going on *dates*?" She said the word like it was a foreign concept.

I grinned. "That's the plan. We can shake things up and

study together occasionally, too. Work on project finance. It'll be fun. Promise."

Her lips curved, her smile blinding. "Okay."

And just like that, I was dating Fleur Marceaux.

11

Fleur

I wasn't sure how it had happened. One minute I was helping Max buy a suit, the next minute we were dating. Okay, maybe I had *some* idea. The kiss in the dressing room had helped a lot. The way he'd talked to me at the restaurant afterward had helped more.

As unexpected as it was, the boy who'd once thought I was an ice queen had sat across from me and looked at me like he saw me in a way that no one else had. He was a force to be reckoned with in a completely different way than anyone I'd ever known before.

It had been a week since we'd started dating, and I was slowly figuring him out.

He wasn't cocky or aggressive, just determined. He left me with no doubt that he knew exactly what he wanted, and for some nearly inexplicable reason besides the obvious physical one, it appeared he wanted me. And something about Max told me that he wasn't the kind of guy to hook up with a girl just because she was hot. There was more there. I just didn't know what I had to give.

"What do you think I should get her?"

I turned my attention away from the eternal puzzle that was Max, and focused back on Samir. We were out shopping for Maggie's one-year-anniversary gift. It was cute, if not a little funny how nervous he was.

We'd gone to Selfridges today to make the trip work with Samir's class schedule. We'd been here for three hours now, taken a break for coffee, and Samir still hadn't come up with anything. I was beginning to understand how Max felt when I'd dragged him shopping.

"How about a purse?" I suggested for what felt like the tenth time. "Or a dress? I'm taller, but she's borrowed enough of my outfits for me to have an idea of what would fit her."

"It's not special enough," Samir replied.

I groaned. "For the love of God, pick something. Nothing has been special enough. Maggie's standards are not that difficult. You could get her a T-shirt and she would love it. I get that you want to buy her something nice, and it's sweet, really, but this is ridiculous. Gift or not, I'm bailing in an hour."

"I want it to be special," he grumbled.

I rolled my eyes. "I get that. You've told me like a dozen times. But I don't know what that means."

"That's the problem. Neither do I," he muttered through gritted teeth.

"What about jewelry?" I suggested, trying to get my impatience in check. I pulled out my phone for what felt like the hundredth time today and scanned my texts. Nothing from Max. Today was his big interview with the investment bank that was at the top of his list. If he did well, he would advance to another interview, and then hopefully another one after that, and then a job offer.

"Earth to Fleur." Samir waved his hand in front of my face.

"Sorry. Distracted."

Samir wrapped his arm around me, pulling me over to the jewelry section. "Yeah, I've noticed. What's up with your constant need to check your phone?"

Part of me wanted to tell him about Max. But he was also Samir, and he was overprotective as hell. Plus, he hadn't been wild about George, so I couldn't help but wonder if he'd think I was just making the same mistake again with Max. But I wasn't, and unlike with George, I knew I liked Max.

"I'm waiting for Max to text me and tell me how his job interview went."

Samir looked confused, like he was trying to place the name *Max* and figure out why it was coming out from my lips. And then he froze.

"Not again."

I shook my head. "It's different this time."

"How? Aren't they friends? Jesus, Fleur."

"Yeah, but that doesn't mean they're the same person." I laughed. "Maggie and I are best friends. Would you say we have the same personality?"

His lips quirked. "True." He sighed. "After everything with George, this is what you want?"

I nodded.

"And you're not just with him because he's a safe, boring guy?"

I almost felt an urge to laugh. Of all the words I would have used to describe Max, *boring* was a joke. Not after that kiss in the dressing room. Not after I'd gone home and lain in bed, unable to sleep, that kiss running over and over in my mind, my body craving his.

"He's not boring at all. He's kind of amazing, actually."

Samir's eyes narrowed. "Wasn't he the guy responsible for the whole Ice Queen nickname? I thought you hated him." His gaze was pointed. "I thought he hated you."

"Yes, and no and no." My lips curved. "We're taking things slow, casually dating." I hesitated. "I thought I'd bring him with me to your little anniversary party in a few weeks."

Samir had booked a dinner at Maggie's favorite Lebanese restaurant for the two of them and rented a table at Babel for all of us to celebrate after. It was all a surprise.

Samir shook his head, a smile playing at his mouth. "Maggie's going to love this. Especially since he's American."

I laughed. "Who would've thought we'd both start dating Americans?"

Samir grinned. "I did set the trend first. Clearly, you had to copy me."

I elbowed him. "You're such an ass. You're lucky she'll have you," I teased.

"I am," he answered, his voice completely serious. He walked over to one of the jewelry racks and bent over, looking at some necklaces in a glass display case. When his head lifted, he studied me.

"You really like this guy, don't you?"

It was a simple question, and yet it did funny things to my heart.

"Yes," I answered.

A ghost of a smile slid across his face. "Good."

We settled on a vintage-style flower pendant from Tiffany. It was elegant, beautiful and classic. She'd love the necklace, and I loved the look on Samir's face when he bought it for her. I gave it a year or two, tops, before they were engaged. I was picking out the ring, and when I told him so, he just shot me a knowing smile.

"Do you want to get dinner?" Samir asked as we walked out of Selfridges. "I'm in a sushi mood. We could go to Nobu."

I pulled my phone out again. Still nothing.

I shrugged. "I told you. I'm waiting to hear from Max."

"You can't do that while we eat? I'm starving."

"I thought he might want to celebrate after his interview."

Samir blinked. "You're totally gone over this guy."

I kind of was. Maybe I'd taken advantage of the cooler weather to change into leather pants that made my ass look amazing. And maybe I was wearing one of my favorite black tops, and a long black coat and my stiletto-heeled boots. Maybe I'd spent an hour on my hair and makeup on the off chance that Max would want to celebrate.

"Yes."

Samir shook his head. "I will never get it."

"We didn't get off to a great start. I'm not going to deny that. But he makes me smile, and he makes me laugh. And he's smart. We're partners in Project Finance, and we're working together. He listens when I talk and doesn't just blow off my ideas."

I didn't add the rest, like how when he kissed me I felt fireworks inside my body, spreading throughout my limbs, or how when he looked at me, I felt special. I didn't add that he made me feel alive, either.

I was still enough of the old me to be embarrassed by that, and Samir, despite his relationship with Maggie, was still enough of the old Samir to probably be freaked out by me saying it. I didn't. Instead I squeezed his hand and gave him what I hoped was my most reassuring smile.

"I know what I'm doing this time. Promise."

"Okay. But he should know, if he hurts you, I'm going to kick his ass."

I laughed. I loved Samir, but Max had to have like forty pounds and several inches on him. "I'll pass that message along," I teased.

He rolled his eyes. "Come on. Let's get out of here before you destroy my ego."

Max

I wasn't sure I could feel my limbs, and no matter what I did, I couldn't keep this stupid smile off my face. I'd made it to the next round.

I'd made it to the next *fucking* round.

I barely resisted the urge to jump, or scream, or do something to release the adrenaline pounding through my body.

I'd been so nervous walking into the interview, and then it was like something had clicked, and a sense of calm had settled over me. I didn't know if it was the suit, or Fleur's words rubbing off on me—*Of course you're going to get a job in finance*—but when I'd walked into that office, I'd believed it.

This was it. Everything I'd worked for. This job was the chance to pay back my student loans, but more than anything, it was my shot at a real future, my opportunity to not have to run back to Chicago as a failure, the chance to silence the doubts that had run through my head every time my parents looked at me like I was foolish for aiming so high. Sure, the competition would only get steeper as I advanced, but at least it was something—the foot in the door I so desperately needed.

I wanted to tell Fleur.

I pulled out my phone, still not used to the idea that I had *Fleur Marceaux's* number in my phone.

I was a nerdy guy from a nondescript suburb outside Chicago whose future ten years ago had seemed like my father's: a boring job I'd eventually grow to hate, a couple kids I'd barely know, a wife I'd know even less, a house and car whose payments would cause a monthly fight and a permanent tightness around my mouth and eyes.

Not anymore.

I lived in London. I'd just advanced to the next round in one of the most competitive investment banking programs in the world. And the hottest girl I'd ever seen, a girl who could make me laugh at the drop of a hat and made everything seem like an adventure, a girl I was completely and totally falling for, wanted me.

I wasn't sure how this had become my life, but all I could do was be thankful for the fact that it was. And pray I didn't do anything to fuck it up.

I found her number and sent off a quick text.

I made it to the next round!

She responded immediately, and my smile spread even wider as I read her message.

Yes! Congratulations! Celebrating?

I wanted to see her. I wanted to kiss her. I wanted everything.

Yes ☺ Leaving Canary Wharf now.

Her text came a minute later.

Meet me at Mist. Drinks on me for the big, hotshot banker. xxxx

I grinned.

Sounds like a plan. xxxx

I figured I'd let her buy me one drink. The money thing between us was a little awkward. Obviously, she had way more of it than I did, and we both knew it. I worked summers, and normally during the school year, although this semester the courses I needed for graduation pretty much made it impossible to do so. And I had my student-loan money, although I'd tried to limit what I took out to what I needed to pay for books, the balance of my tuition and room and board.

Fleur was champagne, and Ferraris and shoes that cost more than my parents' monthly mortgage payment. I didn't want her paying for me. Didn't want her to feel like I was someone she had to take care of. Maybe I couldn't afford big nights out like Costa had been able to, but dates were on me.

I took the Tube, transferring to the Piccadilly line at Green Park, trying to fight off the mad crush of rush-hour commuting. If I got this job, I'd be in London for the foreseeable future. Given the long hours I'd be working, I figured I'd let an apartment in Canary Wharf to be near work. A place that was nice but small, maybe find a roommate from the trainee program. I wanted something comfortable that would help me save money for the next few years so I could pay off my student loans, start saving up to buy a place of my own someday. Start saving up for the life I wanted.

And wasn't it just ironic, that after I'd been the one who'd said we should take things slow, that when I thought of my future, the first person who came to mind was Fleur. Coming home to her after a long day of work and talking about our days. Curling up beside her in bed and watching her sleep. I'd been fantasizing about Fleur for so long now, I wasn't surprised by how much I wanted her—I'd wanted her for years—but I was surprised by how the sexual fantasies had shifted to images of holding her hand, going out on dates with her, or just having her in my arms.

★ ★ ★

I got off the Tube at Hyde Park Corner and started walking toward the bar Fleur recommended. It was located inside of one of the nicest hotels nearby.

The hotel was impossible to miss. Its modern architecture stood out in this part of London that was still largely ruled by tradition. It jutted into the landscape proudly, the building lit up in the darkening night sky. I was more "casual pub" than "flashy bar," but dressed in the suit Fleur had picked out, it felt like the perfect place to be.

Mist wasn't big. The ceilings were low, the room all sharp angles. The bar was black with some metallic accents and flashy lights. Mellow house music played from the speakers. It couldn't have been more different from my favorite pub, with its peeling paint, the constant smell of cider and fish and chips, and the sound of people yelling at whatever football match was playing.

And then I saw her.

As usual, she was dressed to kill. Sexy black top. Black leather pants that were about to give me a heart attack. Black boots...

As usual, the first punch was sexual. I'd just come to accept that it was just Fleur. It was a part of her—a big part. The most noticeable part but not the best part. It would be easy to look at her and just see the sexiness.

And it would be the biggest mistake. Because for as hot as she was, the thing that was the most blinding wasn't her clothes, or her body, or her hair.

It was her smile.

She beamed at me. I'd never seen her smile like that for anyone.

She walked toward me, hips swaying, hair swishing. She looked like she had a wind machine going as she walked, maybe even her own soundtrack, and I still couldn't look away from that smile.

She didn't stop before she reached me; instead, she pressed her body against mine and wrapped her arms around my neck until our mouths fused together. Our tongues tangled, and I forgot everything but the feel of her and the shape of her lips.

Fuck *falling*. I'd fallen.

12

Fleur

Max Tucker shouldn't be allowed to wear a suit. It was overwhelming for women at large. Wasn't fair to other men who could never measure up, either.

I'd been wrong when I'd said Max didn't have swagger. So wrong. He had swagger, it was just his own brand of it, completely different from anything I'd ever known.

Mine.

There was something about him standing in front of me in that suit. He didn't seem to notice; his gaze had been searching for me, but when he'd walked through the bar, people had noticed him. Women had noticed him. And some possessive, jealous streak I hadn't even known I had pushed me to claim him.

He stood there like a warrior who had just come back from battle. Maybe his armor was an exquisite classic black suit and the white dress shirt I'd pushed aside as I'd kissed down his stomach in a cramped dressing room, and maybe his battle was a chance at one of the most prestigious jobs in finance, but there was still something primal that the sight of him evoked in me.

I was proud of him, and so happy, and three seconds away from wrapping my legs around his waist, and I didn't even care who saw.

I kissed him instead.

I kissed him as though my life depended on it, as though it was the last kiss we'd ever have, when really, this felt like the beginning of everything. I kissed him because I had to put this feeling bubbling up inside me somewhere. I gave it to him with my mouth, and my hands and my body.

Max took the gift and returned it in spades.

His hands played at my waist, gripping and stroking, one hand sliding under my shirt and fitting in the small of my back, yanking me even closer to him. It was not a public kiss. It was a private let's-fuck kiss, and right now the last thing I wanted was slow.

He broke away first, still holding my body to his. His head brushed against my hair, his lips teasing my ear. I shuddered and my nipples pebbled.

"One night I'm going to have you in my bed wearing nothing but those boots," he half-whispered, half-growled.

"Yes."

I wasn't sure if I breathed the word or spoke it. I wasn't sure of much besides his body hard against mine. I didn't think I'd ever wanted anyone as much as I wanted him.

Max groaned, reaching down and grabbing my hand, lacing our fingers together.

We stood there, staring at each other, and I knew he was as turned on as I was.

A smile slid over my face as I slowly regained my sanity. "Congratulations on the interview."

He laughed. "What interview?"

My smile widened so much my cheeks ached.

"Come on." I tugged on his hand. "Let me buy you a drink."

Max

We sat in a dark corner in the back, closed off from the rest of the bar with a small table in front of us. Fleur had insisted on ordering a bottle of champagne to celebrate. I hadn't argued because Fleur had also cuddled up next to me, her legs draped over mine, her ass pressed up to my side. I couldn't resist stroking her legs through her pants.

Maybe I had a leather fetish. More likely I had a Fleur fetish.

"Do you like the champagne?"

I took a sip. "It's good." She was better.

I leaned forward and pressed a light kiss on her lips. She sighed against my mouth.

"Thanks for celebrating with me."

She grinned. "I'm glad I could be here with you."

Something thudded in my chest. "Me, too."

I set the glass on the table, my free hand reaching out and capturing a lock of her hair. She stilled as I played with the ends, twisting it around my fingers.

It wasn't even intentional, but I found myself tugging on the strands, bringing her closer to me until her mouth was on mine again.

She tasted like the champagne—cool, crisp, expensive as hell. Her mouth opened against mine, her tongue stroking, her lips hungry. She moved so she was straddling me, her knees on either side of my body on the secluded padded booth, her fingers threading through my hair, pulling, bringing me closer to her. The scent of her perfume teased my nostrils; the taste of her swirled in my mouth as her body filled my hands. When my eyes finally flickered open, desire stared back at me.

I groaned. "I can see taking it slow is not going to be easy."

She tossed me a wicked grin, her body shifting against me, and I went hard as a rock. Her lips brushed against mine.

"I like you," I mumbled between the kisses she planted on my mouth—kisses that were more sweet than sexy, but just as tempting. "I don't want to fuck this up."

She pulled back slightly, her hands drifting down from my hair to stroke my face.

"I don't, either," she whispered, her eyes wide as if the confession surprised her. The intensity in her voice shocked the hell out of me.

"I just think we should get to know each other a little better first." Every part of my body screamed at me that I was being an idiot, that I had the girl I'd fantasized about for years in my fucking lap and I was letting her go.

But I'd rather have more with Fleur than a fling that burned out as quickly as it started.

She sighed, a pout flirting with her lips. "Fine."

I grinned. She sounded as happy about it as I felt. This was going to be interesting.

I coughed awkwardly. "You might want to sit next to me. It's kind of hard to go slow when you're straddling me." I knew she could feel how badly I wanted her.

She tossed me another naughty grin. This girl was going to give me a heart attack, no question, but at least it would be an amazing death.

She moved off my lap, and my body protested, my arms dying to reach out and haul her back on top of me. I took a sip of champagne instead and started counting in Mandarin in my head to distract myself.

Fleur shifted slightly, taking a sip of her drink and studying me over the rim of the glass. "Okay. What does taking it slow entail?"

I brushed a strand of hair away from her face, my eyes hungrily taking in her appearance. "No clue. Getting to know each other. Kissing. Bases."

She blinked. "Bases?"

She killed me. I grinned. "It's an American thing."

"I don't get it."

I wrapped my arm around her, tucking her into the curve of my body. One of my hands drifted to her bare shoulder, stroking the soft skin there. I watched, fascinated, as a line of goose bumps formed.

"Bases?" she repeated, her voice breathy.

"Well, there's first base." My fingers continued, moving downward, teasing the skin right above her elbow with circles and swirls. She bit down on her lip, and whatever hope I had of my erection going down flew out the window. Screw it. We could go slow and still have fun.

"What's first base?"

"Kissing." I grinned at her. "French kissing."

She shook her head. "I don't get why you Americans call it that."

"Maybe because the French do it best," I teased. "You're the only French girl I've ever kissed, but I can definitely get behind that explanation." My fingers trailed lower, shifting her arm slightly, gliding over the inside of her forearm, back and forth, my touch at times featherlight, at other times letting my fingernails skim her skin.

She shuddered against me.

"Then there's second base," I continued, my voice growing hoarse now. I'd never known any girl whose body was as responsive as Fleur's. She sat next to me throwing off heat, and need and want, and I knew without having to move, knew in my bones, that her nipples were tight and she was already wet. Just from the touch of my hand on her arm.

Fuck me.

"What's second base?"

I stifled a groan as I continued, every moment exquisite torture. The words tumbled out, shocking the hell out of me, as I gave voice to my fantasies.

"Touching, stroking, feeling, tasting." I leaned in closer to her, my mouth hot on her ear. "If we were at second base, I'd have you in my room, straddling me, your top off."

She shuddered again, her thigh pressing closer to mine.

"I'd strip off your bra, and I'd spend hours playing with your breasts. I'd use my mouth and my hands to try to make you come. I'd stroke your tits and play with your nipples— sucking, licking. I'd have you ride me, and I'd be so hard that even though there were clothes between us, I'd do everything I could to get you off."

She was so still, I wasn't sure if she'd stopped breathing. I was so hard it hurt. I'd never done this before. Never talked dirty to a girl. I mean, sure, *fuck, that feels good,* and *you're so wet* were normal parts of my repertoire, but this came from someplace darker and deeper than anything I'd ever experienced. We were fully clothed, in public, barely touching, and I was completely and utterly gone.

I pressed a kiss to her ear, letting my lips roam until they reached her lobe, partially hidden by the current of her hair. I sucked her soft skin into my mouth, my teeth gently grazing her flesh.

A moan escaped her lips, and she reached out, her hand shaky as she grabbed her glass of champagne, taking a sip as if to cover what was happening. If anyone came by our corner, they'd just think I was kissing her neck.

Only we knew I was fucking her with my words.

"Then there's third base," I whispered, blowing on the lobe that had just been in my mouth. She shivered, and I hugged her tighter against my body.

"*Mon dieu.*"

"Ask me what third base is," I prodded, the desire in her eyes pushing me further, and the French falling from her lips taking me over the edge.

"What's third base?" Her voice trembled, her accent heavier than normal.

"I'd unbutton those leather pants you're wearing, drag the zipper down, and peel them off your gorgeous legs," I replied, my voice raspy. "Then I'd have you strip in front of me, have you hook your fingers in the lace underwear I bet you're wearing, and watch while you take them off until you were bare. Then I'd have you lie back in bed, legs spread…"

My hand moved to her wrist, stroking the skin there, dragging my flesh against hers, feeling every tremor from her body. It fed my arousal like a drug.

"I don't know what I'd rather do first—taste you or feel you." My mouth moved down her ear, my tongue darting out and tracing a circle against the sensitive skin behind her earlobe.

"Max—"

Fuck me.

I half-groaned, half-laughed. "I'd want to hear you say my name just like that. I'd need to hear how badly you wanted me. And then I'd give you everything you wanted. I'd spend all night between your legs. I'd slip my fingers inside you, drown in your wetness. I'd lick you, kiss you, have the taste of you on my tongue. I'd make you come with my hands and my mouth, over and over again until you couldn't take it anymore."

Fleur turned toward me so I could see her face, and I lost my heart. Her eyes were fire, her skin flushed with arousal, her mouth parted as if begging for my lips on hers. She moved forward and put her mouth on mine. She didn't kiss me, she just settled there, our breath mingling, the taste of champagne surrounding both of us. Neither of us moved. It couldn't even be called a kiss, really. It was everything.

And in that moment I knew it didn't matter who had come before me, didn't matter that she was out of my league.

She was mine.

"Then there's home plate," I whispered into her mouth.

Her voice was soaked with need as if already anticipating my answer. "What's home plate?"

My hand drifted down from her wrist, stroking the inside of her palm. She pressed into me, her breasts rubbing my chest, her nipples hard through her thin top and what had to be a sheer bra. I'd dream of her tonight. I'd dream of this. My fingers moved forward, teasing the space between hers, playing with the flesh there until my hand slid home, and our palms connected, and our fingers laced as she held my heart in her hands.

"Heaven."

13

Fleur

Heaven.

The word filled my thoughts and my dreams. It had been a week since Max spoke that word to me, a week of being busy with school, hanging out with friends and seeing little of Max, yet being constantly aroused. The night at Mist was all I could think about. *He* was all I could think about.

We were still taking things slowly.

For me, sex fell into two categories: before and after. Before the baby, sex had been good, and fun and I'd liked it...a lot.

After the baby? Not so much. I didn't know how to explain it, and I'd tried when Costa had asked what had changed, why the girl who used to skip class to spend all day in bed had suddenly turned into someone who avoided sex.

The part of me that had heard my baby's heartbeat and fallen in love, only to lose it all, couldn't deal. Maybe I should have been stronger. Maybe I should have been better about putting it behind me. But I wasn't, and I couldn't.

I'd been terrified when I'd found out I was pregnant.

The first few days I'd been in shock. Absolutely stunned. I'd thought about my options, repeatedly, and then I'd finally gone for a walk in the Tuileries Garden to clear my head.

And there I'd seen an adorable little baby lying on a blanket with its mother. They both looked so happy together, laughing and gazing at each other like there was no one else in the world. Maybe it had been hormones, or some maternal instinct I'd never even known I had, but in that moment I'd known I was having the baby and that I would love it for the rest of my life. That maybe for the first time ever, I would have that connection with someone.

Then it all fell apart.

My body didn't feel like my body anymore. I mean, on the outside, yes, same legs, same arms, same boobs, same ass I'd always wished was just a bit bigger. But on the inside I felt like someone had gone in and carved everything out. When I'd lost the baby, I'd lost a part of myself, and no matter what I did or how hard I tried, I couldn't seem to get it back.

Sex didn't fix it. Drugs didn't fix it. Alcohol didn't fix it. Neither did shopping, or hanging with my friends, or traveling every time I felt restless. And as much as being with Max was one of the best things I'd ever felt, he didn't fix it, either.

But I wanted to get me back. I needed to. Needed to reclaim the parts of myself that I'd lost when I lost the baby.

The parts that I'd given up somewhere along the way.

"I need a bra," I announced.

Maggie and Mya turned away from the dress racks.

Mya frowned. "I thought we were dress shopping for Maggie's anniversary date with Samir. I have two hours before my next class, and at the rate we're going, we're never going to be done by then."

I waved my hand airily. "We'll have time. I need to pick out a bra. I need you to help."

"You need us to help pick out your bra? Are you having fit issues or something?" Maggie asked.

"No, I don't need a bra, I need a *bra*." I raised my voice and wiggled my eyebrows for emphasis.

Mya snorted. "Well, that clears it up."

Maggie grinned. "I don't understand the subtle distinction."

"I need a bra," I repeated, impatience filling me. "A to-die-for, Agent Provocateur, bring-men-to-their-knees, heart attack-inducing bra. I need a magic bra. I need *the* bra."

Maggie froze, putting the dress in her hand back on the rack and turning to face me. "Okay, share. Now. Why do you need to bring a man to his knees? And honestly, do you really think a bra like that is wise? You're already basically a walking nuclear weapon."

I grinned. "Aw, thanks. And I don't really want to bring a man to his knees. I was just trying to use that as a descriptor," I explained patiently. At least I was trying to be patient. "I need it for bases. Second base to be exact."

Maggie's jaw dropped, and she let out a startled shout of laughter. "Who the hell has been talking to you about bases?"

Mya looked at both of us like we'd lost our minds. "What are bases and what do they have to do with bras?"

"It's an American thing," Maggie and I answered at the same time. We both froze.

Maggie's eyes widened, and her face transformed into the biggest smile I'd ever seen.

"Well, I guess that answers the question of if Samir tells you everything I tell him," I muttered.

"Samir knows?" she screeched.

"Well, not about the bra part," I amended. "He's my cousin. Gross. But the rest of it, yeah, kind of."

"Will someone please tell me what's going on?" Mya interrupted.

"Fleur has the hots for Max," Maggie announced, her tone triumphant. "And judging by the conversation about bases that went on, I'm guessing he knows and is reciprocating."

"He does, and he is."

Mya frowned. "I thought you guys didn't like each other. Am I the only one who remembers all the fighting from last year?"

Maggie snickered. "I'm guessing that was foreplay."

I had to laugh at that one. I had a feeling foreplay with Max would kill me.

"How did this even happen?" Mya asked, still looking like she was trying to wrap her head around the impossible.

I shrugged. "We started working together in Project Finance. Then I went to the library and kissed him the night we all went to Babel to celebrate the first week of school."

Maggie gaped at me.

"So what else happened?" Mya asked.

"We've just been hanging out. Taking things slow. He said he wanted to date, so we are."

Maggie gave me a knowing look. "He's been into you forever."

I stilled. "What?"

"Max. He's liked you for a long time."

I blinked at her. *What?*

"Fleur. How did you not know that?"

"You heard Mya—I thought he hated me. I mean, yeah, I figured he thought I was hot, because…" My voice trailed off as I gestured at myself, and Mya snorted again. "But I think him *liking me* liking me, is a fairly recent development."

Maggie shook her head. "I never said anything to you because you were with George, and you gave Max so much shit, but he used to watch you when we would all go out. A lot. Samir noticed it first, but he pointed it out to me, and he was totally right. The guy is into you. Really into you."

How had I missed this? Had I ever really seen Max before? How had I not known?

"Are you sure?" I still couldn't wrap my head around the fact that Max—genius, Mandarin-speaking, amazing Max— had always been into me.

She nodded.

I might have died a bit. Twice.

"So how far have things gone with you guys?" Mya asked, her expression still slightly dazed, as if she was trying to work this out in her mind.

Maggie flashed me a wicked smile. "I think what she means is what base?"

"Ha ha. Funny. We've just kissed." I gave Maggie a pointed look. "First. Hoping for second."

Mya whistled. "Things are moving slowly, if you guys have just kissed. Is this like it was with George?"

There wasn't judgment in her voice, just cautious surprise. I didn't totally blame her. Maggie and I'd met after Costa and I had broken up, so she wasn't used to seeing me with a guy. But Mya and I had been at boarding school together in Switzerland before coming to the International School, and I knew she was mentally comparing Max and Costa.

It wasn't that Max didn't measure up. He far surpassed Costa. They were just so different, and at this point, with my track record, I could see how *different* worried my friends.

"I'm good. I'm happy. I can't keep my hands off him. Part of me wants to have sex with him now. Part of me is glad we're taking things slow." Part of me was terrified to have sex. Period. I sucked in air. "I haven't been with anyone besides Costa, and sex after I lost the baby…" My chest hurt. "It wasn't so great. I think I need some time to get my head on straight."

Maggie and Mya reached out, wrapping me in a hug.

"I'm fine," I protested. "I'm just telling you guys that I know what I'm doing, and as much as I love you, I have this."

They both nodded, and I pretended that there wasn't a suspicious moisture welling up in Maggie's eyes.

I grinned and squeezed her hand. "So… I need a bra."

It was everything I'd imagined and more.

We'd spent an hour at Agent Provocateur. They'd been having a sale, so Maggie bought lingerie for her anniversary, and I bought what we were all referring to as "the bra."

It was one of those things where the second I saw it, I knew. I could picture Max's expression when he saw me in it, could imagine him taking it off me.

I had to have it.

It was a pale color somewhere between pink and ivory, and the cup of it was so sheer it was basically see-through, my nipples clearly visible behind the fabric. It was edged in scalloped satin and lace, and the cup had pale little flowers and vines embroidered on the sheer netting.

It was a pretty bra, a wisp of a dream. And it was sexy as hell. Maggie and Mya had tried to steer me toward red and black, flashier bras I might have picked a year ago, but there was something about this one. It was so Max; it wasn't obviously sexy on the hanger, but when you put it on… *Whoa.*

It was perfect.

I stared at my reflection in the mirror, my heart feeling like it was beating out of my chest. I'd paired the bra with the matching thong and thrown on my favorite pair of white jeans. In contrast to the bra's mock innocence, I'd gone all out with my makeup and hair—big tumbling curls that screamed bedhead, and dark smoky eyes that smoldered. I kept my lips as natural-looking as possible with a light matte. I grabbed a pair of stiletto-heeled boots, remembering Max's reaction to the black ones, a Hermès belt and a white button-down top. My fingers shook as I put it on.

Max had mentioned that George was having dinner with his family for his grandmother's birthday and wouldn't be back until late tonight. Since we both had roommates, opportunities to be alone were few and far between, and I wasn't letting this one slip through my fingers. Ever since last week, since he'd said those words to me, he'd filled me with an ache I hadn't been able to ease.

It was time to hit second base.

Max

I opened the door and swallowed my tongue. Fleur stood in front of me dressed in white, but for a brown belt and brown knee-high boots, their heels higher and spikier than the ones she'd worn at Mist. Fuck-me boots. Her hair was a wild tumble of curls, her lips full, her eyes a mystery.

"Hi." Her accent curled around me and then slid inside.

I swallowed again. "Hi." I scrambled for words. "You look nice."

Amazing. Mind-blowing. I want to come inside you and never leave.

Her lips curved, and she flashed me an irresistible smile. "Are you going to let me in?"

"Yeah. Sorry." I moved away from the doorway, realizing I'd been standing there like an idiot. She walked over the threshold, her body brushing against mine, her hips against my hips, her breasts against my chest.

I was already hard. I shut the door behind us with a thud.

We were supposed to be working on our project, but the mischief in her eyes told me she had other plans. And she didn't have any books with her.

I bypassed the couch in the middle of the room and sank down on the closest surface, the edge of my bed, my knees suddenly feeling like they needed the extra support.

What was that perfume she was wearing? As if it wasn't enough that she looked and sounded like temptation, she had to smell incredible, too.

"What's up?" Even the words sounded strangled coming out of my mouth.

Her smile widened. "I wanted you to take me somewhere."

I was dressed in a T-shirt and jeans; she looked like she'd just stepped off the cover of a magazine. We weren't dressed for the same party.

"Where do you want to go?"

Fleur didn't answer but kept walking until she was right in front of me. Her hands moved to the front of her white shirt and she began unbuttoning it, starting at the top and working her way down. With each flick of her fingers, another inch of her skin was exposed—her slim neck, the curve of her breasts, her flat, tanned stomach. Finally, she reached the bottom and pulled the shirt off her shoulders until it fell to the floor behind her.

She stood in front of me in a bra that was heart-stopping. It was so sheer that it showed everything, the swell of her breasts, her nipples…

"Holy fuck," I whispered, my words somewhere between an exclamation and a plea.

She moved forward and straddled me.

I lost the ability to speak or string together a rational thought. I went off instinct when it was all I had. I wanted to go slowly. I wanted to be the best she'd ever had. I wanted this moment to last forever, wanted to devour her.

My brain was a series of short circuits I couldn't decipher, as once again, she got the jump on me. I hadn't been expecting this tonight. Sure, neither of us was a virgin, and there was the whole can't-keep-our-hands-off-each-other thing. But still.

Mind blown.

My hands moved to cup her ass, bringing her closer to me as if it was the most natural thing in the world. And then she leaned forward and whispered in my ear.

"Take me to second base."

14

Fleur

I was so turned on I was trembling.

Max's eyes widened at the sight of my bare skin, his Adam's apple bobbing. He looked at me like he couldn't really believe I was in his lap.

I wasn't exactly the nervous type, but this was Max, and everything was different with Max. There was nothing casual about this. It was intense, and desperate and all consuming. I wanted this to be good for him. Hell, I wanted it to be good for me, too.

He felt amazing between my legs, pressing against me as I straddled him on the bed. So hot with his hands molding to my shape, bringing my body closer as if he was never going to let me go.

I fused my mouth to his, giving myself over to the kiss. It was already different from all the other kisses we'd shared. He kissed me like he was lost and I was the key to his being found. He kissed me with a hunger and a desperation I'd never felt from anyone before. His tongue invaded my mouth, as if marking his territory.

We kissed for what felt like an hour, his hands holding me in place, all our attention focused on our mouths. I'd always missed kissing once I started having sex. Costa had stopped caring if we kissed and, instead, focused on the main event. But there was something about kissing, an intimacy that took Max and me out of ourselves and placed each of us in the other's body.

We kissed and kissed until I couldn't take it anymore. Until my hips were rocking against his, my body desperate for release. Until I rubbed my breasts against his chest, my nipples tight and aching for all the things he'd said he'd do to me.

I broke away, moving to unhook my bra, when his hands caught mine.

"Wait." He seemed to force the word out, his chest rising and falling rapidly, his skin flushed, lips puffy, hair mussed, eyes huge.

"I don't want to wait. I can't wait."

"Fleur." Max stilled, his forehead touching mine. We stayed like that for a minute or two as I slowly got my shit under control and his breathing calmed. And then he pulled back, his gaze on my face.

Disappointment flooded me. Was that it? I didn't come here expecting sex, wasn't ready for that, but come on, *second base*. I'd spent three hundred pounds on a bra. I know he didn't know that—and likely would think I was ridiculous if he did—but there were expectations that came with a three-hundred-pound bra.

I started to shift off him, but his hands came down on either side of my hips, holding me in place.

Still hard. Really hard. I swallowed a moan.

"Where are you going?" Max whispered, his eyes wide, his expression slightly dazed.

I shrugged—an art to pull off when you were half-dressed. "You stopped."

His lips curved into a lopsided grin. "I didn't stop for good.

I just needed a moment. I mean, the kissing is great and all, but you said you wanted to go to second base, and I aim to please."

I gaped at him. He grinned at me.

"Babe, I'm just getting started."

His hands, still on either side of my hips, pulled me up with him as he settled back against the headboard. He shifted me on top of his body. My stomach fluttered at the thought of his words—*I'm just getting started*.

His lips curved as his hand moved from my hips to my cleavage. He hovered there, still not touching me, until one finger reached out and grazed the underside of my breast through my bra. I sucked in a deep breath.

"Pretty," he whispered, that wicked smile that called to me on his face. His finger moved over my breast, back and forth, his touch maddeningly slow and light. I arched my back, pushing myself into his palm, not really caring about anything beyond the need to have his hands on me.

"I could play with you for hours like this," he murmured, his expression lazy, his gaze heavy lidded with desire. "Do you know how you look sitting on my lap like this? So damned pretty."

My eyes closed and my head rolled back, giving myself over to the sound of his voice and the touch of his hand. It felt like liquid gold flowed through every vein in my body. I felt heady and rich; I felt weightless.

I felt everything.

His other hand came up from my hip, and I felt his fingertip tracing the same pattern on my other breast, my eyes still closed. For minutes he played with me like that, giving me a preview of what I needed, of what it could be like, without giving me what I really wanted. It was a delicious tease. And then I felt it, the pressure of his palm against my breast.

He groaned. "Do you know how many times I've fantasized about you like this?"

He looks at you.

Maggie's words flew back to me now, and I wondered just how right she was.

How long had this been going on? And how could I have been so stupid to not see what was right in front of me all along? How could I have been with George and Costa, when I could have had this?

Max continued molding and shaping my breast with his palm, each brush against my skin filling me with heat. Finally, I felt the pressure of his fingertips rubbing my nipples through the sheer bra, rolling them between his fingers, pinching—

My eyes slammed open as the moan fled my lips, and my body rocked forward.

"You're killing me," I whispered, my mouth back on his.

His eyes darkened.

"And I haven't even gotten to play yet," I added.

I reached between us, gripping the hem of his shirt, pulling it up until he leaned back and helped me yank it over his shoulders, and he sat before me in all his shirtless glory.

"You get a few minutes to play, and then it's all about you," he warned with a teasing smile.

I rolled my eyes. "Bossy, aren't you?"

He laughed. "Normally, no, but babe, I think I have to be bossy to keep up with you."

"Ha ha," I responded dryly, ignoring the flutters that sprang up at him calling me *babe* again. It was so American, but also sexy and kind of sweet, and it shocked me that I liked it. A lot.

I leaned forward, my lips on his chest, using my hands and teeth and tongue to torment him as much as he'd tortured me.

He was a guy, so it wasn't the same, not by half, but by the way his body jerked beneath mine, he was massively turned on.

Added bonus? The view was spectacular.

For someone who spent most of his time in the library, Max took care of his body. Really good care of his body. His shoulders were broad, his chest a little on the bulky side, his muscles defined. His stomach was ridges and hard planes. The indentations on the sides of his hips were jaw-dropping. I lowered my fingers in the dips on either side, and he rocked against me.

"If you go any farther, you'll be trying to steal third."

I blinked at him. "What?"

He laughed, his hands coming up to thread through my hair and massage the back of my head.

"Come here," he whispered, bringing our mouths together. Our lips caressed, and then he pulled back again.

"My turn."

I wasn't sure how many of his turns I could take.

His hands left my hair and moved down my back, his fingers unhooking my bra strap in one swoop.

I arched my eyebrow in surprise and he burst out laughing.

"As much as it pains me to admit it, that was probably more dumb luck than actual skill. I promise there will be plenty of opportunities for you to bust my balls over my fumbling bra-removing skills."

God, he was adorable.

"Good to know," I replied with a smile.

He grinned back at me, and then I watched as the smile slid off his face and my bra hit the floor.

I didn't have big breasts; I wasn't built that way. But what I did have were firm breasts with a nice shape, and I liked them the way they were. The way Max looked at me made me *love* my breasts. Although, really, I was beginning to realize that with Max it was more about *me* than my body. I was falling so hard, so fast, and with my track record it was probably a dangerous combination.

"Hey." His hands found mine and linked our fingers together. "You okay? Where'd you go?"

I hadn't even realized my body had stiffened. He noticed *everything*.

"I'm fine."

"We can stop if you want." He gave me the sweetest smile that stole my breath. "Believe me. You've already fulfilled enough fantasies to last a lifetime. We should probably stop before I have a heart attack."

I shook my head with a smile. "I'm collecting on your promises."

"See? Bossy," he teased, leaning forward. "Your wish is my command."

The last word got lost somewhere between us as his lips closed over my nipple, and pleasure flooded me.

If his touch had been electric, his mouth was magic. Or maybe it was just that it was Max, and I liked everything he did to me. Whatever it was, my trip to second base had just become the hottest experience of my life.

An hour later, when my breasts were heavy from his mouth and hands, my skin flushed, my nipples tight, my body rocked against his until, finally, my orgasm slammed into me, and I ended my drought.

Max

"Mmm. That was nice," Fleur murmured into my arm, her voice sleepy.

We both lay in my bed on our backs, her body tucked against mine, my arm around her shoulders lazily stroking her side.

After the best time on second base I'd ever had, we put on clothes, ordered takeout Chinese and collapsed on my bed.

She'd changed into a pair of my boxers and one of my shirts, and the sight of her in my clothes had me hard again, even after I'd already come.

I couldn't remember the last time—my first time, maybe—that I'd gotten off from just over-the-clothes touching. If this was what second base was like with Fleur, home plate would be everything.

"I can think of a few other words to describe it."

Fleur giggled. "I can't let you get a big head."

"Babe, you were squirming on my lap, and you moaned…a lot. Let me enjoy the moment."

She hit me in the side playfully, kissing my bare chest. She seemed to like me without a shirt on, and I'd decided I pretty much lived to give this girl what she wanted, so I rocked my boxers and nothing else.

"I don't want to move." She groaned. "I'm sore. I work out five days a week. How am I sore?"

"It was hours," I teased. "Different muscle groups, maybe?"

"Maybe." She lifted up and looked at the alarm clock on my nightstand. "How much time do we have before George is back?"

"A couple hours."

She was quiet for a long time. "I wish you had your own room."

"Me, too."

"Max?"

"Mmm-hmm?"

"How slow is slow?"

"What?"

Fleur moved forward, laid her head on my chest and my heart skipped a beat. "We said we were going to take things slow. How slow is slow?"

I kissed the top of her head, my hand stroking her back,

holding her in place against me. I didn't know what answer to give her. The truth was I already wanted her in my bed, and I wasn't sure I ever wanted to give her up. I wanted to fall asleep beside her and wake up next to her in the morning.

"It probably just sped up a bit," I admitted. "Keeping my hands off you is going to be a big challenge."

She nodded, and tension seemed to fill her body, and then fall away. "Good."

We stayed there for minutes, her head on my chest, my arms around her.

"Max?"

"Yeah?"

"Samir's throwing Maggie a surprise anniversary party this weekend at Babel. They're celebrating one year of dating. I know clubs aren't really your thing, but would you want to go with me?" She hesitated. "As my date?" she added.

I was glad her head was on my chest because I wasn't sure I was ready for her to see the stupid grin that spread across my face.

"I'll be there."

I felt her lips part against my bare skin. "Okay. Thanks."

I waited for a beat. "What should I wear? I know there's a dress code for these things. I can go shopping or something—"

She lifted her head up and kissed me, her lips soft and sweet. She pulled back and stared into my eyes.

"I was an asshole to ever say anything to you about the shoes last year. It wasn't about you. You wear whatever you want. I like you. I don't care what anyone thinks. I'll have the hottest boyfriend there regardless of how you're dressed."

She kissed me again and then pulled back. I'd never seen that look in her eyes. It was fiercely possessive. It reminded me a bit of the way she'd looked at me at Mist right after my interview, and yet it was more.

I only heard parts of what she said, because most of it was drowned out by the one word that had come through loud and clear.

I was Fleur's boyfriend.

My heart skipped and stumbled before it fell headfirst in love.

15

Fleur

I hated the walk back to my room. If I'd had my way, I would have spent the night at Max's. But there was George to think of, and the lack of privacy that came with university. Maggie was lucky Samir had landed a single when he was in school here.

I walked down the hall, not caring that I was in Max's boxers and a T-shirt that advertised some basketball team in Chicago. It was late at night, and kind of quiet, but there were still a few students hanging around the dorms. I ignored the stares and the whispers. No one knew whose clothes I was wearing, but I figured the sports T-shirt screamed "American," and that in and of itself was shocking enough. I didn't care. I was too happy to care.

When was the last time I'd felt this way? When had I ever felt this way?

It was the difference between a fake bag and a real one. One looked good on the surface, from a distance. But the closer you got, the more you noticed the stitching was all wrong, the colors slightly off, some essential mark that should have been there missing. That had been Costa and me. We'd been the shiny couple that everyone had wanted to be, and yet it had never been real. And I'd never been happy. Not like this.

It made a huge difference when you weren't choking on drama.

I liked that I didn't have baggage with Max. He didn't press me about my past besides that one conversation at the burger restaurant, and for the first time in over two years, I felt like I could breathe.

And all the little holes that had been inside me now felt full.

I got to my dorm room and unlocked the door. I walked inside and stopped short as Maggie and Mya both saw me. Their jaws dropped.

"Is there a basketball on your T-shirt?" Maggie asked at the same time Mya blurted out, "Do you know you're wearing plaid boxers?"

I looked down at my outfit in mock surprise. "Ohmigod, I thought I was wearing a Versace dress. How'd this happen?"

Mya rolled her eyes. "At least we know her attitude's intact."

Maggie closed her mouth, opened it again and then her lips twitched. "I take it you went for home plate?"

What was with these bases? I mean the sex part I got, but the rest of it was just weird. Americans.

"I'll have you know that I stayed very firmly on second," I replied airily, sinking down on my bed and pulling my arms up around my knees. I could smell Max on his clothes, and now on my bed, and I decided right then and there that he wasn't getting his shirt or his boxers back.

Maggie laughed. "Um. I don't know what Max has been telling you, but just FYI, second does not usually involve changing clothes."

I felt myself reddening. "It's complicated."

"Did you just blush?" Maggie asked, her expression knowing.

"I hate you both," I announced.

"What did I do?" Mya interjected.

"You're giving me shit about this. We're not talking about it."

Maggie's eyes got as big as saucers. "I never thought I'd live to see the day when Fleur Marceaux was shy over a boy."

"I'm not shy."

"You blushed."

"Fuck off."

Maggie grinned. "Okay, but just one question."

I groaned. "I'm tired. It's late. I want to go to bed. What?"

"Do you like him or do you *like* him?"

Actually, I think I'm falling in love with him.

"Something more than the second one," I mumbled, burying my head in the pillow.

Silence greeted me.

Finally, it was Mya who spoke.

"More than…?"

I knew what she was asking, and it was the easiest question in the world to answer.

"More than anyone."

I woke up the next morning still in my second-base-orgasm haze, dressed in Max's clothes, a silly smile on my face. I'd dreamed about him last night, and while the reality was better than anything, the dream was pretty great.

I grabbed my bathroom stuff to head to the shower on our floor and stopped as I caught sight of a piece of paper taped to our door. I pulled it off, heart pounding. Was it from Max? There weren't words for how adorable that was.

I unfolded the paper and froze at the sight of the black ink. I read the words, once, twice, before I could process them.

I saw your walk of shame. Do you think he'd still fuck you if he
knew who you really are?

My heart clenched as fury poured through my veins. I crumpled the paper in my fist, wanting to make those words disappear, wanting to take the ugliness away from the best night
of my life.

Would Max still look at me like I was everything if he knew
it all? That I'd gotten pregnant, that I'd miscarried, that my
boyfriend had cheated on me and dumped me for someone
whom I'd thought was my friend two weeks after I'd miscarried, that I'd then been so stupid that I'd started hooking up
with Costa again while he was with Natasha, or that when he'd
treated me like shit, I'd taken so many pills that Maggie had to
call an ambulance and I'd nearly died.

Maybe.

But add that to the fact that Costa had shared naked photos
of me with someone and they'd ended up all over the school,
and the situation with George, and I was pretty much the worst
bet ever. Max knew pieces, but not the whole story. The pieces
were bad, but the whole story was so much worse.

Max looked at me like I was special. Like I was more.

When I was with him I wasn't the washed-up party girl,
or the girl who had no clue where her life was going. I didn't
want to lose that.

I couldn't lose it.

Maybe he'd understand, but we were still so new, so shiny,
and I didn't want to tarnish that with the drama that lived inside me. I didn't want him to wake up one day and realize that
I wasn't who he thought I was, that I was broken.

I wanted to hold on to him for as long as I could.

I threw the paper in the trash as if that alone would make
it all disappear.

★ ★ ★

"You look gorgeous." I ran the flat iron through Maggie's long brown hair again. "Seriously gorgeous. Samir is going to die when he sees you."

She grinned. "Thanks. And thanks for doing this. No one does hair like you do."

I smiled. "It's your anniversary. Big date with Samir. I had to make sure you looked your absolute best."

She was my best friend and someday in the not-too-distant future we'd officially be family. I couldn't imagine my life without her. How many times had we done this? Getting ready together in our room for a night out. Sometimes the pre-parties were more fun than going out.

"What do you have planned for tonight?" Maggie asked.

"Just hanging out with Max."

Samir's plan was to take Maggie to dinner and then surprise her with everyone at Babel. He'd ordered a cake for her and everything. It was cute how much thought he'd put into it. I never would have predicted that my cousin would be such a good boyfriend, but he really was. Probably because he loved her so much.

"How are things going with Max?"

"Good. Really good."

Maggie's tone softened. "This is it for you, isn't it?"

"I don't know," I answered, surprised I was even talking about it at all. "I like him. A lot. I could love him really, really easily."

"But?" Maggie prodded.

It had always been the easiest to talk to her. On the surface, we were both so different—she was quiet where I was not—but deep down, we carried similar baggage and recognized that in each other. Neither of us trusted easily, and we each had our walls. I'd watched her struggle with letting Samir in, so I knew on some level she understood. And at the same time—not entirely. Maggie was a mess because her parents had taught her not to trust people. I was a mess because of me.

"I'm a disaster. Is he going to be able to handle it?"

"You're not a disaster. And you won't know until you tell him."

"I don't know how. I don't want to." I fought back against the rising panic. "He's a good guy, and as far as I can tell, he's lived a normal life. I've been a soap opera."

"You made a few mistakes. Who hasn't? You're not the same person you were back then. You were trying to destroy yourself, and you've been picking up the pieces ever since. He's not going to judge you for your past."

"Isn't that what everyone does?" I asked bitterly.

"Isn't that what you're doing to him?" Maggie countered. "It's not fair to judge Max based on how everyone else has reacted. The people who love you are still standing here with you, and Max would be, too, if he knew it all. You didn't do anything wrong. Trust him."

I wanted to believe her, but I'd been burned one too many times.

"I'm not saying I'm never going to tell him. We're just starting out, just becoming a something. We haven't even had *sex*-sex yet."

Maggie made a face. "Do I want to know what the difference between sex and *sex*-sex is?"

I made a hand gesture that simulated penetration, and Maggie cracked up.

"Got it. Thanks for that." Her face scrunched up, and I could tell she was trying to work out the problem that was my fucked-up life. "You want to wait?"

"Yes."

"How long? When is it going to be the right time?"

That was the question I couldn't answer.

Frustration filled me. "I don't know. I can't put a number on it. When it's the right time, I'll know. Would you want to go on a few dates with a guy and then immediately lay every bad thing that ever happened to you at his feet? At what point did you start trusting Samir? And then consider the extent of my baggage versus yours. Then tell me you wouldn't do the same thing."

She nodded after a moment. "Fair enough. Just make sure no one outs your secret before you get a chance to talk to Max about it." Worry filled Maggie's brown eyes. "Have you gotten any more blackmail messages?"

I sighed. "Note on the door."

"Here? When?"

"The morning after I came back in Max's boxers and T-shirt." Which I'd slept in every night since.

"You should confront Natasha."

Costa's girlfriend was never going to take pity on me. There was no point. "Even if she is doing it, we don't know what she knows. So far I've received threats, but I have no actual proof of who they are from."

"What about the picture?"

"Maybe she found it at Costa's. Maybe he hasn't told her anything. I'm not going to let this rule my life."

Maggie frowned. "Aren't you, though? Are you taking things slow with Max because that's what you want or because you're scared?"

"If I'm scared it has nothing to do with my blackmailer and everything to do with the fact that I have horrible judgment at life. It was mainly Max's idea to go slow, but it just feels right. I need this to feel safe so I don't freak out and fuck it up. He's too important for that."

Maggie reached out and gave me a hug. "So are you."

Max

I heard the code being punched in on our door, and panic filled me. This was possibly the last thing I wanted George to see. Well, the second-to-last thing.

The door swung open, and he froze in the doorway, shock all over his face.

"Were we robbed?"

The floor was covered in every shirt, shoe, pair of pants I owned. Even the suit I'd bought with Fleur.

I grimaced. "Not exactly."

George walked the rest of the way into the room, shutting the door behind him with a soft click. "Okay, then why is all of your stuff on the floor?"

Because I was freaking out. The last and only time I'd gone out with Fleur and her crowd, I'd made the apparently unforgivable mistake of wearing actual workout tennis shoes to a club. How the hell was I supposed to know that was the one cardinal rule of London's party scene? Fleur had noticed, of course, and the whole thing was just another searing memory of how out of place I was in her world.

I wanted tonight to be different.

"I'm going out," I mumbled, not entirely sure I should even be discussing this with George. He'd dated Fleur, so he knew better than anyone what these evenings were like. He understood the challenge of keeping up with the girl who ruled London's social scene. Still...

George looked at me, a knowing smile covering his mouth. "With Fleur."

I nodded.

"And you're afraid you're going to make an ass of yourself."

"Pretty much."

He laughed. "Never thought I'd see the day."

Me, neither.

"Well, don't wear those trainers for a start."

I made a face. "Got that, thanks."

"Just wear jeans or something. I don't know."

I nodded again, like it was that simple. Like it was just a matter of throwing on jeans and taking my girlfriend out. But it was so much more.

Not having money had never been a huge deal for me. It was what it was. People like Fleur and Samir Khouri were so far out of my social circle it wasn't even funny. There wasn't anything I could do to change the fact that I would never, ever be able to keep up with them. There wasn't even a point in trying, but I was still a guy trying to impress a girl, and I hated that I couldn't give her everything she was used to. In a decade, maybe. If I got this job and built my career, I could give a girl like Fleur the life she expected. But now I didn't stand a chance. And I hated knowing I'd be sitting at Samir Khouri's table while his money paid for the champagne we drank.

I didn't have thousands of pounds to drop on one night out, didn't have a reputation that got me into London's most exclusive clubs. But I couldn't say no to Fleur. This was her world, these were people she loved, and I wanted her to have a great time. Even if it meant swallowing my pride and hanging out where I didn't belong.

Things between us were good. I knew she was into me; the chemistry between us spoke for itself. But how long would it be before she tired of my kisses, my body? At what point would the sex between us—or the promise of it, at least—start to wear off?

I'd suggested that we take things slowly because it seemed like she still carried a fair amount of baggage, like her reputation and all the things that had come before me wore on her.

But that wasn't the only reason. The other reason was that right now the promise of sex felt like the biggest chance I had of keeping her interested. I wasn't stupid. I knew she liked my body, knew she loved how good things were between us. But what would happen when we settled into a routine, when the new and exciting became familiar? Would the gulf between us then seem insurmountable?

Would she leave?

Fleur

Nerves and excitement jittered in my stomach as I knocked on Max's door.

This was the first night out with my friends as a couple, and I wanted everything to go perfectly. Maggie and Mya already liked him, and Michael wanted to do him, so I figured we were good there. Samir was the wild card.

I knew he wanted me to be happy. And that meant he could go either way—grudgingly accepting Max or going into over-protective mode. Since I was feeling more than a little protective of Max, that was what I feared the most. I wanted tonight to be drama-free so I just hoped everyone could get along. On the bright side, I figured Samir felt the same way, considering how wild he was about Maggie.

The door opened, and instead of Max, George stared back at me.

We'd seen each other since the breakup, of course. At a school like ours it was impossible to avoid it since the campus was small and the student body even smaller. But that still didn't mean I relished facing the boy whose heart I'd broken.

"Max is in the laundry room." A smile slipped on to his face as if he was trying not to laugh. "He's been getting ready for tonight for a while."

So awkward. I nodded, my throat still tight.

"I think he texted you."

I winced inwardly. Nice to know I could have avoided this. "I didn't check my phone. I was in a hurry and didn't want to be late for him."

George's eyes widened slightly—apparently, my tardiness was legendary—and then he stepped back. "You can wait for him here, if you want. He should be back soon."

I hesitated.

"I'm on my way out," he added, obviously aware that his presence was making me uncomfortable.

There was no graceful way to get out of this, so I followed him into the room, sinking down onto Max's bed.

Not only were they roommates, but George was also Max's best friend. And more than that, George was a good guy. He'd treated me well when we were together, and last year, when we'd broken up, I'd pretty much avoided him. I took a deep breath and decided it was time to do the right thing.

"I'm sorry about everything."

George grabbed his wallet off the dresser and turned to look at me. His face was an unreadable mask. "Everything?"

I nodded. "Everything that happened between us last year. I'm sorry it didn't work out. It wasn't anything about you. It was me." I realized how that sounded the second it left my mouth. I grimaced. God, I was bad at being nice to people.

George's lips curved again, as if he'd reached the same conclusion I had and thought it was hilarious.

"It's okay."

I shook my head. "It's not. I hurt you, and it's what I do, and I'm sorry. It's not okay. You deserved better." This just kept getting worse. "And I'm sorry to put you in this awkward position with me and Max. I don't want to hurt you again, and I don't want to make things uncomfortable between the two of you. He's a good guy and—"

"Fleur."

I stopped talking. George sat down on his bed, opposite Max's.

"We didn't work out. It happens. You didn't cheat on me, you didn't lie to me, you didn't do anything wrong. We didn't work together, and that's not on you, it's just the way it is. I knew from the beginning that I was more into you than you were into me."

I felt like such an asshole.

"And I didn't care," he continued. "I thought maybe you would come to feel that way for me in time, and I wanted to be there for you. But you didn't, and that's okay."

I didn't even know what to say.

"I'm sorry," I whispered.

He shook his head. "I'm fine. I'm dating a girl I met in my history class. She's sweet, and she seems to like me, and I'm happy. You're right, though, Max is my best friend, and the last thing I want is for things to be weird between us. Everything's good. Don't worry about it."

Like I said, George was a nice guy.

Relief flooded me. "Thank you."

He grinned. "No problem." He rose from the bed, but instead of leaving, he hovered there.

"He's happy with you."

I stilled.

"Really happy. Happier than I've ever seen him."

The words set off so many feelings inside me—terror, joy, the urge to vomit from some combination of the two. And underneath all of that, I heard the unspoken question and the point George was trying to make. He wanted to know I wasn't going to hurt his best friend, and I didn't know how to tell him that I was more afraid that Max would break *my* heart.

"He makes me really happy, too."

George's smile deepened. "Good."

16

Max

"Let's get out of here," Fleur whispered in my ear, her arms wrapped around my neck, her body swaying against mine. We'd been at Babel for a couple of hours, and thanks to her dancing and kissing, I'd been turned on practically the entire time.

I buried my face in her hair, drawing her tighter against my body.

"Are we supposed to leave the party early?" I asked.

Fleur pulled back slightly, pointing to where Maggie sat on Samir's lap making out. "We've been here long enough. Trust me. They won't even know we're gone."

My hand lowered, stroking the skin exposed by her open-backed dress.

"Besides, Maggie and Mya will be here for a while." She flashed me a wicked grin. "We could go back to my room and have some privacy."

"I think I've created a monster," I teased.

She trailed a fingertip down my chest, tracing a line down

the center of my stomach, her expression sultry. "Is that a bad thing?"

After a night of watching her dance, of slow kisses and holding her, it wasn't a bad thing at all. I was the luckiest guy in the world to have Fleur on my arm.

She wore black tonight—a tiny dress that highlighted every single one of her physical assets—and mile-high heels. Her hair was long and straight, her eyes shining, her lips painted red. She'd walked into Babel like she owned the place, like she was coming home. I supposed it was like home with as much time as she and Samir spent here.

It was interesting watching her with her friends. She'd danced with Maggie, laughing and joking around, the two of them in their own world at times. Maggie had always seemed a little quiet to me, but when she was around Fleur, she really relaxed. Fleur was still the ringleader, but Maggie seemed to enjoy letting her take the lead. Mya joined in, floating in and out of the group, content to go off and do her own thing. I liked them.

I wasn't sure about Samir.

He wasn't rude to me, but he was the least friendly. He gave me a head nod when we arrived and then, for the most part, ignored me for the rest of the night. Or at least he pretended to. I couldn't help but notice that every time his gaze settled on me he looked like he was wondering if I was going to run off with the family silver. And because I could tell he was special to Fleur, that their relationship was perhaps the most important one she had, I'd noticed.

I'd always thought he was a dick. Before Maggie, he'd had a reputation for being a player, but now it was easy to see he wasn't interested in anyone else. He looked at her like she was everything, like he never wanted to look anywhere else.

He was equally protective of Fleur, albeit in a different, big-brother sort of way. He checked on her throughout the night, making sure she had a drink, leaning down and whispering in her ear and making her laugh. And the few times he looked at me with an expression that said something other than that I was going to run off with something I shouldn't have, his eyes screamed, *Hurt her and I will fuck you up.*

Which would have been funny considering I had a few inches on him, and more than a few pounds, but then again, the guy was fierce. And Fleur loved him, so I tried.

"Come on," she whispered again, leaning up to press her mouth to mine. She gave me slow, drugging kisses, her lips seducing me.

I reached down, my hand grasping hers, twining our fingers together. I held her like that, one arm around her waist, pressing her against me, the other holding her hand. She was a little tipsy, and I could taste the champagne on her lips, something I would forever associate with her mouth. She continued kissing me, her body plastered against mine. My hand moved down from her waist to her lower back, and then lower still until I had her ass in my hand, just above the hem of her dress.

Maybe I was a little drunk, too.

"We have to actually stop kissing in order to go back to your room," I murmured in between mind-blowing kisses.

"Mmm-hmm."

She thrust her tongue into my mouth, and I couldn't resist the urge to suck on it, drawing her deeper inside. She moaned as I pulled her hips forward. She swayed into the curve of my body, dancing, the beat of the music throbbing around us.

I pulled back slightly, breaking the kiss, staring down into her gorgeous brown eyes.

"Your mouth is amazing."

She grinned. "Yours, too."

I loved how puffy her lips were, loved the flush covering her skin, loved seeing how turned on she was from my kiss. I remembered the look on her face when she'd come on my lap, the sounds she'd made, the feel of her body. It was all I'd been able to think about all week. I wanted it again, wanted her again.

"Let's get out of here."

We said our goodbyes quickly, her hand clutched in mine. I didn't miss Maggie's knowing look of glee or Samir's speculative one. Or the eyes on me—curious, envious—as I led Fleur through the crowded club, her body close to mine, her hand in my palm.

And while the attention would have made me uncomfortable at one time, I accepted it now as part of the ride and walked next to Fleur, pride running through my body, my head held high. I might not have come from money or been dressed in designer jeans, but I was with the girl everyone wanted. And she only wanted me.

Fleur

I wished I could have said I played it cool when we got back to my dorm room. That I hadn't spent the cab ride from Mayfair to Kensington making out with Max like a horny teenager. Or that I hadn't pretty much attacked him as soon as we stepped over the threshold of my room and closed the door behind us. But fuck it. He made me feel like a horny teenager, so yeah, I totally acted like one.

I threw my arms around his neck, locking my mouth on his. He met me move for move, his hands gripping my hips and lifting me up, wrapping my legs around his waist, walking me over to the bed until the mattress hit my back and he came down on top of me.

We kissed for an hour, teasing each other with our hands and lips and tongues. Most guys would have tried to move things further. He'd already had me straddling him with my top off, so I'd expected him to at least start there. But he didn't. Instead, we just made out. For an hour. And it was amazing. *He* was amazing.

Max rolled over onto his back, bringing me with him. I broke away from the kiss first, pulling back so I could see his face, look into his eyes.

He smiled up at me, reaching out and grabbing a strand of my hair and wrapping it around his fist. "So pretty," he whispered.

I grinned. His tone was sleepy, his gaze heavy. It was late. We'd left Babel around midnight and it was almost 2 a.m. now. I figured we had about an hour before Maggie and Mya would be back.

"I had a good time tonight." He released my hair and stroked my neck.

I arched into his touch. He'd learned what I liked, what made my body respond. And he was a very quick learner and more than a bit of an overachiever.

"Me, too." I reached down and laced my fingers with his. "Thanks for being my date."

His smile deepened, and his dimple popped out. "Anytime."

I leaned into him, tracing my tongue against his lips until they parted and he was kissing me back, openmouthed, his hand cradling my head, bringing me closer. He gripped my hair, pulling back slightly, his lips leaving mine to trail kisses down my neck while I shivered and trembled on his lap.

"I used to fantasize about your hair," he whispered in between kisses.

His tongue slid down to my collarbone, and I rocked forward, his hardness pressing against me, wondering just how much foreplay could be considered too much.

We hovered around the line between pleasure and pain. I wanted him so badly that the touch of his hands, his lips, his body, was the most amazing thing I'd ever felt; I needed him so much it hurt to not have him.

"I used to fantasize about touching you like this," he continued.

His free hand moved to cup my ass, holding me against his erection while his hips thrust against mine. But it was his words, not his body, that wound their way through me like a silken caress. I remembered everything Maggie had said, and suddenly I wanted to know when this started for him, how long he'd wanted me. I needed to know.

"When?"

"What?"

It took me a second to formulate a sentence. "When did you start fantasizing about me?"

He groaned, his mouth moving down to my cleavage, kissing the skin there. "Always."

I stilled, his mouth and hips momentarily forgotten. "What do you mean, *always*?"

He leaned back, his gaze on mine. His hand tightened on my hip.

"Always," he repeated, as if it was the most obvious answer in the world. "Since the first moment I saw you. Years. When I was in China." His gaze darkened. "When you were with my best friend. Always."

I couldn't speak. Couldn't do anything but stare at him in shock.

"The first time I saw you was in English Lit. It was the first day of classes, my very first class, and I was sitting in the front row. I was so nervous, first day of university and all that, and Lit was never one of my favorite subjects. The teacher was just about to start class, the room was so quiet you could have heard a pin drop and then the door opened."

I didn't remember it, not really. I was mainly impressed that I'd made it to class during the first week.

"You walked into the room and I swear my heart fucking stopped. You were wearing this dress…it was bright pink and short. You were so tan, and your hair was down, falling straight. You had on these pink shoes with a monster heel and a strap that tied around your ankle. Your eyes scanned the room, and I sat there, hoping you'd see me, hoping you'd smile at me. That you'd notice me. That this thing I felt inside me was something you felt, too.

"And then you saw Costa, and your eyes lit up and you smiled, and suddenly you were so beautiful it hurt, like someone had stabbed me in the chest. And that was it. I dreamed of you that night and so many nights after. And even when I didn't like you, even after all that stupid Ice Queen shit, I still got that feeling in my chest every time I heard your voice, or someone said your name, or I saw you. Every time."

It was like I was having an out-of-body experience. I heard the words, remembered the dress, remembered the shoes and yet it felt like his words, his emotion, must have been meant for someone else.

The thing about being beautiful was that everyone assumed men were constantly falling in love with beautiful girls. That being beautiful paved a way for you that somehow made life easier. It was such bullshit. Sometimes men yelled things out when I was walking down the street. Occasionally, they'd offer to buy me drinks at bars. But it didn't *mean* anything.

No one had ever wanted me the way he described wanting me. No one had ever made me feel special the way he made me feel special. Not my parents, not Costa. Just Max.

"I dated a girl while I was in China."

I felt an irrational stab of jealousy at that one. She'd probably been brilliant, and argued about politics with him or something.

"She was awesome, and I was really into her," he continued. "But I would still dream about you. I hated it. I hadn't even seen you in months, and yet you were there in my head, and I couldn't shake you out no matter how hard I tried."

There was a boulder in my chest now. All I could do was sit there, his body beneath mine, my heart in his hands, and listen as he bound me to him with each word that left his lips.

"I hated Costa. From the first moment I saw you smile at him, I hated him. I used to see the two of you together..." He grimaced. "He treated you like shit."

Oh, God.

"I know you loved him, but he did. I know all the girls thought he was hot and mysterious, but he was an asshole. He was never good enough for you. I used to sit there and wonder why you put up with it."

The boulder moved from my chest to my throat. It was too much. It was not enough. It was everything.

"I hated you with George. He was my best friend, and I knew he'd had a crush on you, too. I should have been happy for him. I wanted to be happy for him. But seeing you together was like a constant knife through my heart."

Disgust filled his eyes. "I used to wonder if you'd slept together. It used to consume me, wondering if he'd had his hands on you, if he'd been inside you."

Oh, my God.

"I hated myself. I had no right to care. He was your boyfriend... and my best friend." He shook his head. "And then one day he let it slip that you hadn't had sex and I could breathe again."

I couldn't breathe now.

"I'm sorry for the Ice Queen nickname. So sorry for all of it. It was easier to think the worst of you than it was to live with the fact that you were the thing I wanted most, and the one thing I couldn't have because you never even looked at me. Easier to tell myself that you weren't everything I thought you could be, and that I wasn't missing out on everything I'd dreamed of."

"What did you think I could be?" I asked, my voice sounding foreign to me, as if the words and the tone belonged to someone else. As if this moment was happening to someone else.

"Funny. You laughed a lot freshman year." His gaze held mine. "And then you stopped laughing. When I got back from China, your laugh had changed."

How many details had he collected over the past few years? How many things had he picked up on that others had missed? Was that why things were so good between us? Because he'd been paying attention all along?

"Maggie told me you were loyal. That you'd do anything for your friends. I didn't want to believe that, didn't want to believe you could be that. But I saw you with them—saw how much you loved her—and I understood you weren't what everyone said you were. What I thought you were.

"You're beautiful, and funny and loyal, and even though I know you think you aren't, you're smart. You get things other people don't. Maybe you don't care about math. Maybe you hate being in a classroom, but you're perceptive. Maggie told me what you did for her and Samir. How many people would hop a plane to play Cupid? How many people would succeed? You have amazing instincts. You're creative and artistic. You're walking art."

I felt myself blushing but still no words came. He'd done the impossible and made me speechless. This was the romance I'd always wanted. This was the fire and the passion.

"So yeah. It's always been you. Even when I thought I could never have you. Even when this was all just a dream."

My heart lurched, and suddenly the words tumbled from my chest.

"You have me. I'm yours."

His gaze darkened, and emotion vibrated between us, and then he captured my mouth with his, using his lips to prove my words.

I pulled back first, my mouth puffy and swollen, my head swimming, heart full.

"Be mine."

The second I said the words, it vaguely registered that I'd just broken every piece of advice I'd ever given anyone about dating and playing hard to get, and I didn't care.

For a moment he didn't answer me, and then the moment stretched into a minute. But I wasn't nervous. It took him a minute to say the words, but the emotion in his eyes, swirling around us, had answered for him before I'd even asked the question.

"I always was."

And then we were kissing again, until Maggie and Mya came home and found me fully clothed, making out with my boyfriend.

17

Max

A foot slid up my leg, moving past my knee. I struggled to concentrate on my Derivatives reading. The foot slid higher.

I groaned, tearing my attention away from the book in front of me. Fleur's foot moved up until it settled in my lap under the table.

"Stop distracting me."

She smiled sweetly. "I don't know what you're talking about." Her tongue swept across her bottom lip and Derivatives flew out the window.

"We're studying, remember?"

It was Friday night, and Fleur sat across from me in the library, books spread out around her. We'd finished going over stuff for our class project and were now catching up on work. I was prepping for my next round of interviews, and she was doing her reading for the week. She'd been into it for the first two hours, but by the foot currently caressing me, I could tell she was starting to get restless.

She made a face, her foot stilling. "How can I forget?"

I grinned, trying to fend off the aching arousal. "You need a break?"

"God, yes."

I gestured toward her books. "Which class are you reading for?"

"Marketing."

We had different majors; I was studying finance, and she was studying fashion marketing. We'd had a couple classes overlap last year and Project Finance this semester, but that was it.

"How's it going?"

She shrugged. "Okay, I guess. At least it's the least mathy out of my classes this semester."

I laughed. "Mathy?"

That teased a smile out of her. "Don't give me a hard time. English isn't my first language."

Her English was perfect and we both knew it.

"Have you given any more thought to interning next semester?" I asked her.

One of the benefits of the International School was its amazing internship program. They had international opportunities like the one I'd done sophomore year in China and London-based ones, as well. With how big the fashion industry was in London, there were a ton of possibilities for Fleur.

"My adviser thinks it's a good idea. We're meeting later this week to talk about it."

Her tone clued me in. "You don't think it's a good idea?"

She sighed. "I do. I know I have to do something after graduation. And I do like fashion."

I knew she wasn't wild about school, and yet it was still strange to see her like this. Insecurity didn't fit on Fleur.

"But?"

"I just don't think I have a chance. My résumé is basically

blank. I've never even made one. Never had a job. I'm so out of my element here."

"You've modeled."

"I don't know how impressive that's going to be. I had my picture taken and walked a runway. How is that going to look against people who interned at fashion houses and worked with designers?"

"It shows that you know the industry," I countered. "That plus your degree might be enough."

That same uneasy look filled her eyes as she bit her lower lip. "Maybe."

"I know you think you aren't ready, but trust me. You aren't the only one who feels that way. The nerves are normal. I still feel like I'm going to throw up every time I go into an interview. You just have to remember why you're doing this. You might have to work your way up, but once you do the internship, your résumé won't be blank anymore."

Her look was skeptical at best. "Do you really see this working out for me? I mean, does anything about me scream model employee? It's different with you. You've been working for this for a long time."

I waited a beat before answering because the look in her eyes told me just how important my answer was. The last thing I wanted to do was let her down. Enough people had already done that.

"If you'd asked me that question last year, I don't know what I would have told you. But now? You're not the girl you used to be. You didn't care before, and that made all the difference. Bottom line, you're smart and you have style. Fashion is your art. So yeah, I think you'll be great at this. But honestly, it doesn't really matter what I think. More than anything, you must believe it."

She shook her head, her eyes wide. "How did I end up

with you? You're a good guy, aren't you? I mean a really, really good guy."

I didn't know about that, but I did know I'd do anything to keep that look in her eyes. She seemed happy and settled, and as much as I hated that she'd never had that before, I couldn't help but be glad that I was able to give it to her. Maybe I couldn't shower her in diamonds or designer outfits, but at least I could make her feel safe.

"I like making you smile," I confessed. "I like seeing you happy. You light up the room when you're happy."

She leaned across the table, closing the distance between us, putting her mouth on mine. It was a quick kiss, and a sweet one, and I knew her well enough by now to know that while she didn't always say what she felt, she always showed it. This kiss was thanks for making her smile. I could have told her the smile was enough.

Fleur pulled back. "Will you help me with my résumé?"

I grinned. "Absolutely."

Fleur

I gnawed on my lower lip, waiting for the door to open. In three years at the International School, I'd visited my adviser once and that had been when I'd finally been unable to keep ignoring the letters from the university telling me it was time to declare my major. I'd had a few classes with her, but I wasn't one to make a positive impression in the classroom.

I clutched the paper in my hand, staring at the bits of black and the sea of white. Max and I had spent an hour last night working on my résumé, trying to figure out a way to take my pathetic lack of experience and make it seem like more.

The result wasn't going to get me an internship at Gucci, but I hoped it was enough to open doors for me somewhere.

The door opened, and my adviser, Professor Green, greeted me with a smile.

"It's nice to see you, Fleur. Come in."

I followed her into the small office, my attention momentarily diverted by her black peep-toe pumps. She had excellent taste in shoes for a professor, although I figured that came with the territory.

"Sit." She gestured toward the empty chair in front of her desk. "Nice dress."

Her gaze ran over me with professional scrutiny. In this, at least, I wasn't nervous. I might not know much, but I knew fashion.

"Thanks."

She leaned back in her chair, studying me over the rim of her eyeglasses. "So have you given more thought to doing an internship next semester?" she asked.

I nodded, willing the tremor in my hand to stop as I slid my résumé onto her desk.

"It's not much, but that's all of my educational and fashion experience."

I held my breath as her gaze skimmed over the flimsy piece of paper, and I said a little prayer that Max had done a good job spinning things.

I cleared my throat. "Do you think I might be able to find something next semester?" Nausea rolled around in my stomach. "I know my grades aren't great, but I was hoping I could find an internship that would be willing to overlook that."

She set my résumé on her desk, her gaze softening. "I think this is a wonderful start, Fleur. We'll enter it into our internship database so prospective companies can see if you match what they're looking for. I can also make a few phone calls. I'm friends with some designers who are up-and-coming talent. That would be an excellent way for you to get a start."

The kind of excitement that had previously been reserved for getting bumped up on the Birkin wait list filled me.

"That would be amazing. Thank you."

"My pleasure." She smiled. "I know school isn't always the most exciting thing in the world. And here in London?" She laughed. "Let's just say the professors aren't oblivious to the many distractions in a city like this. I've looked at your transcript, and I can tell that you've had a hard time finding something you're passionate about. But that doesn't mean that you should write yourself off. You have an eye for fashion and a sense of style that can't be taught. And I know I'm not supposed to be telling you this, but there's so much more to having a career than what we teach you in the classroom. An internship will give you valuable skills that will set you up for a career in fashion when you graduate.

"You can do this. And remember I'm always here to chat during office hours."

I was speechless. The professors had always intimidated me a bit. Okay, maybe a lot. They saw the work I did in class, gave me grades that barely squeaked by as passing. I figured if anyone knew I was an airhead, it was the teaching staff. And yet, here I was, sitting with the head of my department, planning an internship.

"I really appreciate you giving me a chance," I answered, wondering if she knew how much this meant to me, that she was one of the only people to really make me believe I had a shot at something other than looking pretty.

Besides Max.

Max

Fleur stood outside my classroom, grinning from ear to ear.

I wrapped my arms around her, kissing her forehead, the same excitement I always got at the sight of her filling me before I pulled back. "So how did it go?"

She beamed at me. "It went well. Really well. She had some internship suggestions, and she thought I had a shot at getting one of them."

Relief flooded me. "That's awesome."

Fleur nodded. "I still can't believe it."

I loved the excitement in her voice and the hope in her eyes. She'd been so nervous about this meeting, so sure that an internship was out of her reach. It was the best feeling to see her realize she could do more.

"We need to celebrate," I decided, taking a cue from her book. "Go out for drinks or dinner or something. Maybe get dressed up and make a night of it."

"That sounds like a great idea," she replied.

"Where do you want to go?"

"I've been dying to go to my favorite restaurant," she answered. "It's romantic and the food is incredible. You'd love it."

I could do that; anything to keep the smile on her face and to show her how special she was. There wasn't a lot of room for romance on a college student budget, but at least I could splurge occasionally.

"Sounds like a plan."

Fleur's smile deepened. "Okay. Don't get mad."

"Why would I get mad?"

"I sort of already made plans for us to go there. I figured you wouldn't care, and I wanted to take you to my favorite place." She looked hesitant, and I immediately wanted to make sure the smile returned. "We normally do a big trip for fall break, but Maggie has plans with Samir, and Mya talked about visiting her mom in Nigeria. I know you have interviews then, too, so I figured a fall-break trip is out. But I thought we could get away for a bit. Just a few hours. Nine hours to be exact."

I still didn't get it. "I thought you wanted to go to dinner? What dinner takes nine hours?" Was this some fancy new restaurant or something? I had no clue what the mega-rich found normal, although nine-hour meals seemed ridiculously excessive. But what the hell did I know?

"I want to go to Paris for dinner," she answered.

I was convinced I'd misheard her.

"Paris?"

"I got us really cheap, student Eurostar tickets, and it's a fast train ride," Fleur added. "We can spend a few hours in the city and then be back late tonight so you can still make your 8 a.m. class tomorrow morning."

"You want to go to Paris for dinner? As in France?" I figured if I said it enough it would sink in.

There was that smile again, the one that stole my heart. "It'll be an adventure. Are you in?"

So far I wasn't ever sure I was climbing out.

Apparently, I was going to dinner in Paris.

The whole night was surreal—the city, the food, the girl. Most of all, the girl. I'd been to Paris before, done the touristy stuff, the Eiffel Tower, the Louvre, Notre Dame. It was a great city, and I'd always enjoyed my time there. Seeing it with Fleur took things to a whole other level.

We sat huddled together at a little café, her body tucked against mine. Dinner had been amazing. Fleur had ordered in French for both of us, and there was something about listening to the words roll off her tongue—even if she was saying things like *fromage* and *poisson*—that sounded sexy as hell.

She was so different from anyone I'd ever known before. She made every day an adventure. Only Fleur would think of going to dinner in another country just for the hell of it. There was a passion to her that was irresistible, and as much as it was sometimes that same attitude that drove me wild, it might have been the thing I loved most about her.

She was a roller coaster, and it was the best ride I'd ever been on.

The dinner was amazing. I'd expected her to want to go somewhere fancy, but instead, she took me to a small restaurant in the Latin Quarter.

We sat at a table in the corner, getting drunk on wine and feasting on the different courses Fleur had ordered. I didn't recognize half the dishes, but they were all delicious.

I even tried the escargot at Fleur's urging, and as unappealing as the idea of eating snails was, it was surprisingly good.

We finished the meal off with a selection of cheeses and coffee.

"This was a great idea," I admitted, taking a sip of my drink, my free arm wrapped around her body, pulling her closer to me. Her hair tickled my face, the scent of her shampoo teasing my nostrils.

She grinned. "I've been homesick for good French food."

"Why don't you come home during the semester? It's an easy enough trip for the weekend."

She shrugged. "I'm not close to my parents. I love Paris, but sometimes I need the space. London's close enough without being too close."

"Do you think you'll come back to Paris for work?" I asked, trying to keep my voice casual. We'd never talked about her plans after graduation. I didn't know much about fashion, but even I knew Paris was a big deal. She could easily find a dream job here. As much as I hated the idea of her being far away, two hours wasn't terrible. Worst case, we could see each other on weekends. It would be hard for me to take vacation in the beginning, but we could work something out.

Fleur was silent for a moment, and I knew she heard the question behind my question.

Do we have a future?

"I love Paris," she repeated, her voice careful, as if each word she uttered mattered. "But I've lived in London for so long now that it feels like home, too. Samir's there, and Maggie and Mya. They're my family in a way that my parents never have been."

My heart raced, but I had to know. "And me?"

She shifted slightly so we faced each other, our lips nearly touching. There was a chill in the air around us, and I could feel the warmth from her cappuccino between us. I wanted her mouth on mine, but I wanted her answer more than I wanted her kiss.

She flushed slightly. "I like you. A lot."

I love you.

"I like you, too." I reached out, linking our fingers together. "This isn't casual for me. Or temporary."

She sucked in a deep breath. "Same."

"So we're doing this."

Her lips curved slightly. "We're doing this."

I wanted to tell her the rest. Wanted to tell her I'd fallen for her. But there was something about Fleur… We hadn't even had sex yet, and I still sensed that there were parts of herself she wasn't ready to give me, parts she wasn't ready to share. It wasn't just her body; it was like there were orange cones surrounding her, keeping the rest of the world at bay. On one hand, she'd let me in more than anyone else—except for Maggie and Samir, maybe—but I still wanted more. I tried to tell myself to be patient. She wasn't going anywhere, and neither was I.

"Do you want to walk around for a bit?" Fleur asked.

We had another hour left before we had to catch the Eurostar back to London.

We left the restaurant, our hands linked, heading toward the Seine. Fleur was bundled up in her coat, her nose and cheeks pink from the chill in the air.

"What do you think of Paris?" she asked, pride evident in her voice.

I grinned. "It's gorgeous. I've been before, but not gonna lie, it's different seeing Paris with you. I feel like I'm getting the complete French experience."

Her eyes twinkled. "Not quite." She moved into my arms effortlessly, raising her face up to meet my lips. We kissed by the river, strands of a saxophone playing somewhere in the background. She tasted like coffee, and adventure and a desire I didn't think I'd ever get enough of.

She pulled back, her lips rosy, mischief all over her face. "There. Now you've had the complete French experience."

I groaned, pulling her tighter against me, burying my face in her hair. I didn't think she realized how badly I wanted the complete Fleur experience.

I loved her. Completely.

18

Max

I stood in the hall, waiting to pick my girlfriend up from class. *My girlfriend.*

It had been almost two months since we'd started dating, and the feeling of being the luckiest guy in the world still hadn't worn off. I wasn't sure it ever would.

The more time we spent together, the more I liked her. She wasn't easy, not by a long shot. She had a temper the likes of which I'd never seen before. And she felt *everything*. For the most part, I was a pretty calm guy. Things pissed me off, other things made me happy, but my moods were usually pretty even. Fleur was something else entirely.

When she was happy, she was the most dazzling thing I'd ever seen; when she was upset about something, it was like a thunderstorm had rolled in and threatened to obliterate everything around it. She could be sweet and playful; she could be high-maintenance and difficult. I never knew exactly what I was going to get with her, and I'd found I didn't care. I took whatever came my way and had even learned how to handle her moods—if anyone could be said to handle Fleur. If she blew, it was a short explosion; she wasn't the type to hold grudges. And even when we did fight—usually about the project—she got over it quickly. And we got to make up. A lot. Which was awesome.

With George, she'd been a shell of herself. She'd rarely lost her temper. But she was completely different with me, and I loved that she was comfortable enough to be herself.

"Hey, Max."

A girl from my Multinational Corporations class walked over to me, a smile on her face, books in hand. We'd talked a few times; she was American, too, and her name started with a *J*—Jules, or Jamie, or Julia. Something like that.

"Hey."

"Are you ready for the final?" she asked.

Most of our classes came down to one grade for the whole semester—a final exam, or a massive paper, or project. It made it hard to know where you were in the class until everything was on the line, but it also meant that you didn't have to stress until the very end.

I nodded. "Yeah. I've been going through an old outline I got from a friend who took the course from our professor last year. And his lectures have been helpful."

I checked my watch. Another minute or so before Fleur was out of class. We were going to grab lunch in the cafeteria and then work on our project in the library. So far the app was going well, but I was still nervous. It wasn't just my future on the line; it was also hers.

"Maybe we can study together?" she suggested. "I'd really love it if you could explain some things to me. You always seem to know what's going on, and I'm a little lost."

"Yeah. Sure…" My voice trailed off as my gaze fell on Fleur a few feet away.

It was mid–November and the weather was already cold. She was dressed in a pair of white jeans, a black top, those same black boots from that night at Mist and a black vest. Her hair was up, her lips pink, and I loved her.

Fleur

I knew I was supposed to be one of those girls who didn't get jealous. I was supposed to be all, *It's fine if he hangs out with other girls. I trust him.* And yeah, that part was true. I did trust Max.

But I was possessive in a "Don't even think about stealing my man" sort of way. I hadn't missed the way the girl had asked him to help her study in that syrupy-sweet tone. Or played with her hair while she spoke, which everyone knew was the universal, international symbol for *Let's get it on.*

So I staked my claim and sent the message loud and clear that a) he had a girlfriend, b) he had a girlfriend who ate girls like her for breakfast and c) he had a girlfriend who was already giving him everything he needed to get. There wasn't anything left for her to give.

I walked up to Max, ignoring the girl completely. I wrapped my arms around his neck, pressing my body flush against his. It sent the message that we were intimately familiar with each other's bodies, and the second we connected, I knew he didn't see anything but me. My lips came next, and his mouth opened immediately to meet my kiss, his tongue brushing against mine, his hands tightening around my waist. It was a fast kiss but a deep one, a quick imprinting that was partially a claim-staking and partially me just missing him. I hadn't seen him all day.

I pulled back slowly, his hand on my ass, my body still wrapped around his.

I flashed him a wicked grin. "Hi, baby."

His eyes sparkled with humor. I wasn't the kind of girl who called a guy *baby*, and he knew it. He had also definitely picked up on the claim-staking, and by the way I felt him hardening against my hip, he liked it.

"Hi, gorgeous," he whispered.

I moved to the side, his arm firmly around my waist. I laid my head on his shoulder, and I smiled as I registered the look of surprise on the girl's face. And by surprise, I meant shock.

We hadn't advertised the fact that we were dating, and a lot of the student body didn't live on campus, so I guessed she hadn't seen us around together and didn't know.

Now she did.

Max broke the silent pissing contest. "This is my girlfriend, Fleur."

I felt a flutter at that. A big flutter.

She nodded, her lips tightening. "Hey, I'm Jules."

I granted her a nod and a bigger smile.

She looked uncomfortable, and then she mumbled something about having to go study and left.

Max turned to face me, pulling me against him again. Laughter filled his voice. "What was that?"

I shrugged. "I can kind of be a bitch."

He grinned.

"And I can be possessive." I was silent as it built inside me. "Especially with you."

I looked down, not sure I was ready to meet his gaze. Part of what had just happened was totally ego, but a bigger part of it was that I felt like I'd finally found a guy whom I wanted to be with. Who was good to me and gave me what I needed. I didn't want to lose him.

He was like a gorgeous Fendi bag at the bottom of a bin at a sample sale. Maybe you hadn't been looking for it, maybe you hadn't even wanted it, but the second you saw it and realized the deal you were getting, you had to have it. And you carried it around with you like your life depended on it, afraid to set it down for even a second because you worried that if you did, someone else would see it, realize its worth and snatch it away from you.

It was a miracle that he had been single when we'd hooked up. I wasn't taking any chances.

A better woman would have probably been all, *I just want him to find someone who makes him happy. I just want him to be happy.* And I did. More than anything I wanted him to be happy. But I wasn't altruistic. Not by a long shot. I wanted to be the one who made him happy. I wanted to be the one who made his face light up. Wanted to be the one he kissed. The one whose hand he held.

Jules could fail Multinational Corporations for all I cared. Seduction by studying was not happening on my watch.

His fingers lifted my chin, holding me in place while our gazes collided. The expression he sent me was a combination of desire and affection that had me melting.

"Do you know how hot that is?" Max whispered.

I moved forward an inch, feeling him against me. "I think I have some idea."

He groaned. "How hungry are you?"

God, he was amazing.

"I could skip lunch."

His eyes closed. "Good. George has class."

Yes.

"What about studying?" I teased as he grabbed my hand and started pulling me down the hall.

"Fuck studying."

Max

I fumbled with the door lock, the lust pounding in my brain making it tough to concentrate. I was so hard it hurt. It didn't help that Fleur had her arms wrapped around my waist, her breasts pressed against my back. Her hands moved down and stroked me through my jeans, and my hand slipped on the metal keypad.

We'd had weeks of foreplay now, and I basically existed in a state of agony. I was constantly turned on, constantly wanting, perpetually distracted. She was everywhere, and try as hard as I could, I couldn't see past her. She was everything.

I got it on the third try, opening the door and pulling her into the room as I slammed the door shut behind us.

Thank God George was in classes all day.

I turned, grabbing her arms and pulling them around my waist, putting my mouth on hers. I used my tongue to show her what I wanted to do with my body. My hips rocked against hers, my cock desperate to sink inside her warmth. We were hurtling toward sex each time our lips touched, and my body knew it. I was shocked we'd lasted this long.

Every time I kissed her she gave me another piece of herself. Each time I learned something new about her, something she didn't share with anyone else.

My touch gentled from demanding to soothing. On the surface this was sex—the potential for great sex—but this feeling inside me wasn't just about sex. It was everything.

And then need took over.

Our hands were a mad tangle in a desperate race to touch. She gripped the hem of my shirt, tugging it up my back, over my head. She groaned as we had to pull apart for it to come off, and then it was on the floor, and her mouth was back on mine, and her hands were everywhere.

She stroked my skin, kneaded my muscles. She broke away from my mouth and began pressing kisses along my collarbone, on my pecs, down lower, kissing the ridges of my stomach, her tongue tasting me there.

I groaned, my hands fisting in her hair. I pulled her vest off her shoulders. Then her top. I stepped back to take in her bra.

I'd learned that Fleur loved lingerie. I never saw her in the same thing twice, and every piece she had seemed designed to elevate my blood pressure and raise my heart rate. Today was no exception. Her bra was lacy and hot pink, and it pushed her cleavage together in a way that made me want to pay tribute to the lingerie gods.

I moved forward to unhook her bra, but she evaded my grasp as she sank to her knees in front of me.

My heart stopped.

Her hand at my belt, I watched, mesmerized as she unbuckled it, unbuttoning the top button of my jeans, the sight of her bright pink fingernails on my zipper mind-blowing. She unzipped my pants, and then her hands were on my hips, pulling my jeans down. All thoughts had fled, so I stood there in a stupor while she handled me. She moved lower, tugging off my boots and socks until I stood before her in just my boxers.

Fleur looked up at me, her eyes shining, a naughty smile on her lips. I heard the words *third base* leave her mouth, and then my boxers were gone and I was naked in front of her.

The energy swirling around us became something heavier, deeper.

And then she took me between her lips, sucking me deep, and my brain shut off.

She felt so good—warm and wet—and the sight of her on her

knees in front of me was hotter than anything ever. I stroked her hair while she sucked on me, while she ran her tongue along my cock, while she fisted me, her hand and wrist twisting, creating an amazing friction. There were moments when it felt like I'd drifted in and out of consciousness, moments when I almost feared my knees would buckle with pleasure. She held me in the palm of her hand, and there was no question I was hers.

She used her hands and her mouth, her movements getting faster, harder, as if she could time my orgasm better than I could. And when I came, when my release slammed into me, carrying my body away, she looked up at me, and our gazes locked, and I knew I'd dream of her for the rest of my life.

Fleur

We lay on our sides facing each other in bed. Max was naked. I'd taken off my clothes and only left on my bra and lace boy shorts. He'd hooked an arm around my waist, pulling me against his body. His expression was slightly dazed.

I'd never loved giving blow jobs. They were fine; they just weren't my favorite thing on the menu. Not anymore. There was something about the way Max had looked at me—the awe and desire on his face—that had just bumped them up an item or two. I liked them with Max. I liked everything with Max.

"You okay?" he whispered, burying his face in my hair as his fingers lazily stroked patterns on my stomach. Each touch sent a tremor through me.

I grinned. "Way better than okay."

He rolled over to his stomach, pressing a kiss onto my chest. "You're amazing."

"Because I give good blow jobs?" I teased.

"You give fucking amazing blow jobs," he corrected. "And no, that's not why."

I stretched my arms over my head, back arching, and tossed him a lazy grin. "Well then, don't let me stop you. Please tell me all the ways in which I'm amazing. Just so you know, examples are always welcome."

He laughed. "There it is. You always make me smile. And laugh. It doesn't matter what's going on in my day or how stressed I am, you always make me feel lighter. You bring smiles everywhere you go."

I cracked up at *that*. "I find that hard to believe. Just so you know, it hasn't escaped my notice that I have a bit of a temper, that I can be difficult."

He shrugged, and it was so adorable I had to kiss him.

"I like your moods," he mumbled against my mouth.

"No one likes my moods," I corrected.

"I do. Everything with you is exciting. You keep me on my toes, babe."

My expression turned serious as I gave voice to one of my biggest fears. "What if you get tired of exciting? What if you just want normal or boring? What if you decide you want easy and calm?" I paused. "I can't give you that. I can try, but I'll probably fail. It's not who I am, and if I've learned anything about myself, it's that I suck at faking it."

Max shook his head. "Don't you get it? I know that. I've had over three years to figure out who you are. And I was stupid for a while, only seeing parts of you, not all of you."

His gaze met mine.

"You make a guy work for it. You don't give all of yourself. You give pieces. And the pieces you give are the ones you think are the toughest to love. You test people. I'm not going to fail."

Mon dieu. He could read me like a book.

"I think you're scared. It's easy to love the beautiful, sexy girl who's every guy's fantasy. You think it's harder to love the real girl—the one who is still beautiful, and sexy and smart, but has a hot temper. The one who could kiss you or kill you depending on her mood. But you're wrong. It's just as easy to love that girl as it is to love the perfect girl. Maybe even easier. Because she's real. I want you, exactly as you come. I want the parts of you that you don't give to anyone else."

I bit back the emotion rising in my throat.

"No one's perfect, Fleur. We all have our flaws, our own shit we're dealing with. Whoever told you yours wasn't lovable was so wrong. I want you. Only you."

Max

She stared at me, eyes wide, lips parted. I was so in love with her. She was mine, and I'd meant what I said. I wanted all of her, even if I had to work for it.

I shifted in bed, moving lower, the need for her building inside me. I didn't hesitate. I just pulled her underwear off and tossed them on the floor, and she spread her legs instinctively as I settled my weight there, and then my mouth was on her.

I tasted her, my lips and tongue teasing until her body was trembling and her wetness surrounded me. I fucked her with my fingers, drowning in her warmth, in her tight, wet heat.

After she came, I wrapped her up in my arms and held her, tucking her against the curve of my body.

"Max?" she whispered, her voice sleepy.

"Yeah?"

She cuddled back against me, her ass brushing my cock.

"I can't wait for home."

I smiled so wide my face hurt as I remembered our earlier conversation about bases.

"Neither can I, babe."

I set my alarm for an hour before George would be back in the room, and then we fell asleep, our bodies spooning, and even though I'd just had her, I dreamed of the girl in my arms.

19

Fleur

A week passed, the London weather turned colder and things with Max kept getting better and better. We didn't have sex, not full-on anyway, but we continued with the world's best foreplay.

Despite the lack of sex, there was still a familiarity with us. I'd never been friends with a boyfriend before, never just enjoyed hanging out together. With Costa it had been physical from day one. With Max, the heat was there, but the slow burn gave us the chance to build a friendship at the same time. I discovered I liked spending time with him, even if it meant doing things I'd never imagined myself doing before.

Like celebrating American holidays.

"I need you to come to Paris with me this weekend," I told Maggie. "You and Samir," I amended. It would be better if there was a big group involved. Especially if Maggie was there to show me what I needed to do. "And I need you to explain to me about Thanksgiving."

Maggie gaped at me. "Thanksgiving?"

I nodded. "Max mentioned that it's Thanksgiving this week-end and that he's homesick for American things. I've decided to host Thanksgiving in Paris. My parents are in Argentina, so our flat will be empty. There are plenty of bedrooms for ev-eryone, and I figured we could make it a big group—you, me, Samir, Max, Michael, Mya and George. Maybe George's girl-friend, so he doesn't feel awkward. I went online and started looking at menu options, but I couldn't decide what to go with. I mean, turkey seems to be standard, but all the sides started to get confusing and—"

"You're cooking Thanksgiving dinner for seven people?"

"Kind of? We have a chef who can help, but I figured he wouldn't know traditional American recipes. I want to make sure we get it right. I figured you could help. Maybe Mya." Mya prob-ably knew as much about cooking as I did, but surely we could muddle our way through it. "We could go for a night or two."

She just kept staring at me with that look, like I'd finally lost it.

"What?"

Maggie shook her head, a soft smile playing at her lips. "Does Max know you love him?"

I froze. Considering I'd just started getting used to it myself, that was a huge negative.

"No."

Maggie gave me her most no-nonsense face. "But you know it, right?"

I nodded.

"Is this your way of telling him?"

I shook my head. "No, it's just Thanksgiving." I shrugged, trying to keep the embarrassment out of my voice. "He said he was homesick, and I wanted to do something to make him feel better."

"You really love him."

"I do."

Maggie sank down onto the bed across from mine. "Have you talked to him about everything?"

"No."

"Fleur."

I groaned. "Look, I don't want to do this. I know I have to tell him eventually. But right now we're just enjoying spending time together. It's only been a few months, and it's nice not having to deal with drama. I don't want to dump all my problems into his lap. Not yet. We haven't even had sex yet."

Maggie's eyes widened slightly. "What's the deal with that?"

I sighed. I'd been doing such a good job of avoiding this conversation, and now I wasn't sure if I was grateful to have someone to talk to or if I wished I could put it off longer.

"We both agreed to take things slow." I hesitated. "I think he wanted to make sure things weren't just physical between us. I think he was worried that if we jumped into bed together then we wouldn't get to know each other or give ourselves a chance at a real relationship. Especially since we started out in such a weird place."

"For the record, I love Max," Maggie added with a grin.

"Me, too," I whispered.

"Are you worried it's just physical?" Maggie asked. "'Cause I gotta tell you, the idea of you cooking Thanksgiving dinner for him makes it pretty clear to me that this isn't even kind of *just physical*."

I snorted. "Yeah, I figured that out somewhere between the first time we kissed and looking up recipes for green beans an hour ago."

"Green bean casserole. Definitely green bean casserole."

I grinned. "Well, that's one thing down. Are you guys in? I want this to be a surprise for Max. I want it to be special."

Maggie nodded. "We're in. You do know Samir's going to give you so much shit for this, right?"

I rolled my eyes. "Please. He's one to talk."

She laughed. "I'll make sure to tell him you said that." The smile changed, her eyes suddenly serious. "He's happy for you, you know. We all are. I think he was originally worried about Max. He didn't get it, but you're so much happier lately. It's good to see you smile. Good to know that he makes you smile. That's all we ever wanted for you."

"Me, too."

"Then listen to me. You had a front-row seat to my relationship with Samir. You saw how much time we wasted playing games, afraid to tell each other how we really felt. Don't chicken out with Max. He's not with you because you're hot, or because he cares about how much money you have, or what VIP list you're on."

All of them.

"He cares about you because he's a genuinely good guy. He's kind of shy."

I had to laugh at that one. "Trust me. Max definitely isn't shy."

Maggie shook her head, a small smile playing at her lips. "You don't get it, do you? Max *is* quiet. Max *is* shy. He's spent three years blending into the background. Max isn't shy *around you.* He trusts you in a way I've only ever seen him trust George. He lets you in, and he doesn't let a lot of people in. Don't fuck that up, Fleur. You need to trust him."

"I don't—"

"You do. You get it. You know how I know you get it? Because you're the same way. Maybe you don't hide in the background, maybe you're hiding on that pedestal you and everyone else put yourself on, but you're hiding just the same. You're brave when it doesn't matter. You don't let anyone put you in your place. But you're scared in a way that makes it impossible to let anyone in. If you don't get over that, you'll lose Max the way I almost lost Samir. And trust me… Nothing hurt as much as it did the morning Samir walked out of here and left me behind."

She was right. I couldn't imagine losing Max.

Max

I walked into Fleur's family's apartment in Paris and froze in shock.

Arms wrapped around my neck.

"Surprise," she whispered.

Maggie, Samir, Mya, Michael, George and Amy—George's new girlfriend—sat at an enormous table beneath a huge, glittering chandelier. The table was covered in expensive-looking dishes and glasses, and candles flickered against the setting Paris sun as it shone through the big windows lining the room's back wall. I blinked. A giant turkey sat in the middle of the table. Next to a bowl of mashed potatoes. And a bowl of cranberries. And…was that a green bean casserole?

I turned away from the food and stared down at Fleur. She beamed back at me.

"Happy Thanksgiving."

I blinked again, momentarily stunned and unable to process what was going on.

"You…you gave me Thanksgiving."

She nodded. "You said you were homesick. Maggie helped with the menu. I wanted it to be a surprise. Henri, our chef, helped me cook." She leaned in closer, her voice dropping to a whisper. "I'm not sure about the sweet potatoes, to be honest. I made them, and they seemed a little lumpy, but Maggie said that—"

I wrapped my arms around her, not caring about the fact that six pairs of eyes were staring at us. My mouth found hers, her lips immediately opening beneath mine, and then I was inside, desperate for more, needing it all. I kissed her with the smell of Thanksgiving around us, with the sound of laughter, and eventually clapping, and whistles and catcalls in our ears. Fleur pulled back first, her lips swollen, her eyes sparkling.

"Do you like your surprise?"

I shook my head, my voice hoarse. "Love. Love my surprise, babe."

Her eyes shone, and even though I hadn't imagined it could be possible, I fell more in love with her right then and there.

"Are we going to eat or what?" Michael called out.

Fleur answered back in French, something that had Samir and Mya laughing and me hardening against her.

An answering smile spread across her lips that she only directed at me. Her voice lowered slightly. "So the French thing works for you?"

I groaned, shifting so I blocked us from the rest of the group. I needed the moment to get my body under control. It was a little embarrassing to have a visible boner in front of your girlfriend's cousin and friends. Although, in all fairness, given the intense kiss I'd interrupted between Maggie and Samir last year when we'd gone bowling, I figured he'd understand.

"You have no idea how much the French thing works for me."

Fleur's gaze turned sly as she shifted her body against mine. "I think I have some idea."

"You're killing me. You know that, right?"

She laughed. "I have to keep you on your toes."

"Done."

★ ★ ★

It was, hands down, the best Thanksgiving of my life.

Fleur had been right about the sweet potatoes, but the rest was perfection. The girl at my side was even better.

I hadn't spent a lot of time around Fleur's friends, but it was surprisingly easy to slip into the rhythm of their interactions. They were a funny group, and as much as I had been prepared not to like him, I even found myself enjoying Samir's company. He wasn't the guy I'd seen hanging around with Costa freshman year, looking down on the rest of the student body like we weren't good enough to breathe the same air. I wasn't sure if it was Maggie or what, but the guy who sat across from me at the table wasn't a dick. Maybe not a ringing endorsement, but I didn't think we'd ever be best friends. He was still a bit much, but he wasn't the asshole I'd imagined he was.

And I couldn't believe Fleur had invited George and Amy. The fact that she cared enough to have my best friend and his girlfriend here despite the awkwardness that could have come up made me love her even more.

And surprisingly, there wasn't anything awkward about it.

George looked like he was genuinely having a good time, and Fleur definitely tried to make sure he was enjoying himself.

We'd been together for two months now, but I wasn't sure I'd ever felt as much like I was hers, like we were a couple, than I did at that moment.

I was building a future with Fleur.

After dinner the group broke up a bit. George and Amy weren't staying the night; they were heading back to London. Mya and Michael decided to go see a French movie I'd never heard of about some fashion designer I'd never heard of, either. Maggie and Samir went out for drinks with a friend of Samir's.

"Alone at last," I teased, sinking down next to Fleur on the couch in her parents' living room—probably a fancier thing than a *living room* considering how much crystal and gold was everywhere. I tried to ignore the paintings that looked like they should be in museums. I'd gotten to the point where I'd pretty much accepted that the wealth was just a part of her. I could have been dazzled by it, intimidated by it, could have used it as an excuse, or proof of yet another reason she was probably out of my reach.

I didn't.

I'd wanted her for forever. Now I had her. Nothing else mattered.

Fleur snuggled into the curve of my arm. *Luckiest guy in the world.*

Her gaze tipped up to meet mine. "Good day?"

"Best day ever," I answered with a smile.

20

Fleur

I wasn't sure if it was all the food I'd eaten, or the turkey, or the way he looked at me with those languid, naughty eyes, but an almost sleepy, post-orgasmic haze filled me.

I'd never been more aware of anyone than I was of Max sitting next to me, his large body dominating the small couch. He was close enough that I could just barely smell his cologne—an earthy scent that was so male, so *him*.

I leaned forward a bit and sniffed, inhaling his scent like a drug. I vaguely remembered reading something about pheromones and attraction in last month's *Cosmo*. Whatever it was, my pheromones wanted to jump his pheromones, like, yesterday.

Max's head whipped to the side, nearly colliding with my face. His lips quirked.

"You okay?"

I nodded, as though I hadn't just been trying to smell him. I was officially losing my mind.

"Did you just sniff me?"

"Of course not," I lied.

"You sure about that? Because it sort of seemed like you were trying to smell me."

"I was not trying to smell you."

He grinned, wrapping his arm around my shoulders, pulling me tighter. "It's okay if you were, babe. A little weird, but mostly cute."

I elbowed him in the side.

He laughed, holding me even closer. *God, he did smell amazing. Fuck it.*

"Okay, fine. What kind of cologne do you wear?"

"I don't. It's Old Spice."

"Never heard of it."

He smiled again, and I got the sense that he wasn't laughing at me as much as he thought I was cute. "I'm not surprised. They don't sell it at Harrods," he joked.

I rolled my eyes. "Are you always going to give me shit for being high-maintenance?"

His dimple popped out. "I'll let you in on a little secret. I like that you're high-maintenance." His tone was wry. "And as much as I definitely shouldn't admit this, part of me kind of gets off when you're high-maintenance." He leaned in, and his lips caressed my ear. "It's a little sexy, in a fiery, passionate sort of way," he teased.

I blinked. "Are you serious?"

"You in a temper is hot, babe."

My eyes narrowed playfully. "You didn't seem to think it was hot before."

"You weren't mine before."

I stilled—at least on the outside. On the inside a flutter started in my belly and spread through my body, a million flutters beating as one.

"Babe…"

His hands drifted to my waist, resting on my hips, holding me in place, anchoring my body with his.

I wanted him. But I wasn't ready.

I didn't want him to think I was leading him on or that I was trying to be confusing. I just wasn't at a point where I trusted myself. Not entirely. I was nervous and scared. Scared that all I was to a guy was sex. In the rational part of my head, I knew that wasn't true. I knew Max wasn't Costa and that he looked at me in a way Costa never had. But I'd been burned enough to question my own instincts.

"I need more time."

Max was quiet, and I waited for the argument, waited for him to try to convince me that I was wrong. Instead, he nodded.

"Okay."

I waited.

"Okay?"

He nodded. "Yeah. Okay."

Relief flooded me.

"Are you really this good of a guy?"

He laughed at the disbelief in my voice. "I don't know, Fleur. I'm a guy. I'm hard as a rock sitting next to you right now. I spent half of dinner thinking about how I wanted you for dessert."

I died.

"I spent the other half thinking about how amazing you are. What you did tonight? Not just the dinner and the surprise of it, but inviting George and Amy, making my best friend feel welcome despite the weirdness between you guys? That means so much more to me than whatever my body wants. I'll do anything to make this work. If that means we keep taking things slow, then okay." He grinned. "And to be honest, it's not that altruistic, because your slow is better than every other girl's supersonic."

The last word was swallowed between our mouths as I closed

the distance between us, kissing him until we were both breath-less with it.

"Do you want to do something totally cheesy and touristy?" I asked when the kiss ended.

"If it means I get to spend the evening with you, yes."

I stood up, holding my hand out. "Come on."

Max

Fleur took me to the river, our hands linked.

"What's the plan?"

She pointed toward a dock and a large boat. "We're going for a ride on a Bateaux Mouche."

"What?"

She repeated the words a little more slowly this time.

"We're going on a boat cruise of Paris." She flushed a bit, and I was momentarily surprised at the fact that she seemed embar-rassed. "It's touristy. They play 'La Vie en Rose' like twenty times, and it's always packed, but it's a cool view of the city."

I blinked. "You've been on it before?"

Somehow, this didn't fit with my view of the perpetually cool Fleur.

She turned a pretty shade of pink. "Yeah."

I waited for the rest of it. Waited for her to give me more of herself.

"Sometimes I need to think. It's the kind of place where you can disappear in the crowd. No one looks at you or cares. It's best at night. The city is beautiful, and there's something about being on the water, the wind in your hair. You can forget your-self for a while." She turned an even deeper shade of pink. "And it's totally a clichéd song, but I kind of like 'La Vie en Rose.'"

"Why?"

"The words." She fumbled for a bit, and I let her, because in a few minutes she'd painted another picture of herself, so different from the one I'd had. "It's romantic." She shook her head. "It's stupid."

"Stop. It's not stupid."

Her gaze lifted, met mine and held, and something vibrated between us. Her eyes gave me all the answers I needed.

She wanted—no, needed—romance.

It was surprising, and at the same time I felt like a complete idiot for not realizing it sooner. The thing about Fleur was that her persona was predicated on the idea that she didn't care what anyone thought. It made her seem like she had a hard shell. But I realized now how wrong I'd been.

There was a softness to her—one you had to crack through layers to get to. It was so deeply protected that it was easy to miss it. But wasn't that the point?

For all that she acted like things didn't matter, like she was all flash and no substance, she kept the most important parts of herself hidden away. She made you work for it in a way that had nothing to do with expensive presents or fancy dates.

She wanted romance, because what was romance, really, if not showing someone else that you cared?

She needed to know someone cared about her, and given the way Costa had treated her, and the relationship she'd described with her parents, I doubted she'd ever had that.

I wanted to give it to her more than anything.

Fleur

Somewhere between the Place de la Concorde and the Eiffel Tower, I knew I'd go to bed with Max tonight.

He held me the entire boat cruise. They played "La Vie en

Rose" so many times the words ran through my head on a never-ending loop, and still, each time I heard the music and Max squeezed me tighter, I felt like a champagne bottle had exploded inside me.

When he kissed me, I saw fireworks.

I pointed out the sights to him, loving the way he responded. As much as I no longer wanted to live in Paris, the city would always have a piece of me. It was like I was giving him parts of my past, and he loved every one of them.

It was magic.

At Les Invalides we asked a group of German tourists to take a picture of us with my cell phone. The image that stared back at me shocked me.

Max sat behind me, his arms wrapped around my waist, his head on my shoulder pressed against mine.

My lipstick had long since rubbed off from kissing. My hair was a tangled mess, my mouth puffy, my cheeks red from the wind and the cold and the man. My smile was blinding. I looked happier than I'd been in years. Happier than I'd ever been, maybe. And Max looked at the camera like he couldn't be prouder than he was at that moment with his arms around me.

And just like that, I couldn't hold it back anymore.

"I love you."

I wasn't going to say it first. But then I realized that Max told me he loved me every time he kissed me, every time he held me. With every smile, every look, every word.

So fuck it. I felt it, so I said it.

"I love you, too."

My eyes closed as I drowned in his words.

My eyes flickered open, and the look shining back at me was beyond anything I'd ever imagined.

"So much," he whispered, capturing my mouth. "It's always been you. Always."

We made out in front of a school group of German students until the boat stopped and people started getting off. Until I was close to getting off.

I grabbed his hand, pulling him toward me.

"Home?" I asked.

He grinned. "Home."

21

Fleur

I made it to the front door before I began stripping, my need for him overwhelming. It was late and the staff was likely sleeping, and even if not, I just didn't care anymore. I was too far gone.

My coat landed on the marble floor as I walked down the hall toward my bedroom, looking over my shoulder at Max behind me, staring at me like he wanted to eat me up in big, all-consuming bites.

My sweater joined my coat a few steps away from my door. The cold air hit my skin, sending a chill through me that had my nipples tightening. I reached back to unhook my bra when Max's body collided with mine, holding me against the door, surrounding me with his warmth.

He pressed my front into the cool wood, his chest rubbing against my back, his erection pressing into me from behind. His hands on either side of my hips, he pulled me toward him until I could feel every inch of his desire. His head came down, his face buried in my hair, his lips caressing me. We stayed still like that for a moment, the night silent around us.

Max lifted my hair, gathering it in his hand and pushing it forward, exposing the bare skin at my nape. He bent his head, his lips stroking down my neck. His fingers glided against my back, and then my bra came unhooked and slid off my arms.

His big hands covered my breasts, heating my skin, his palms brushing my nipples as he held my body to his. I fumbled for the door handle, my fingers slipping against the cool metal as Max teased me with his lips and tongue, tracing the path his mouth had taken. A tremor slid over my skin and crawled inside me.

I turned in his arms, grabbing the collar of his coat, pulling him toward me, over the threshold and into my bedroom. Without breaking away, Max kicked the door behind him with a thud. He cupped my bare breasts, his thumbs rubbing my nipples, sending sparks through me as he kissed his way down my chest, his mouth leaving a trail of goose bumps in its wake. I arched into him, craving his touch, needing him closer, wanting to take him into my body until he filled me completely.

His mouth closed over my breast, and my head rolled back as I gave myself over to pleasure. His tongue stroked me and I swear I saw stars. The warm, wet tug of his lips, the feel of his teeth grazing my flesh... Incredible.

We stumbled over to the bed, our bodies wrapped around each other. My hands dove under his shirt, stroking at the muscles there, at the skin I'd spent hours exploring. He groaned against my breast, the sound sending another tremor through me. Despite the cold outside, he was burning up, and suddenly I was, too, and I needed the rest of our clothes off.

Now.

I moved out of his grasp, another shiver ripping through me at the desire that darkened his eyes. I fumbled with the button of my pants, dragging the fabric down over my legs, working my boots off my feet. I sank down to the bed, on a mission to get undressed, and then suddenly I was bare before him except for my lacy blue thong.

Max stood in front of me, still wearing his shirt and jeans, staring down at me.

"Are you going to get naked?" I asked, my voice slightly breathless from the stripping, and the kissing and the way his mouth had felt on my breast.

He blinked, and then his lips curved, slowly, lazily.

"Yeah."

I tried to stifle the frustration. I figured it would look bad if I threw myself at him, but it had been a few months of foreplay, and a couple years of celibacy, and I was kind of dying here.

"Soon?"

Max grinned. "Yeah."

I waited.

"Tu me rends fou." The French came out before I even realized it, but in my defense, he *was* driving me wild.

He shook his head as if he were looking at something he couldn't believe.

"I've thought about this a lot. Dreamed about it." His voice set off another pull of lust. "I couldn't have imagined this. You blow every fantasy out of the water."

Tension slammed into me as each word gutted me. I'd made the mistake of assuming that after a while he'd stop looking at me like I was special. That eventually I'd just be another girl.

I'd been wrong.

"You're not supposed to get everything you ever wanted." His voice was thick now, and I wasn't sure if he was talking to me or thinking out loud.

Emotion filled his eyes and flooded my heart. "I love you, Fleur. So damn much."

He knelt in front of me, and my arms wrapped around his body as if they belonged there.

"Je t'aime," I whispered back, my eyes welling up with tears as the words spilled out in the language of my heart.

And then I got it.

This was what had been missing from sex. *This* was what I'd always wanted and never found. I'd had good sex; I'd had bad sex. I'd had orgasms and spent more time chasing them than I'd like to remember. But I'd never had this. I'd never seen love shining back at me, and I'd never felt it bursting through my body like a light that couldn't be contained. I'd been so empty and dark for so long, and with three words Max lit me up like a Christmas tree.

The air simmered with emotion, and then it swelled, cresting to a breaking point.

My mouth found his, my heart taking over when my mind ceased to function.

His clothes came off in a blur, and then his body—the body that I'd gotten to know almost as well as my own—was pressing me back against the mattress, covering me with his warmth.

He kissed me while we explored each other, while our hands traversed now well-traveled paths. He tore sighs from my lips and took them into his mouth as easily as he pulled my heart away from me.

Although it wasn't really taking when I gave it away as though he'd won this part of me—every other part, too.

Max peeled my thong off my hips, and then his fingers slipped inside, stroking, possessing. I was so wet, so ready, and yet the feel of his hands against me was enough to send me into a whole other state of need.

"I love touching you," he whispered against my mouth. "Nothing has ever been like this."

I couldn't. I tried. Tried to put words to the emotions raging inside me. And then just when they seemed out of reach, I realized I had all the words I needed. He'd given them to me.

"I love you."

I sobbed it, my voice full of want, and need and love.

I'd never understood why Maggie made such a big deal about being a virgin or waiting for the right guy. I didn't get the American puritanical view on sex. It felt good, and it was life and that had always been enough for me. But now I understood that while that was fine, and even hot at times, it wasn't everything.

This was everything.

It was scraping out a part of yourself—the barest, most intimate part—and handing it to someone else with an unspoken plea...

Please don't break my heart.

It was amazing and terrifying and still really hot. But this time my orgasm came with the knowledge that I'd given my heart to the one person I trusted to keep it safe.

Max rolled off me, grabbing his discarded jeans from the floor. He fumbled with his wallet, pulling out a foil packet.

His cheeks turned red. "I don't always carry a condom around ready to have sex at a moment's notice. It just seemed like it was a good idea to have with us. Just in case. Not that I was expecting—"

I couldn't have kept the smile off my lips if I tried. "Max?"

"Yeah?"

"Come here."

He moved so quickly, I barely registered it. One moment he was standing in front of me, condom in hand, the next he was there on the bed, hovering over me, in between my legs, yanking his boxers off his hips, ripping the foil packet open.

God, he was beautiful.

He rolled the condom on, and then he was naked against me, each touch of skin leaving a kiss of fire in its wake. He reached out, grabbing my hand, our fingers linking, and my heart clenched. And then he slid inside me in one smooth stroke, and my hips arched to meet him.

For a moment we were still, Max buried deep inside me, hard, and thick and big. It felt right and oh, so good. So much foreplay, and now we were here, and it was better than I'd ever imagined.

Our gazes locked.

"I love you," he vowed, his eyes fierce.

I shivered, my body clenching around him. A groan escaped his lips. And then he began moving, and I knew what he meant by *heaven* when we'd talked about bases.

It wasn't technique. He didn't have any wild moves, and the feel of his body sliding into mine wasn't the feel of a body that'd had one hundred women and knew exactly what it was doing. It was the feel of a man who only cared about pleasing one woman—me. And while it took a few moments for us to adjust to each other, to mimic the motions of each other's hips, to learn the rhythm of what worked, we did.

Max held my hand the whole time he thrust into me, his body filling me, stretching me. Sweat covered his skin, and I leaned forward, my mouth on his shoulder, needing to taste him. My teeth sank down into his flesh as his hips jerked, and he hit the right spot, and I felt the beginning of an orgasm coming on strong.

His hips kept moving, hitting that spot *every single time*, and my head rolled back, my hand squeezing his as my back arched, pressing my breasts into his chest, our bodies colliding until I came with a shudder, my body tensing and then falling into the delicious slide of oblivion.

When he came, buried deep inside me, he came with my hand in his, and his gaze locked with mine, love between us. And then his eyes closed, and his body collapsed and we came off the most incredible high I'd ever had, joined…

One.

Max

I couldn't stop touching her. Or looking at her. It was as if I was afraid that if I did anything to break the connection between us, she'd disappear. She felt more like a mirage than a flesh-and-blood girl, and yet her breath against my chest, her lips brushing against my skin, her head over my heart, told a different story.

"I love you." I'd never get tired of saying those three words to her.

"Love you, too," she answered, her voice sleepy, her hand trailing down my chest.

I'd just had her, and yet that lazy caress was enough to have my body waking up again.

"We were kind of amazing at that, weren't we?"

I bit back a laugh. Trust Fleur to be arrogant about how good we were at sex. Although in all fairness, she was right.

"Yeah, we were."

She kissed my pec, her tongue circling my nipple, and I began to wonder just how tired she really was.

"Did I ever tell you how much I love your muscles?" she murmured against my bare skin.

I grinned. "No."

"Well, I do." She lifted up on her elbows and pressed a swift kiss on my mouth. "I'd always thought boys who spent all their time in libraries would have scrawny bodies. I am so glad I was wrong."

I laughed. "I did. I wasn't big when I was younger. I spent all my time in the library or playing computer games, so the guys at school started giving me a hard time. I got sick of getting picked on and I started working out, tried out for some sports teams. Bulked up."

Anger flared in her brown eyes at the words *hard time* and my heart clenched. I loved how protective she was over the people she cared about. God, she was intense in the best possible way.

"Babe, it was a long time ago. It's okay now."

She sniffed. "I don't care. Assholes." She broke off in an angry burst of French before her face calmed slightly. "Well, look at you now. You're hot and smart and everything they'll never be."

"And I have you." Which made everything better.

"And you have me."

Fleur shifted, wrapping her long legs around my waist, her arms locked around my neck.

"When did you know?" she murmured.

My body was waking up.

"When did I know what?"

"When did you know you loved me?"

I thought about it for a minute, trying to remember when this feeling had begun. She'd been such a part of me for so long, I wasn't even sure.

"I think I've been falling in love with pieces of you since the first moment I saw you."

I knew how it sounded, and I struggled to string the words together to make her understand how I felt. She was like a puzzle, and I'd loved each piece as it came to me, even if I hadn't been able to see the whole picture or understand it. But with

each one, I'd gotten a clearer sense of who she was, and I'd
fallen more as each part slid into place.

"I fell for each piece you gave me. In the beginning, it was
just a crush, but you stole my heart as soon as you walked into
that classroom freshman year. You were the most beautiful thing
I'd ever seen. I didn't know you then, but I loved the idea of
you first."

Her gaze clouded slightly. "I'm not the girl you thought I was."

"No, you're not. I fell in love with the image first, but that's
only part of you, and that changed as soon as I got to know
you. I fell in love with your attitude. The first time you kissed
me, I loved your passion.

"I fell in love with the girl who cared enough to make sure I
had a nice suit for my job interviews, the girl who played Cupid
for Maggie and Samir, who cooked Thanksgiving dinner for me
because I was homesick, the girl who likes to go on boat rides
to clear her mind. The girl who apologized to my best friend
because she didn't want either of us to get hurt. The girl whose
mind fascinates me because it works so differently from mine,
who makes every day an adventure. I've been falling in love
with you all along."

She didn't speak. I tipped her chin up, studying her face.
Tears shimmered in her eyes.

"Don't cry," I whispered, kissing her cheek. A tear fell, trick-
ling down until it hit my lips on her skin. My tongue darted
out, licking the moisture, taking that part of her inside me.

I held her tight, showering her face with kisses until our
mouths found each other, and her lips devoured mine.

"I don't know what I did to deserve you," Fleur whispered
between kisses as another tear fell. "And I'm afraid I'm going
to lose you. Afraid you're going to meet some girl who reads
comic books and has, like, a genius IQ or something."

I laughed. I didn't know how she could ever think she was in danger of me falling out of love with her.

"I'm not going anywhere. Are you going to leave me for some tool who wears designer shoes and spends twenty minutes doing his hair?"

She grinned. "No."

"Good. I feel the same way. Whatever I had in the past doesn't compare to what I have now. Doesn't compare to you."

Fleur shifted on my lap, kissing her way down my chest. I played with a handful of her hair, reveling in the feel of silk in my hand. She grabbed a condom and rolled it on me, adjusting until her body was positioned just over mine, and then she sank down until I was buried to the hilt, filling her, surrounded by her warmth.

Her hips began to rock, her body moving in a slow rhythm that had me unable to do anything but watch her, following her lead as she rode me. Her brown hair spilled over her shoulders in a tumble of thick curls, her back arching, her tits thrust forward. I reached out, capturing her hand, locking our fingers together as her hips rocked faster and faster, taking me over the edge until we both exploded and her body collapsed on top of mine, our hearts beating against each other.

22

Fleur

November blurred into December, and the end of the semester neared and things with Max continued better than ever. I kept waiting for something to happen, for the novelty of each other to wear off, and yet, surprisingly, it didn't. Things were perfect. For the first time I was in a healthy relationship that felt right. Max was solid and he was always there—steady and reliable. It was everything I never knew I needed.

When we'd come back from Paris there'd been no doubt in anyone's mind that we were together. We were pretty much inseparable, studying together and spending most of our free time hanging out. I still saw Maggie and Mya, but it was different now. They were still my best friends, but our lives were changing, going in different directions.

Maggie was moving in with Samir next semester, and it would just be Mya and me in the dorms. As much as I'd miss having Maggie around, I was happy for her. I got it now. In our own ways we were each preparing for graduation and going out on our own.

I'd loved the camaraderie of college—pregaming in our rooms and doing each other's hair and makeup. As an only child, I'd never gotten to experience having siblings, and Maggie and Mya felt like sisters. We'd been through so much together, good and bad. Much of it had felt like one big party, and there was a part of me that wished it would never stop, a part that was still scared of the changes that would come.

But it was time. I was starting to look forward to life after graduation.

Today was the biggest day, though—Max's final job interview. I wasn't sure who was more nervous, him or me.

If he made it past this round, they'd offer him a position in their investment banking training program after graduation. He'd spent most of the week studying in the library, preparing for any questions they might throw his way. I wanted this for him because it was important to him, but selfishly, I also wanted it for myself.

If he got a job in London after graduation, we could stay together easily. Being French, I had the luxury of an EU passport and could stay in the UK. If he went back to the United States, things would be way more complicated. I'd seen how tough it was for Maggie and Samir to sort out their living situation, and while I didn't have a political dynasty waiting for me, I couldn't imagine myself living in America.

London was the perfect compromise.

I was still waiting to hear if I'd gotten an interview for an internship next semester, but if I did, maybe I'd have a chance of finding something more permanent.

I had a future to plan for now.

I dressed quickly, throwing on jeans, an Armani sweater and Max's favorite pair of boots. We were meeting for a good-luck breakfast before he headed to his interview. I put on mini-

mal makeup and pulled my hair back in a ponytail. I snagged
a leather jacket from my armoire, closing the door behind me
with a thud.

Max was always punctual and I was perpetually late, so I'd
been working on doing a better job of trying to make it places
on time. Or beat him there. Strangely enough, it was helping
in other areas of my life, especially with class. I rarely skipped
anymore—Max *might* have worked out an incentive system—
and I'd become a regular fixture keeping him company in the
library. Sometimes I brought the latest issue of *Vogue* instead
of a textbook, but I figured getting there was half the battle.

Finals were just a week away, our project nearly due, the
moment of reckoning upon us. For the first time in my entire
academic career, I felt confident going into exams, and our
project kind of kicked ass.

I hit the staircase, the day full of possibility, heading toward
the cafeteria, and stopped dead, the blood draining from my
body.

Pictures of me lined the walls. One picture, over and over
again. It was one of the ones Costa had taken on his phone—
easily recognizable by the fact that I was topless and he stood
behind me, his arm around my waist. He'd taken it freshman
year, whispering something in my ear about how hot we looked
together or some stupid shit like that.

I was going to throw up.

Last year when this had happened, I'd been angry and a little
embarrassed. Now my thoughts immediately went to Max. He
would see this. See me half-naked, see the look in Costa's eyes.
And every time he looked at me, would he see this picture?
What guy wanted to be reminded that his girl had fucked another guy? Especially when it was Costa. Especially when the
whole school would see.

This wasn't a coincidence. Everyone knew we were together. If someone were going to hit me, they'd just chosen the perfect time.

I ripped the pictures off the walls, grateful the halls were empty, my nails like talons as every civilized bone in my body fled. My temper exploded until all I saw was red...and my breasts taunting me in all their digital glory...

Max.

I struggled to calm down, to handle my temper so I could focus on damage control. As much as I wanted to explode right now, I needed to keep my shit in check so I could deal. Somehow.

My hand shook as I grabbed my phone from my purse, typing a text to Max. I had to contain this.

Sorry, running late. Not going to be able to meet for breakfast. Why don't you just go ahead to Canary Wharf? Good luck with your interview xxxx. We'll celebrate tonight.

Since the good-luck breakfast had been my idea, hopefully he wouldn't bother going to the cafeteria if I wasn't meeting him. The last thing I needed was for him to see this on one of the most important days of his life.

That was what pissed me off the most. Whoever was responsible for this—and I knew it was Natasha—hadn't thought about how this would hurt him. All she cared about was taking me down. She wanted to mess with me? Fine. But not when someone completely innocent was caught in the crossfire.

I stormed down the steps, letting the temper I was famous for have its way. I hadn't confronted Natasha because I didn't want to give her the satisfaction of seeing me react. And if it wasn't her, I didn't want to tip her off to all the drama swirling around me. But that was before. This was Max.

Nobody messed with someone I loved.

I hit the cafeteria, my gaze trailing the crowd until it locked on Natasha sitting at a table with a group of my old friends. Friends who'd been friends with Costa and me, and then traded me in when he got a new girlfriend. For a moment I regretted not having spent more time on my appearance, regretted that I didn't look my absolute best. And then that moment disappeared.

I walked toward her, using my "watch me" walk, and our gazes met, all eyes on me now.

If there had ever been any doubt that Natasha was responsible for the photos, the blackmail and everything else, it was gone. Satisfaction flashed in her eyes, and I knew she knew she'd gotten to me.

I'd held on to my pride for so long, and now I knew it didn't matter. I didn't care what everyone else thought of me, if they judged me or pitied me.

Only Max mattered.

I stopped a foot away from Natasha's table. Five pairs of eyes settled on me. One smirk.

"What's your problem?" I snapped, hand on my hip, crumpled pictures in my other hand.

For a second Natasha's smirk faltered, and I wondered if she'd been expecting this, if she'd been prepared to deal with my wrath.

Her smirk slipped back into place. "Looking at you, I would say you're the one with the problem."

I didn't even bother trying to keep my voice low. This would be all over the International School as soon as I walked out the door—if people weren't already texting on their phones, Fleur's losing it in the cafeteria.

Screw it.

"You're right. I do have a problem. Apparently, I have a stalker whose own life is so pathetic that she has to mess with mine. Would you know anything about that, *Natasha*?"

Her face colored. "I don't know what you're talking about," she snapped. "It's not my fault you're such a mess."

"Really?"

I was so sick of everything that had happened the past few years. It registered through the red haze in my brain that the cafeteria had gone completely silent, that I had just given everyone a front-row seat to my drama, and I was only getting started.

"Let's go through all the things *I've* done. He was my boyfriend. For years before you even met him. And you were my friend." I gestured at the table. "All of you were my friends."

Four pairs of eyes looked down at their trays. Only Natasha stared back at me.

"I was your friend. I was so lucky to be the great Fleur Marceaux's friend," she sneered. "Please, explain to me how we were friends because all I remember was you wanting someone to trail after you like a dog."

I flinched, her words hitting their mark. Fine, I'd been an asshole. That was fair. But I didn't see how that justified her fucking my boyfriend.

"So you had to get me back, didn't you?"

I'd thought it would hurt more, but I realized now that whatever sense of betrayal I'd felt was gone. I'd been a bad friend back then. We'd been bad friends to each other. I'd thought losing these friends had been such a blow, and now I realized it was the best thing that had ever happened to me. I'd found Maggie and Mya, people who cared about me. And I'd found Max.

"If Costa had been so happy with you, he never would have slept with me," Natasha added. The smirk returned with a vengeance. Her voice rose. "Do you know how easy it was to get him in bed? I barely had to smile in his direction and he was taking off my clothes."

That one pricked my vanity but missed my heart entirely. Did I know Costa was an asshole who had probably been screwing around on me since the beginning? I did now. Too bad eighteen-year-old me hadn't gotten that message.

My eyes narrowed. "So that makes it okay, then?"

Natasha rose from her seat, stepping toward me, her voice lowering. "You really want to talk to me about what's right? Do you think I don't know? Do you think I couldn't tell when he came back to me, that he'd been with you? You're going to blame me when you ended up doing the same thing? You had sex with him sophomore year when he was my boyfriend. Don't take the high road with me. Maybe you've fooled everyone else, but I see exactly what you are."

Well, that answered the question of if she knew about Costa and me. And explained a bit about why she hated me so much.

"You're right." The anger sifted out of me little by little, the impending adrenaline crash coming. I was so tired of this, so sick of it defining my life. So tired of carrying it around with me, letting it be a part of me. I wanted to carve it all out like the poison it was.

"I should never have gotten involved with him. What I did wasn't any better. There's no excuse." And there wasn't. I'd made a stupid, selfish decision, and the irony was that I'd hurt myself more than anyone, over a guy who wasn't even worth it.

"I'm sorry. I should have told you that a long time ago. I should have settled this sophomore year. Tried to at least. I'm sorry I messed around with Costa when you were together. But the rest of it? This?" I raised the hand holding the pictures. "This stops now. You want to hate me, fine. Hate me. I don't like you very much, so it's not exactly a hardship to be hated by you. But the emails and the photos and the threats end now."

Natasha's cheeks reddened, her eyes flashing with anger. "Right, because Queen Fleur said so. We're all just supposed to do exactly what you want. You don't care about me or anyone else. You walk around here like you think you're better than everyone else, like you own the place."

Her smile turned cruel.

"Could you hold your head up if everyone knew all your secrets?" Her gaze trailed down to my stomach, lingering there, and I knew she knew, or at least suspected. I kept my expression carefully blank, refusing to give her the satisfaction.

"Do you think Max Tucker would still kiss you, and hold your hand and look at you like you're perfect, if he knew just how dirty your past really is?"

"Fuck you," I snapped.

"You don't get it, do you? We aren't even. We will never be even. I've spent years watching you flaunt yourself in front of everyone." Her face scrunched up as pain filled her eyes. "Costa still has pictures of you on his phone, on his computer. Did you know that? That he looks at them? That he still talks about you?"

No, I didn't. I wasn't sure what I felt. Disgust. Sadness. We'd been together for three years. Fooled around for another year. And together we'd wrecked everything we'd touched. She was punishing me for Costa. And I understood, really understood, that this wasn't going to go away with a confrontation in the cafeteria. She wanted to see me destroyed, and she wouldn't stop until she did it.

"I told him about your new boyfriend. How is it that even you can bounce back from all of this? Sure, he's a step down for you, but how do you keep finding these guys stupid enough to fall for you?"

A new wave of anger filled me as I faced off with her. "You're the one whose boyfriend is still hung up on another girl. You're the one who found naked photos of another girl on her boyfriend's computer."

I glared at her, holding her red-hot gaze with my own. "Here's a little newsflash I found out a little too late. Costa is an asshole. He has always been an asshole. He might be good at hiding it, he might be good at convincing girls that he cares, but he doesn't. He's cheated on you, and I can promise you, he'll do it again. You know it, too. You wouldn't be doing this if you were happy, if you were in a good relationship, if you were with a good guy. Want to know how I know this? Because this vendetta you insist on doesn't really matter. I don't care about Costa, or you, or any of it. All I want is for you to leave me alone.

"You're right. I have found someone. And Max is a million times more of a man than Costa ever was."

I could feel the weight of the entire cafeteria's gaze on me, but I ignored them, all my attention on Natasha.

"Back off. You aren't going to win this. And you know what, more than anything, I feel sorry for you. Rather than moving on, you're wasting your life on this. For what? Costa's not worth it. He never was."

Embarrassment filled Natasha's face, and her mouth opened to speak, but I didn't bother waiting for a response. I was done here. I turned and headed out of the cafeteria. At least I intended to. But then I saw him.

Max stood in the doorway, dressed in his suit, looking hotter than ever, staring at me, his face completely unreadable. I offered a prayer to the heavens that he'd just walked in, that he hadn't watched the colossal drama play out. That all he'd heard was me saying he was amazing. But then his eyes changed, and the emotions swirling in them were a punch in the stomach.

He'd heard everything.

23

Max

I headed for the staircase, not sure if I was going to my room or hers, not sure of much of anything besides the need to breathe. I held the crumbled picture in my hand, the anger I'd felt since the moment I saw it on the wall building to a stunning crescendo. I knew Fleur was behind me, but I didn't turn around.

I'd never been out of control before, never felt this way. The fury gathering inside me had started with the picture and grown with every word that had come out of that fight. I needed a moment to get my temper in check. Needed a moment to deal before we talked. She had enough to handle, and I'd figured out that our relationship worked best when I could be calm for her.

But I couldn't get calm. With each step I took, I just became more pissed off, until I stopped and realized I was standing in front of my room.

Fleur laid her palm on my back, her body brushed against me and my eyes closed.

"Max."

I shook my head, my voice raw. "I need a minute."

"I'm sorry." I could hear the unshed tears and panic in her tone. "I'm so sorry. I know you're angry with me—"

I whirled around so quickly I collided with her chest. "I need a minute," I repeated, my teeth clenched.

I wanted to put my fist through the wall. I hated Costa with every fiber of my being, and right now Natasha wasn't too far behind.

And I was pissed with Fleur. I didn't do drama, didn't do secrets. And right now it felt like her entire persona was wrapped up in this shit. Why couldn't she have just talked to me about this from the beginning?

I gave her my heart, and what did she give me in return? She said she loved me, but what was love without trust?

I turned back, unlocking the room. I didn't want an audience for this, hated that she'd had an audience earlier in the cafeteria. I hated the way everyone talked about her like she wasn't even a person, like she was just a freaking drama for them to watch.

Fleur followed me into the room.

I sank down onto the edge of the bed, and she sat down next to me, our knees nearly touching. A minute passed, and then two, before she spoke.

"How much of that did you hear?"

"I walked in when you were going up to her table."

She swallowed. "Fabulous." She reached out, touching my hand and the crumpled picture that lay there. Her voice was thick. "I didn't want you to see it."

I didn't want to see it. I wanted to push it out of my mind. I wanted to pretend I hadn't seen it.

"I hate him," I admitted, my throat raw as the words scratched their way out.

She nodded. "Sometimes I do, too. Other times it just makes me sad."

I tried to clear my throat, tried to push the anger away so that the words would leave.

"I didn't know you guys hooked up after you broke up with him."

She paled slightly, and her voice became even smaller. "Yeah."

"For how long?" Knowing that she still had secrets from me, that there were parts of herself she refused to share, hurt more than I'd ever imagined, like someone was peeling layers of my skin from my body.

"Pretty much all sophomore year," she admitted.

"Why?"

I didn't think it was possible for her to get any paler, but she did.

"It's complicated."

I made a noise of disgust. "You broke up over two years ago. He's an asshole. He cheated on you. What's complicated about that? I don't understand why you would get involved with him again."

"Because my head was fucked back then," she burst out, leaping up from the bed to pace the floor in front of me. "Because I made stupid decisions, and I was hurting. I don't know why I do half the things I do. Sometimes I just feel something and I act on it. Sometimes I don't think until it's too late and the damage is already done. I'm trying to be better about it, but I was a mess then."

"Is he the reason you overdosed?" I asked, hating myself for the question, sick over what her answer would be. We'd danced around all of this, but we hadn't really talked about it. In the beginning I'd gone along with the idea to take things slowly, agreed that we could get to know each other with time. But I loved her, and if this was going to be something, then I needed to know where it was headed.

As much as I loved her personality, the passion that made her at times dramatic and unpredictable, it also scared me. She danced so close to the edge, and I worried she would fall.

I was so far out of my comfort zone. My past was boring. She was a walking soap opera. I didn't know how to live in her world, how to play her game. I wanted to learn, but we spoke a different language, and just when I'd thought I understood, I realized how little I knew after all.

She shook her head. "This isn't about Costa. It's complicated."

Frustration bubbled to the surface like a geyser on the brink of explosion.

"You keep saying that, but what does it mean? How is it complicated? Do you still have feelings for him?" It hurt to speak. "Are you still in love with him?"

She pulled back, shock filling her eyes. "No! How can you ask me that? I love you."

"Then why won't you talk to me? Why don't you trust me? What was Natasha talking about when she said you had secrets? What else aren't you telling me? I listened when you said you didn't want to talk about your past, but Fleur, it feels like this isn't just in the past. It's here between us, and it's still hurting you."

"I don't want it to affect us," she whispered.

"It already is affecting us," I answered, suddenly exhausted. It wasn't even 10 a.m. and I already felt like I'd packed a lifetime of drama into a few short hours.

"We're amazing together, and I love you more than I've ever loved anyone, but I can't have a relationship with someone who doesn't trust me. I don't want to feel like I'm desperate for you to let me inside."

She froze.

"Tell me I'm wrong."

She was silent for an eternity. "You're not wrong."

"Then talk to me, Fleur."

She leaned forward, her head in her hands.

"I can't. Just give me a little more time. I promise. Let's talk tonight after your interview. I never wanted any of this to happen today. The last thing you need is to be distracted. I promise you, everything will be okay. I love you. I'm not going anywhere."

I wanted to be patient for her, wanted to give her space and time. But she was the most stubborn person I'd ever met, and if we didn't bring it up now, would we just dance around it forever?

I got up from the bed, that same restless feeling coursing through my body. This was the absolute worst time for this. My mind was everywhere but where it should be. And time was running out.

"I have to go. I'm going to be late for my interview."

She nodded. "I'm so sorry."

I met her gaze, my voice strained. "We need to talk later."

"I know," she answered, getting up from the bed and standing in front of me. "We will. Good luck with the interview."

I left her in my dorm room as I struggled to clear my head and my heart and prepare for the biggest day of my life.

24

Fleur

I headed back to my room on shaky legs, a stabbing pain in my chest.

Was this it? Had I just screwed everything up with Max?

Maybe I should have just told him. I'd thought about it when I'd seen how upset he was, but today was too important for him to be caught up in my problems. I didn't want to drag him down with my drama and bad decisions.

But what if I already had?

I needed to do something, needed to change the way I was handling everything. Clearly, avoidance wasn't working. It hadn't worked when I'd used alcohol or drugs, when I'd dated George to get my mind off Costa and everything else. I wanted to say that falling in love with Max had been enough to save me, to erase the pain of everything I'd been through, but it hadn't.

I was beginning to realize that no one could take that pain away from me. And maybe that was the point. I would never be the girl I'd been before. Would never go back to a life where my biggest worries were what outfit I'd wear or how I'd do my hair. I carried the loss of my baby around with me always.

I'd been running for so long. Now it was time to face it.

I pulled out my phone, staring at the number, wishing I didn't have it. I wanted to delete it, wanted to pretend he'd never existed. But more than that, more than anything, I wanted to let go. The old me would have gotten drunk or gone shopping. I would have taken the easy way out, rather than face my problems.

It was time to grow up.

I sat in bed, curling my legs against my chest, staring at his name in my phone. We hadn't spoken in over a year. I pressed Call, my heart pounding in my chest.

He'd graduated from a different university last year and he was back in Milan now, probably working for his family's company.

He answered on the third ring.

"Fleur?"

It was the strangest thing to hear my name on Costa's lips. On one hand, it was so familiar. Like we'd traveled back in time and I was at school in Switzerland calling my boyfriend, the one all the girls were jealous of. And yet, it felt like a stranger said my name now. Maybe it was that I'd moved on or maybe it was the realization that despite everything I'd thought I knew about him, I hadn't really known him at all.

"Are you okay?"

It would have been easier if I hadn't heard the concern in his voice. It would have been easier to hate him, to not allow even a flicker of the happy memories spill inside, if I could just convince myself that he was truly evil.

But I couldn't. He was a cheater and a player. He'd treated me terribly for a lot of our relationship, and unfortunately, I'd let him. But the universal thread among good liars was that there was always a thread of truth. And for all his flaws, there was a part of Costa that had loved me in his own way. It hadn't really been *love*, it had been his version of love, and now I knew it hadn't been nearly enough, but hearing his voice still made everything worse.

I wasn't sure how two people could screw everything up as much as we had, how something could have started in kisses and affection, and ended up as this ugly, mangled mess.

But it had.

I took a deep breath and spoke my first words to him in over a year. "Natasha just put a naked picture of us up all over the school."

Costa cursed in Italian, and whatever doubt had existed trickled away. Despite his many flaws, he hadn't done that. Some part of me felt a thread of relief to know that despite my stupid choices, at least I hadn't dated a complete and total monster.

Just someone who had never really deserved me.

"She did it last year, too."

He cursed again. "Why didn't you tell me?"

"I didn't want to talk to you then."

He didn't speak for a beat. "And now you want to talk to me?"

"If I had my way, I'd never talk to you again," I answered honestly. "But I need to know something because things are getting ugly here. Did you tell her about the miscarriage?"

"No. She knows I got someone pregnant and that she lost the baby. She doesn't know it was you."

My chest tightened. "Do you really think it would be that hard for her to figure out? The rumor has already been quietly circulating the International School. At least now I know where it came from."

"Fleur—"

"No. It's my turn to talk. I was a good girlfriend to you. I wasn't always perfect, but I cared about you, thought I loved you at the time. I never cheated on you, only ever tried to make you happy. If you ever cared about me, if you have any shred of decency in you, then you will lock this down. You know what losing the baby was like for me." I had to push through the lump in my throat. "You know what I've been through and have done to myself. You need to handle your girlfriend."

"She's not my girlfriend anymore."

Well, that explained why she didn't care how messy this was getting… She had nothing to lose. I was the one with everything hanging in the balance.

"I miss you, Fleur," Costa continued, as if the past two years and everything in between hadn't happened. "I was thinking maybe I could come to London and see you. Or maybe you could come here. We need to talk about this, deal with it together."

He had to be kidding me. Of all the things for him to bring up now, after everything we'd been through, the fact that he wouldn't just let this die made me the angriest. Any hope of dignity was gone. We'd both obliterated it.

"That's not going to happen."

"We were good together."

The saddest part was that I'd believed that once. And I finally understood who Costa was. He was rich, gorgeous and used to having everything he could ever want. But he only wanted things when they were just out of his reach. Once he got them, they lost all their value. He was like a spoiled boy who only wanted to play with a toy if someone else had it.

It had never been about me; it was always about the chase.

"We weren't good together. We were young, and we didn't know any better."

I hadn't known any better.

"I still love you."

I closed my eyes, wondering why this hurt so much. I didn't love him. I didn't even like him. But there was too much history there for me to ignore the feeling completely. Maybe I regretted the time wasted, the tears shed. I hated that he'd almost destroyed me when he wasn't worth anything.

I thought the anger and regret would consume me. I could feel the darkness closing in, the desire to do something stupid, to release all these feelings building inside me.

I fought for control, tried to channel a sense of calm. I wanted more. I wanted to be happy. I wanted a chance at a better life, and I wouldn't get it unless I took it.

I needed to let go.

"I've moved on. I've met someone else. I'm happy. It's over."

"Do you really think that? After everything we've been through? How can you turn your back on the years we've spent together? I love you, Fleur."

I cut the last cord that had bound me to him—the sadness, the pain—I let them float away until there was nothing in their place but my present and my future.

"Goodbye, Costa."

I hung up the phone and closed the door on my past.

I sat in my room, trying to figure out what I was going to say to Max when someone pounded on the door.

Maggie and Mya were both in class, although they'd sent me frantic texts telling me they were willing to skip. I'd promised them that I was okay and it wasn't necessary. We had finals coming up in a few days, and the last thing I needed was for this to be another "drop everything, Fleur's having a crisis" semester for them.

I padded over to the door, opened it, and saw Samir standing in the hall.

"Is everything okay?" I asked as he walked over the threshold and closed the door behind him.

His voice was tight, his accent heavier than normal. "No. Everything is not okay. I'm going to kill Costa."

I groaned. "I'm guessing Maggie told you about the picture." I sank down onto my bed, exhausted from all the drama this morning. My body was drained, and all I wanted to do was take a freaking nap. "I'm okay. I'm handling it."

Samir shook his head. "No. This isn't okay anymore. This is the second time someone has pulled this. What the hell is going on? If that asshole thinks he's going to get away with spreading pictures of you around the school—"

"It wasn't Costa."

His eyes narrowed. "What do you mean it wasn't Costa?"

I shook my head. "I called him."

"You what?"

"I called him. I needed to confront this. Needed to talk to him. He was as shocked as you are, albeit not as angry."

"Then who put those pictures up?" His gaze darkened as he realized the answer to his own question.

"We had an incident in the cafeteria. It was Natasha."

He sat down next to me, leaning forward, his elbows on his knees, his face in his hands. "What are you going to do, Fleur? You can't live like this."

"I know."

"Why aren't you doing something about this? Fuck. Go to the administration. Fight back. Something. You can't let her get away with this. If you want, I'll go talk to the administration with you. Or I'll handle her."

Tears rose in my eyes. I loved him so much. He was always there for me, always ready to do battle to protect the people he loved. I loved him, and he worried about me and finally I did what I should have done a long time ago.

"I need to tell you something."

Samir looked up, his eyes clouded with worry. "What?"

"Last year I started receiving threatening emails."

"Threatening how?"

I could feel the anger coming off his body.

"Emails threatening to expose some of my secrets if I didn't pay them money."

"Blackmail," Samir uttered in disbelief.

I nodded.

"Why am I just now hearing about this? Why didn't you tell me last year?" His voice rose until he was nearly at a shout.

I winced. "I know you're pissed, and I know you're scared for me, but you have to calm down if you want me to tell you the rest."

"There's more?"

I nodded. "I didn't pay, but after today I now know it was Natasha. She was behind the photos, all of it."

"Did you get emails like that this year, too?"

"Yes."

Samir stood up, pacing the room, Arabic flying out of his mouth. He'd taught me enough that I recognized the angry curse words. I waited while he got his temper under control.

He came back and sat again, the pain on his face breaking my heart. I stared down at the floor in front of me, unable to look at him as I told him the rest of it.

"I was pregnant at the end of freshman year. I had a miscarriage."

Shock flashed across his face.

I couldn't look at him while I told him everything. At one

point he put his arm around me, and we sat there as I cried and spoke of the baby I'd loved and lost.

I realized then that each time I spoke of my loss, it became a little easier. It was still so hard, but there was a strange comfort in being able to share this part of myself with Samir. When I'd finished, his face was pale, his eyes pained.

"I'm so sorry, Fleur. So sorry you had to deal with that." His voice cracked. "I hate that I wasn't there for you. I hate that you were alone."

I hesitated. "I wasn't always alone. Don't be angry. I swore her to secrecy—"

His eyes narrowed. "Maggie knows."

I nodded. "I told her when I was in the hospital after my overdose. She was so upset when she found me in our room. So scared. We told Mya last year when the picture came out."

"I'm glad you guys had each other. I just wish I could have been there for you, too." Emotion filled his voice, and I almost wondered if he was going to cry. "I love you, Fleur. You've always been more like a sister than a cousin, and you don't know what it's been like seeing you in pain for so long. I would have given anything to make it better for you."

I hugged him. "I know. I just didn't know what to say. I knew how you felt about Costa, and you were right. I just wish I'd learned my lesson earlier."

He sighed. "How are you now?"

"It's hard to explain. It's like everything fits into these little boxes. I love my friends, and I love Max and I'm finally starting to think I might get a job after graduation. Hell, I'm starting to think I'll graduate. But the other boxes?" I tried to think of the best way to describe it. "The baby box is like this dark place I try not to go. Whenever I think of it, I just feel this emptiness inside and nothing seems to fill it."

"Have you tried talking to someone?"

"What do you mean?"

"Have you gone to therapy?"

"My parents sent me to that spa after sophomore year to 'fix me.' It was basically holding hands and talking about our feelings. I hated it."

"Maybe you just didn't find the right person to talk to."

"Do you think I can't handle this without professional help?"

Samir leaned forward, pressing a kiss on my forehead. "No. But I think everyone has things in their life that they need to sort out, and there's no shame in it. You don't always have to be invincible. It doesn't make you weak just because you show someone your softer side. If anything, putting yourself out there is the scariest thing in the world, but it only makes you strong."

He smiled softly at me, all the love between us shining through. "A very smart girl told me that one day when she flew to Saint-Tropez and told me to get my head out of my ass before I let the best thing in my life go.

"You're the toughest person I know. You've been through hell, and you're still standing. Take the time you need to fix what you need to fix, because you'll never find peace if you don't figure out a way to keep this from dragging you down. It's okay to be sad, okay to mourn. But you have to find a way to be able to move forward. You need peace."

"I know," I whispered.

"And Fleur? I'm here for you. Always. No matter what. Nothing could change that."

Another tear fell. "I love you."

He hugged me tighter. "Love you, too."

I went to Mrs. Fox's office to report Natasha. She was the Residence Life director and had been there with me in the hospital when I'd overdosed sophomore year. The rest of the administration could be a little aloof, but Mrs. Fox had an open-door policy with all her students, and I'd always felt comfortable with her.

Samir had wanted to come with me, but it was one of those things I needed to do on my own.

She greeted me with a smile. "Fleur. It's good to see you. What can I do for you today? Come in and sit down." She closed the door behind us. "How are things going this semester?"

I clutched the folder in my hands that contained the printed-out emails, the note that Natasha had left on my door and the pictures.

"Not great." I took a deep breath and started talking.

The best thing about Mrs. Fox was that she was calm. She was the first person I'd seen when I woke up from my overdose, and as scared as I'd been, she'd made it better. When I told her about Natasha now, she just sat there and listened until I'd finished.

"I'm so sorry you've had to deal with this, Fleur." She nodded at the folder on my lap. "Let me take that to the dean, and we'll go from there. You'll need to meet with him at some point, and I'd be happy to go with you. We'll also have to look at the evidence to see if this could turn into a criminal matter beyond any administrative steps the university would take. We'll have to speak with Natasha, as well, regarding these allegations."

I nodded.

"You might want to talk to your parents about hiring legal representation to help with this. You haven't done anything wrong, of course, but it might help you to have a professional taking care of some of the workload." She gave me a kind smile. "I know you've been through a lot lately, and I don't want you to have to worry about this, too."

I didn't want to think about it anymore. I was here because

I wanted this to stop, but honestly, I didn't even care if Natasha suffered for it. I just wanted to be left alone.

I handed Mrs. Fox the folder with the assurance that I'd hear from her soon, and I walked away.

25

Max

The morning went by in a blur of nerves and frustration. No matter how hard I tried, I couldn't focus. I wanted to kill Costa; I was pissed at Fleur for not letting me in. For not trusting me with her secrets from the beginning.

How could she think anything would change the way I felt about her?

I took the Jubilee line to Canary Wharf, my mind on Fleur the entire time. I tried to push her out, tried to focus on the interview rather than the drama, but it was impossible. I was beginning to realize that it was hard to be happy when she was dealing with so much.

I just had to get through the next few hours.

This last interview was an audition of sorts. I'd passed their tests, answered their questions. Today was a meet and greet with all the candidates and the partners. If this went well, we'd been told to expect calls with formal job offers. There were twenty of us that had made it this far, and about half would be admitted into the training program.

I wore the suit Fleur had picked out for me and a new gray tie that she'd bought me as an early Christmas present. In true Fleur fashion, the tie was Gucci.

I got off the Tube and was caught up in the sea of I-bankers headed to lunch. Nerves rolled around in my empty stomach, and I instantly regretted skipping breakfast. I hadn't been hungry after all the drama with Fleur, but now I needed the extra boost.

If things didn't go well today, it wouldn't be the end of the world. There would be other jobs. My GPA was pretty much perfect, I spoke Mandarin and I had some solid internships on my résumé from both summer jobs and my time in China. Plus, I'd worked through three years at the International School. I'd find something before graduation.

But I wanted this job.

I was the first person in my family to go to college. When I'd told my parents I wanted to study in London, that I wanted to work in finance, they'd laughed at me. For them, the idea of me working with millions of pounds was ludicrous. We'd never been poor, but I hadn't grown up with many luxuries. They hadn't understood why I wanted to go overseas, why I wanted more.

Hell, I wasn't even sure myself.

I loved numbers. I always had. And more than that, I wanted to prove that I could do this. To myself more than anyone. Since I was usually so quiet, I think it surprised people to know that I was competitive as hell. But I was. I'd worked my ass off all through high school, all through college, and now I was here. And as much as I loved Fleur, and as much as I was worried about her, I couldn't afford to choke.

I walked into the impressive glass building, and my focus began to return. This part of London was so different from Kensington, where the International School was located. This was the more modern part of the city. This was where deals were made, fortunes won and lost.

It was my future.

I checked in and waited until the receptionist told me to go up to the twenty-second floor. With each step, the nerves began to fade. In the beginning, when I'd started interviewing, the wealth surrounding me had been intimidating as hell. But of course, that had been pre-Fleur.

I'd spent enough time with her and her friends to no longer feel out of place. I understood now what she'd been telling me all along. It was all about attitude. Maybe I didn't have a million-dollar portfolio, or a Rolex, or drive a fancy sports car, but I had my shit together. I was smart, and I was determined. And I knew without a doubt that I would be willing to work harder than anyone else in the room to succeed.

I channeled my inner-Fleur and something clicked inside me.

I worked the room, drink in hand, making conversation with the partners, laughing and joking around with the other candidates. I was no longer the skinny middle schooler who got mocked for playing video games and belonging to the Chess Club. I wasn't the guy who wore the wrong tennis shoes to a London club, or the guy who had a crush on a girl he was too shy to talk to.

I was the guy I'd become this semester—the one who'd learned to go after what he wanted, who wasn't afraid to put it all on the line. I was still me; I just didn't feel the need to hang on the sidelines anymore. Fleur had shown me the confidence I needed to get into the game.

I rocked the meet and greet.

"We've been very impressed with what we've seen from you, Max," the head of the training program remarked as we stood in the corner chatting about basketball. He was American like me, and apparently a huge Chicago fan.

"Thank you, sir. I've really enjoyed this opportunity. There's nowhere else I'd rather work."

Some people would have probably played it cool, but I'd never be one of those guys. So far being direct had served me well. I wasn't the smoothest guy in the world, but I was honest.

He smiled. "Glad to hear it. I think you'll be an excellent addition here. We're not just looking for smart candidates but also individuals who will fit in with the work culture. We're in a client-focused business and your ability to interact with our clientele is just as important as your investment knowledge."

I nodded, really understanding what he meant for the first time in my life.

That had always been the biggest hurdle for me. I'd always been a numbers guy, but I hadn't been the most social. But little by little, Fleur had helped bring me out of my shell. I realized now how much she'd done for me. The whole time I'd thought I was helping her get more serious about school, encouraging her to study, giving her the confidence she needed to believe that she had a shot at getting a good job after graduation.

I just hadn't realized how much she'd been doing the same for me.

She made me a better person. She did it with everyone, and it was so effortless, it just happened. She supported Samir, made Mya laugh when she was dealing with family drama, gave Maggie the love and encouragement she needed. And she gave me confidence.

She gave the people around her the best parts of herself and made us better for it.

And suddenly, all I wanted was to see her, to talk to her.

I finished up the interview receiving smiles, handshakes and the promise that they would call me soon.

Then I went home to my girl.

I found her alone in her room.

"How did it go?" Fleur asked when she opened the door.

I barely let her get the words out before she was in my arms and I was kissing her.

We were so different, and yet, when we were together...it worked. We brought out the best in each other, learned from each other, made an amazing team. Our differences were what made it special. We challenged each other. It was rarely easy, it meant work and patience, but it was completely worth it.

And if there had been any doubts about whether I would fight for her, they'd been completely erased. I'd stand by her through anything.

She pulled back first, her mouth swollen, her eyes red-rimmed. I wrapped my arm around her, following her into the room and shutting the door behind us.

"Are you okay?"

She nodded. "Yeah. You didn't answer me before. How was it?"

Worry filled her beautiful brown eyes, matching the strain in her voice.

"It was great. I think they're going to offer me a spot."

Her whole face transformed as she broke into a huge, beaming smile. She launched her body at me, throwing her arms around my neck, and I caught her, pulling her body to mine, lifting her feet off the floor.

"I'm so happy for you." She buried her face in my neck. "I was so worried that you would be distracted, that I'd messed everything up for you. I'm so glad it went well."

I ran my free hand over her hair, stroking gently. "Babe, you didn't mess anything up. I never would have gotten this far without you." I set her down on her feet. "It went well because of you. Because you gave me the confidence I needed to prove that I belonged there. I didn't even know I needed it and you gave it to me anyway. You knew. You've been showing me what I needed all semester, and I didn't even realize it."

"Max—"

"Let me finish." I took my hand in hers. "We work. It's weird, and we probably shouldn't work and yet when we're together we're both better. We make each other stronger. We support each other. We're a team, and that means we stick together through the good times and bad."

I took a deep breath.

"I don't make promises I can't keep, and if I say something, it's because I mean it. There is nothing you could do or tell me that would change the way I feel about you. I love you. I will love you until the day I die. Whatever you're dealing with, we will deal with together. I'm not going anywhere, Fleur. You're so lodged in my heart I couldn't carve you out even if I wanted to. And I don't. So let me in. Please."

Tears fell down her cheeks.

"Please don't cry," I whispered, closing the distance between us, kissing each tear as it fell.

I kissed her until she stopped crying and pulled back. "We need to talk," she murmured.

"I know."

She pulled away and sank down onto her bed, staring up at me.

"I was pregnant freshman year." Her voice cracked as the first wave of shock hit me.

"Fleur…"

"It was Costa's, obviously," she continued, not meeting my gaze. "I was terrified at first when I found out. Wasn't planning on having a baby. Ever, really. But then I began to love it. I don't even know if it was a boy or a girl. It was too soon to tell."

A tear trickled down her face. "I woke up one night when I was home in Paris for spring break and there was blood in the bed. I knew something was wrong. We went to the hospital, and the doctors told me I'd had a miscarriage."

"Fleur…"

I knew parts of the story—knew Costa had cheated on her, knew he'd broken her heart, had just learned that they'd hooked up sophomore year. I'd heard about her overdose and seen the ugly feud between her and Natasha. Had seen firsthand the fury and humiliation she'd felt when her naked body was exposed for the whole school to see. All along, I'd thought those things had created the pain inside Fleur.

But when I heard the words *I was pregnant*, I knew. For all her swagger and attitude, for all that she pretended she glided through life, as soon as she spoke of her miscarriage, I finally understood that her heart had been broken, and it had nothing to do with Costa.

She loved so deeply, intensely, passionately. She had the biggest heart of anyone I knew, hidden under the layers she employed to keep it safe. She had loved her baby with everything she had, and my heart broke for her.

"That's why I missed so much school at the end of freshman year," she continued. "My parents told me not to tell anyone. They were angry about the whole situation. They said it was just another example of me screwing up. I was the party girl who always took things too far. They didn't say as much, but I know they thought I deserved what happened."

I gathered her in my arms, rocking her as she cried. I could only imagine how scared she must have been and how brave she'd been to survive it. When she spoke of her guilt, of the way her parents had treated her, tears welled up in my eyes.

Her pain filled the room, sweeping us both up in its wake. It was impossible to love someone and not feel like her hurts were a part of you, too, to not wish you could take away her losses.

"Two weeks later Costa cheated on me and then broke up with me. He said everything was too 'intense' for him." Her voice cracked. "I thought he'd be there with me to mourn our baby. I kept waiting for him. I thought he was just scared. I didn't realize until the end of sophomore year that he never really cared at all."

She reached out and squeezed my hand as if she was holding on for strength. "I guess I haven't been okay since then. I kept waiting to get over it. For this hole in my heart to disappear, but it never did. Natasha found out about the miscarriage and figured out it was me, and she's been threatening to spread it around school."

"Why didn't you tell me? Why didn't you tell anyone about it?"

"I didn't want to be the girl everyone looked at like she was a train wreck. Maybe it was stupid, but I didn't want the pain of hearing people gossip about the miscarriage. Didn't want to let it be real. It was easier to just pretend it never happened, that it happened to someone else." She shook her head. "I was a coward—"

"No. Costa was the fucking coward." I wanted to kill him for what he did to her. "You deserved to have someone by your side. You shouldn't have gone through that on your own. God, Fleur. Don't ever say you're a coward. You're the best person I know."

I wished I knew what to do for her, how to make it better.

I wanted to give her a baby, even though I knew that wouldn't erase the memory of the one she'd lost.

She'd be such an amazing mother. I knew she still didn't see it, still didn't understand that her greatest strength was the depth with which she loved, but I knew it.

I wanted a daughter with her spirit. A daughter who would probably bankrupt me if she had a fashion habit like her mother's. We were so young, and yet I wanted to give her the family she'd never really had. Maybe not now, but I knew without a doubt that she was my future, that we'd build a life together.

She already had my love.

When she finished speaking, we both just sat there, wrapped up in each other.

"What can I do?" I asked, my voice hoarse. "Just tell me what I can do. I'd do anything for you."

Her gaze met mine. "I know," she replied softly. "I don't know how to fix this. I'm trying. Talking about it seems to be helping. I told Samir earlier."

I nodded, not sure I trusted my voice enough to speak.

"Just be patient with me. I wish I could be the girl you need me to be, but I'm still fixing myself. It's going to take time."

"I can do that." I tried to clear my throat, pushing out the knot that had been lodged there. There would be time later for me to process all of this. Now I had to be strong for her. "Have you thought about talking to someone?"

"Yeah. Samir suggested it."

Who would have thought Samir and I would agree on something?

"Since school's almost out, I found a therapist in Paris. I'll go during break, and then when I come back in January I'll find someone here."

"Sounds like a good plan. I'm here for you, Fleur. For whatever you need."

She squeezed my hand. "I know. I went to the administration and filed a formal complaint about Natasha. Told them about the pictures and the blackmail. I saved everything, so that helped. I'm not sure what they'll do to her, and honestly, I don't even care, but I just needed to feel like I was doing something."

"Good."

"I can't stop this from getting out, and it might." She sucked in a deep breath. "I've thought about it a lot, and if it does get out, I'm not going to deny it. It's no one's business, but I'm also not going to hide like I'm scared or like I did something wrong." Worry filled her gaze. "It could get kind of ugly. I understand if you don't want to deal with it."

I shook my head. "I'm not going anywhere. And if it does get ugly, I'll be here. It'll be okay, I promise." I squeezed her hand. "We'll get through this."

And then I kissed her, giving her everything I had. I'd only intended for it to be a kiss, didn't want to push her into sex when she was so upset, but even sad, Fleur wasn't one to shy away from taking the lead.

She began stripping off my clothes, seducing me with her hands and mouth, wrapping her legs around me.

"I need you," she whispered, arching her hips and offering her body to me. "Please."

I'd never been very good at saying no to her, so I gave her what she wanted, what we needed, until our bodies joined and she was crying out my name.

I got the investment banking job. And news of Fleur's miscarriage didn't come out. Natasha had her hands full with the investigation after Fleur turned over all her proof to the administration, so I figured she didn't want to press her luck. No one wanted to get expelled with a semester to go until graduation.

Fleur didn't seem to care.

We both focused on exams, cramming in the library. We presented our fashion app in Project Finance and received an A. Fleur joked that it was the first A she'd ever received in school.

We'd get our final grades in the rest of our classes next semester, but she was no longer worried about graduating and had even managed to line up an interview in January for an internship.

At the end of the semester, I took her to St. Pancras to board the Eurostar to Paris. I was headed back to Chicago for Christmas break and Fleur was going home, too. I'd been worried about her spending the holidays by herself, but Samir and Maggie decided to go to Paris, as well, so at least she would have them to keep her company. They were taking a later train after Samir finished his grad school exams.

Fleur held my hand at the station, her other arm wrapped around my waist while we waited for her train. It was only a month, and still it felt like four weeks too long.

"I'm going to miss you."

She kissed me, cuddling closer. "Me, too."

"Are you sure you're going to be okay?"

She nodded. "Yeah. Promise. I have my first therapy appointment set up for Monday."

"Okay. You know if you need to talk while you're there, I'm just a phone call away. We can Skype. And email. And chat."

She grinned. "We'll talk every day. And I promise I'll be okay. Just enjoy being home and don't worry about me."

Not likely, but I gave her what she wanted.

"Okay."

An announcement came over the loudspeakers calling for first class to start boarding. My girl traveled in style.

"That's you."

I looped my arms around her waist, leaning down to capture her mouth. She threw her arms around my neck, putting everything she had into the kiss. Her mouth opened, her tongue teasing mine, and then the kiss exploded.

It wasn't the kind of kiss you'd typically have in public, but Fleur wasn't typical. She kissed like she did everything else—exactly the way she wanted it, not caring if anyone saw.

We broke apart when the announcer came on the loudspeaker again.

I groaned. "You can't kiss me like that and then go away for a month."

She gave me an arch look and a knowing smile. "Just making sure no American girl stands a chance."

I cracked up, pulling her back into my arms. "Never."

I couldn't resist the opportunity to kiss her again, making her mouth mine just like she'd done to me.

She leaned back, breathless, staring up at me with wide eyes.

"Just making sure you stay away from guys named Pierre or Jacques," I teased.

She grinned. "I love you."

I reached out and squeezed her hand, pulling it to my heart. "I love you, too."

I let her go, standing on the platform, watching as she did "the walk," the one that had ensnared me for years. Her stride lengthened, her mile-long legs eating up the pavement. Her hips swayed, her long brown hair flipping over her shoulders in a tumble of curls and silk. She walked like she knew everyone in the train station's eyes were on her, wanting her, wishing they had her. And then she turned, and our gazes connected across the platform, and I *knew*...

She did the walk for me.

I watched my dream girl walk away, carrying my heart with her, a smile on my face.

Because this time I knew she'd be back. And she was mine.

26

Fleur

"How are you feeling today?"

I shifted on the couch, tearing my attention away from the window and the snow falling on the ground, to the elderly woman sitting at the desk across from me.

I'd been home for three weeks now, and this was my sixth therapy appointment. In the beginning it had been awkward, but I was surprised at how easy it had become to talk to her. She was quiet for the most part, occasionally asking me questions about how I was doing. She let me lead the conversations, and little by little, I'd started opening up to her.

"I'm doing well. It gets a bit easier each day. The pain is always there. I think I'll always feel it, always think about the baby, but now I feel like I can live with it whereas before I felt like it was killing me."

She nodded. "You're dealing with it. And the guilt?"

I didn't know how to explain it, but I'd lived with the pain for so long, through all my stupid decisions, that I think it had become a part of me. And on some level I'd thought I deserved what happened. That my parents were right.

That was the hardest part: learning to forgive myself.

Or more importantly, perhaps, learning that there was nothing to forgive.

"I understand now. Maybe I held on to it for so long because it was all I had. But I don't want to be that girl anymore. I don't want to screw up the good things I have in my life."

My friends. Max. My future.

"I'm taking it a day at a time, but I feel better. I feel like I can breathe."

She smiled. "Good. The holidays can be difficult. Do you have plans with your family?"

"I'm spending Christmas with my cousin and his girlfriend—my best friends."

"Wonderful. And your parents?"

We'd already talked about how I wasn't close to them, so I knew she wouldn't be surprised by my answer.

"They decided to go to St. Barts. I didn't feel like it, so I stayed behind."

"With the holidays, this will be our last formal session before you go back to London, but I want you to know that I'm happy to counsel you over the phone if you'd like. Or if you'd prefer, I can help find someone for you to speak with in London."

"Thank you. Maybe we could try the phone consultations and see how that goes?"

She smiled. "I think that would be an excellent plan."

I nodded.

In the beginning, I'd been skeptical about how this would work, but it was helping. The pain was still there, but she'd taught me how to handle it better. I no longer felt like my emotions were out of control, but instead like I had a chance at learning how to deal with this.

I felt hope.

"Do you feel ready to go back to London? You must be excited to get back to your friends and your young man."

God, I missed Max. I thought about him constantly, even though we talked every day. Things would happen and I'd find myself wanting to tell him. Sometimes it would be the middle of the night with the time difference, and I'd have to wait to get a chance to talk to him. He was the best part of my day.

"I am."

We talked for a bit longer about things I could do when I started to feel depressed or stressed. Coping mechanisms.

She glanced up at the clock. "Well, I'm afraid our session is almost over."

I nodded. "Thank you so much for everything."

"It was my pleasure, Fleur. Really. I'm so proud of how far you've come. You're a very strong young woman, and you've made so much progress in the short time we've worked together."

"Thank you."

She smiled at me. "And I hope you have a wonderful Christmas."

"You, too."

I curled up in bed, flipping through the TV channels, looking for something to watch.

It was Christmas Eve and every station seemed to be playing a holiday movie. I wasn't a holiday person. Even when I was younger, the holidays hadn't been great. My parents were rarely in the same place, so I could probably count on one hand the number of Christmases we'd spent together.

I was used to being on my own. Last year I'd gotten drunk and spent all day reading fashion magazines, judging celebrity outfit choices. This year Maggie had thrown herself into planning a traditional Christmas for Samir and me. I think she was a little horrified at our festive indifference.

Tonight they'd gone out to listen to carolers, and I'd put my foot down. The fact that she'd forced Samir, and the image of him listening to a bunch of carolers, was too bizarre for words.

I'd gone along with the giant tree in the entryway and agreed to help her cook. I'd gone shopping—not exactly a hardship—and wrapped gifts, and we were all going to church at Notre Dame tomorrow. But no carolers. I had to draw the line somewhere.

My phone went off and I grabbed it, expecting a text from Max.

Maggie's name flashed instead.

We're going out for crepes. Come join us.

I groaned. It was snowing outside, not heavily, but still. Crepes were good, but I wasn't sure they were worth ruining my hair over.

No.

My phone pinged a minute later.

Yes.

God, she could be stubborn when she wanted to be.

It's freezing out.

Throw on a coat, she replied.

It was almost 9 p.m., and maybe I was getting old, but the last thing I wanted to do was trudge out in the snow for a fucking crepe.

My phone pinged again.

Come on, it's Christmas Eve. We let you out of caroling, but we're supposed to be spending the holiday together.

My phone pinged again.

Samir says you owe him for Thanksgiving.

Way to guilt trip. He had been good about coming over for Thanksgiving dinner even though he'd totally thought I was ridiculous when I'd invited him. I groaned, burrowing farther under the covers. Yeah, there was no way I was getting out of this.

Fine. Where are you?

She texted me the location and I groaned. My cousin was turning into such a sap. They had a thing about this crepe stand by the Eiffel Tower since they'd gone there when they were falling for each other Maggie's freshman year. The crepes were good, but it was literally the most touristy part of the city.

The worst part about spending the holiday away from the guy you loved and instead with a couple who couldn't keep their hands off each other, was that it was tough to not feel like the third wheel. Even when that couple happened to be comprised of your best friends. I had zero desire to be around a bunch of couples taking pictures of themselves kissing in front of the Eiffel Tower on Christmas Eve.

The things I did for my friends.

I trudged over to the Eiffel Tower, muttering curse words under my breath. The streets were full of people, and I was suddenly longing for last year when I'd spent my holiday judging ugly dresses and drinking a bottle of Cristal.

I found them in front of the crepe stand, Maggie's cheeks pink, Samir's arms wrapped around her. Snow was falling, sprinkled through her hair, a flake settling on her nose. It was really fucking cold.

"I'm here," I announced crossly.

Samir grinned. "Happy Christmas Eve to you, too."

I flipped him off.

His grin deepened. "Someone's in a bad mood."

I groaned. "Did you drag me here to torture me, or are you going to feed me?"

"What do you want?"

"*Chocolat.*"

He nodded and ordered for me while I waited with Maggie.

I sighed. "Sorry. Maybe you guys should just do your own thing. Have a nice romantic Christmas without me ruining it."

"You aren't ruining it."

"I am. I'm not a big holiday person, and I miss Max. I wouldn't want to be around me tonight, either. You guys go off on your own. Seriously. I really appreciate you wanting to make this Christmas special for me, but I'm just not in the mood."

I expected her to agree with me, but instead she just smiled. "Eat your crepe."

Samir came over to me and handed me the chocolate crepe and a hot chocolate. "This will warm you up."

My eyes narrowed. "Are you guys trying to boss me around now?"

Maggie laughed. "Yes. Wonder who we learned that from?"

"I'm not bossy," I muttered. I took a bite of the crepe. Fine, it was kind of amazing. I practically devoured it.

"Okay, we've had crepes. Can we go back to the flat now? We can even watch a Christmas movie if you want."

Was it my imagination or did a look of pain cross Samir's face? I grinned. I guessed he'd hit his limit after the caroling.

Maggie shook her head. "I want to watch the Eiffel Tower sparkle. It's almost time. Then we can go."

Samir just stood there, a smile on his face.

My eyes narrowed. This was not the Maggie I knew. Maggie was always easygoing. Now she sounded…well, like me.

"We're standing here, waiting for the Eiffel Tower to sparkle?" I looked at Samir for help.

He just stared back at me with that same knowing smile.

Maggie nodded.

I stuffed my hands into my pockets, struggling to ward off the cold, the snow beginning to fall heavier now.

And then I heard it…the sound of "La Vie en Rose" playing nearby. I closed my eyes, remembering that night on the boat, how Max had been so romantic and sweet with me. And how it had given me the courage to tell him I loved him.

I missed him so much it hurt.

I opened my eyes, ready to make some excuse so I didn't have to stand here, having this romantic moment completely by myself. I turned away from the Eiffel Tower, shining in the dark Paris sky, trying to block the song out, when Maggie hugged me.

"We didn't know what to get you for Christmas, but we knew we wanted it to be special. It was hard to know what to get the girl who has everything," she teased, "so I figured we'd just get you the thing you wanted most."

I pulled back, staring down at her, confusion filling me. "What?"

Samir leaned over, kissing my cheek. "Turn around."

Awareness slowly dawned as I turned, my body in shock, everything around me feeling like it was in slow motion.

The song burst through first, taking me back to the night on the Bateaux Mouche, and then it registered that the Eiffel Tower was indeed *sparkling* as Maggie had described it, the lights twinkling like a giant Christmas tree in the night sky, snow falling around us. And then I looked—really looked—and saw the beauty around me, breathed in the magic of the moment.

Because I saw him, the shape of a boy walking toward me— *Max*—and then I was in his arms, and my lips were on his, and the rest of the world disappeared, the faint sounds of my friends cheering, and "La Vie en Rose" playing, lingering in the background.

And just like that, I finally got my happy ending.

Epilogue

Three Years Later...
Fleur

"Can I look yet?"

I shook my head, grabbing the veil from the back of the chair. "Give me another minute. Almost perfect."

I slid the veil into her dark brown hair, adjusting the lace around her flowing curls. The material was a long, sheer panel of lace that trailed down to the floor. It fit into her hair with a comb adorned with crystals and pearls. Mya handed me a few bobby pins and I used them to hold the comb in place, sectioning off Maggie's hair so it wouldn't move during the ceremony or the reception.

Mya and I worked together while she put the finishing touches on Maggie's makeup. Mya had flown in last night from Nigeria for the wedding. She was working for a think tank in Lagos and was in the middle of a huge project, so she couldn't get away until the last minute.

I'd come over from London early in the week to help Maggie with the final preparations. I'd loved having the opportunity to be part of the wedding details.

"Can I look now?" Maggie asked, her tone impatient.

My gaze narrowed as I studied her appearance—her hair and makeup were flawless, her gown an elegant lace sheath with a small train that we'd found at a little vintage shop in Paris. She wore the necklace Samir had given her on their first anniversary in London and a pair of my diamond chandelier earrings. Her bracelet had been her grandmother's. She wore the cushion-cut diamond Samir had put on her ring finger last year.

My eyes welled up at the sight of her. It felt like just yesterday that I'd watched them fall in love at the International School. They'd moved in together the spring of my senior year and had been living together ever since. Samir had proposed in Hyde Park at Christmas, halfway through her master's at the London School of Economics. They'd both called me, so excited, Maggie asking if I'd be her maid of honor.

A year later here we were.

I grabbed a tissue from the vanity, dabbing at my eyes before my mascara began to run. Part of it was seeing Maggie like this; part of it was how emotional I'd been lately.

I squeezed Maggie's hand. "Okay. You can look."

She stood up, turning toward the mirror and froze midstep. Oh, God, I was going to cry again.

"Samir is going to have a fit when he sees you walk down the aisle," I predicted, my voice thick with unshed tears. "You look like a princess."

Mya grinned. "You really do."

Maggie turned back to face us, her eyes shining, her expression dazed.

"I can't believe this is happening. Can't believe this is my wedding day."

At this rate I was going to sob through the entire ceremony.

I grabbed another tissue, passing one to Mya, as well. Her eyes were filled with suspicious moisture.

I sucked in a deep breath. "Okay, we can't keep crying. Our makeup's going to start clumping and we'll look like raccoons walking down the aisle."

Maggie nodded, turning away from the mirror. "Okay. No more crying. Let me look at you guys."

Mya, Jo—Maggie's friend from home—and I were her only bridesmaids. Thankfully, she'd let me pick out the dresses, so we'd been spared heinous ruffles and poofs. My job in fashion PR gave me the opportunity to work with a lot of young designers, and I'd spent months finding the perfect person to design our gowns.

Maggie's wedding colors were pink and gold, so the three of us wore floor-length sheaths in various colors of pale pink.

Jo's was the darkest, then Mya's and finally my dress was the softest shade, somewhere between pink and blush. The dresses were similar in style, but all cut a bit differently to fit our builds. Mine was fitted down to my knees where it flowed out into a modified trumpet shape. It was a little tighter than it had been when I was fitted for it, but you couldn't really tell by looking at me. And the bouquet of pink roses I'd carry down the aisle would hide my stomach.

"You look amazing." Maggie's eyes teared up. "I love you guys. Thank you so much for being here for this."

I reached out and hugged her, trying not to get caught up in her veil. "There's nowhere else I'd rather be."

"Okay, seriously, let's get this party started," Jo interjected. "We have ten minutes to go before you have to walk down the aisle, and we can't spend it getting mopey. It's time for a toast."

Mya nodded and moved away from the group to pour champagne into waiting crystal flutes.

We were standing in the church's small changing room. They'd decided to get married in a little chapel near the Eiffel Tower with a small reception afterward at the Hotel Georges V. Maggie and Samir had moved to Paris after Maggie graduated LSE. Samir found a job working for an international organization, and Maggie was working on her French and interviewing for jobs. They'd rented a nice flat in the fifteenth district.

Samir's parents were pissed about the marriage and hadn't come to the wedding, but Maggie's family was here. I hurt for him, but I knew that in their absence, Maggie had become his family now.

Jo lifted her champagne glass in the air. "To Maggie and Samir, and a lifetime of happiness."

We all clinked glasses. I held mine to my lips, trying to look like I was drinking without having to. I set it down on the vanity, hoping no one noticed, keeping busy by gathering our bouquets. Maggie's father would be here in a few minutes for their walk down the aisle.

The girls drained their glasses, and then Maggie's eyes narrowed as she looked at me. "Are you going to drink your champagne?"

I shrugged. "I had a sip," I lied. "I figured I shouldn't be tipsy walking down the aisle," I joked. "Don't want to trip in my heels."

"Since when do you pass up expensive champagne?" Mya asked. "Samir sprang for the good stuff." She shot me a strange look and a pause filled the air.

Maggie's eyes widened, her gaze traveling down to my stomach, and her entire face transformed. "Fleur…"

It was barely anything, the faintest of bumps that I stared at in the mirror in amazement, but it was there.

I fought to keep the smile off my face.

"Am I going to be an aunt?" she shrieked.

We'd decided not to say anything until after the wedding—I didn't want to take the attention away from Maggie and Samir—but the joy on Maggie's face told me she was almost as excited as I was.

I nodded, unable to speak for the fear of the floodgates it would unleash.

"Ohmigod."

Maggie and Mya threw their arms around me.

"Tell me everything. How far along are you? Does Max know?" Maggie bombarded me with questions, hugging me until we were both crying.

"Just over three months. We wanted to wait until after the wedding to tell everyone. And I was nervous about the baby since I'd miscarried before. But my doctor says I'm doing well and we're past the first trimester."

Mya smiled. "I bet Max is thrilled."

"He is."

Max had been amazing. I'd been nervous to tell him I was pregnant. We lived together in London in an amazing flat in Canary Wharf, but it wasn't exactly kid friendly. We both worked long hours, Max especially, and even though he'd paid off his student loans and was saving up to buy a flat, he was the kind of guy who liked to have a plan in place. A baby hadn't been on our agenda. He seemed to like kids, but I hadn't been sure how he would handle the news that he would be at dad at twenty-five.

I'd been so nervous when I told him, but the second I had, the nerves completely disappeared.

I couldn't have predicted how happy he'd be or how excited. It was like I'd given him the best gift ever. We spent so much time talking about the baby now—looking at flats in central

London, talking about nannies and day-care options since we both worked. It was unexpected, and overwhelming and every dream I'd ever had.

"Are you guys going to get married?" Maggie asked suddenly.

"Maybe, eventually?"

"If he asked you to marry him, though, you'd say yes, right? You do want to him marry him?"

"Of course I'd say yes. It's just not something I'm thinking about right now."

"Why?"

"It's not that big of a deal to me. I love him. I will always love him. He feels the same way about me. We're having a baby and starting a family, and I don't know that we need a piece of paper. It won't change anything between us."

A determined glint filled Maggie's eyes. "You should get married."

I grinned. Some of my stubbornness had rubbed off on her. Although, to be fair, she probably needed it to handle Samir.

"We'll see. Let's just focus on getting you married right now."

Max had talked to me about it when I'd told him I was pregnant, but I didn't want him to marry me just because of the baby. Maybe it was a French thing, but I didn't think we had to get married to be a family, and if we did, I wanted it to be because he wanted to marry me, not out of obligation. I knew what Max and I had; a ring wouldn't change that. Neither would reciting vows in front of our friends.

He gave me those promises every single day.

We spent a few more minutes fussing over Maggie in the changing room, and then her father came in. I hadn't spent a lot of time with her family, and I knew her relationship with her father was rocky, but it was obvious by the look of pride that came into his eyes at the sight of her, that he loved Maggie. And she was thrilled to have him there.

The bridesmaids moved to get into position to walk down the aisle.

Maggie's little half brother was the ring bearer so he would go first, then Jo and Mya, then me. I waited in the back of the church with Maggie and her father, hidden from view until the wedding planner signaled that it was time for me to get ready to walk.

I squeezed Maggie's hand. "Love you."

She beamed back at me. "Love you, too."

I waited for my cue, and then I was walking down the aisle to the sound of the most gorgeous pipe organ I'd ever heard. The second I hit the ivory runner, I looked to the front of the church where Samir stood with his three groomsmen—Tarek, his childhood friend from Lebanon, Omar and Max.

Despite their different personalities, and largely due to my stubborn insistence that they get along, Max and Samir were close now. They were a strange pairing, and I knew sometimes Samir annoyed Max, but they'd become family. I couldn't have asked for more.

I walked down the aisle, my gaze on the two most important men in my life. Samir looked nervous, but the second our eyes met across the church, his face relaxed a bit, a lazy smile on his lips. As much as he'd pretended that it didn't bother him that his parents hadn't come, I knew it wasn't the same.

She looks hot, I mouthed to him as I neared the altar, and I watched as he fought the urge to laugh, his head shaking, and then the rest of the tension slid out of him.

My job done, my gaze traveled to Max, who looked like the

hottest thing I'd ever seen in his custom tux. He was laughing, the pride in his eyes making me fight back tears.

Love you, he mouthed to me, and then he looked down my body, and his gaze settled on my stomach, and I knew he wasn't just talking to me.

I took my place at the altar next to Mya and Jo, waiting for the bride, and my gaze scanned the crowd. I caught sight of Michael sitting near the back, and he winked at me and flashed me the thumbs-up sign. George sat next to him.

I smiled at Maggie's grandparents sitting in the front pew of the church. Maggie's stepmom sat next to them with her son in her lap, looking adorable in his little tux.

Another wave of emotion hit me as I imagined us having a little boy who looked like Max. I honestly didn't care if we had a boy or girl; I just wanted a healthy baby. But that didn't stop me from daydreaming about the baby we'd made.

The music changed, and the guests rose in the pews. Everyone turned to catch a first glimpse of the bride.

I waited a beat, and instead of looking at the entrance of the church, I glanced across the altar and caught the look on my cousin's face the first moment he saw his bride.

And then I started crying again.

It was a beautiful ceremony.

Maggie and Samir spent the whole time staring into each other's eyes and laughing, and it was impossible to not feel like they were in their own private world.

Afterward, we all went to go take pictures near the Eiffel Tower before heading over to the reception. We did a bunch of group photos, and now we waited while the photographer took some shots of Maggie and Samir alone.

"How are you feeling?" Max whispered in my ear, pulling me away from everyone else. It was chilly outside, and we were all bundled up in coats in between photos.

I grinned. "Amazing."

"Are you doing okay with the cold?"

I loved the protectiveness in his voice. He'd been so worried about me in the beginning of the pregnancy. I'd had a bit of nausea and been tired, but otherwise things had been good. He was there for the food cravings and basically wouldn't let me carry anything heavier than my handbag. It was sweet. He was going to be an amazing dad.

"Yes, Daddy," I teased.

His arms wrapped around me, his hand settling over my stomach. He stroked the tiny almost-bump.

"I love you."

"I love you, too."

"The ceremony made you emotional."

I groaned. "Hormones." It was kind of embarrassing that I cried constantly now. I was losing major street cred over this.

He turned me around to face him, his hands rubbing back and forth over my arms as if to warm me. His gaze turned serious.

"Have you ever thought about what our wedding would be like?"

I froze in a way that had nothing to do with the cold outside.

"Our wedding?" I squeaked.

Max nodded, his gaze intent. He had that determined look in his eyes now, the one that had taken the financial world by storm.

I struggled for nonchalance, even though my heart was suddenly racing. Had I thought about marrying him?

Maybe. Every day. Always.

But I'd already sprung a baby on him. We were young...
what if this was too much responsibility?

I hesitated. "Kind of."

"Are you saying you don't want to get married?"

My mind raced. "No, I'm saying that I don't want to put too
much on you. We've talked about this."

"Babe. We're having a baby together."

I blinked. "I don't want you to marry me because we're having a baby. We can have a baby together without getting married. You love me, and I love you. We love this baby. That's
enough for me. I'm not worried."

Max smiled at me. "I want to marry you because you're my
world. Because I love you more than anything, and I will love
you until the day I die. I want you to be my wife because you're
the most incredible woman I've ever known. And while I'm so
grateful that you're giving me the greatest gift of my life with
this baby, I promise you, I'd want to marry you even if you
weren't pregnant. I love you, Fleur."

I was crying now, and I was pretty sure it had nothing to
do with the hormones and everything to do with the man
standing—*ohmigod*—kneeling in front of me.

"What are you doing?"

Max grinned, pulling a black velvet box out of his pocket,
and then the tears really started falling.

"Marry me, Fleur."

I laughed through my tears at the fact that he didn't *ask*. Apparently, that was what three years together had done to him.

My answer came out in a rush of excitement and joy, somewhere near a shout.

"Yes."

Max stood, pulling me into his arms and kissing me until I

was breathless, until my happy tears mingled with the moisture of our mouths.

I pulled away first and stared down at my left hand, getting a good look at the ring he'd put there. It was an eternity band of emerald-cut diamonds. I probably shouldn't have cared about the ring, but yeah, I kind of did. And it was *gorgeous*. It wasn't a traditional style, which suited me perfectly. And it was big.

Max shot me a knowing look. "Did I do okay?"

I stared at it sparkling on my hand, dazzling me, then back at my future husband. "It's better than anything I could have ever imagined." I bit my lip. "Maggie knows about the baby, but do you think maybe we should wait to tell them we're engaged? I don't want to take the attention away from their wedding."

Max grinned. "Babe, who do you think helped me pick out the ring? She made me promise that I would propose where everyone could see. We came up with the compromise to do it here where it would still be private and away from the rest of the wedding celebration, but she and Samir could be a part of it. They're your family. They love you. I figured you would want them here."

I was so incredibly lucky. Tears spilled over my cheeks. "Maggie helped you pick out the ring?"

He laughed. "Actually, no. Let's just say her taste is a little more modest than yours. She went with us, but Samir helped me pick out the ring."

Surprise filled me. "You went with Samir?"

"I'm old-fashioned. I had to ask someone for your hand in marriage."

God. More tears. He'd known exactly what to do, even when I hadn't thought of it. And now I knew who would walk me down the aisle.

"And for the record, I bought the ring before you told me you were pregnant. I've been carrying it around for months, waiting for the right moment. The Eiffel Tower has been lucky for us. And it had to be in Paris. You first told me you loved me in Paris."

And I felt that love burst through me right then. "Have I ever told you that you're absolutely perfect for me?"

He smiled. *"Tu es l'amour de ma vie."*

I froze as the French tumbled out of Max's mouth. He turned red as the words came out, his accent slightly off, but his delivery full of all the love in the world.

You are the love of my life.

He'd given me the words in the language I'd teach our child, given me the words in the language etched in my heart.

He gave me the world.

Max leaned forward, and our lips connected, and I felt the same click I always did when we kissed. And then he broke contact and turned to face our friends, who were no longer taking photos but were standing there expectantly, watching us.

Clearly, he'd filled them in on his plan.

"She said yes!" he yelled, a huge grin on his face.

Cheers went up in the group, and then we were surrounded by Mya, Samir, Maggie, George and Michael. The photographer snapped pictures as we hugged, and laughed and cried, Maggie in her beautiful white wedding dress, Samir with a platinum wedding band on his ring finger, George, Mya and Michael beaming at us. And in the middle, Max with one arm around me, the other on our future.

It was my favorite photo of all of us.

One that sat on a desk in Mya's office in Lagos, in the living room of Samir and Maggie's cozy flat in Paris, in Michael's chic Tribeca loft, in George's office in Surrey.

And when our daughter was old enough, I pulled the photo out and showed her the picture of her father and me surrounded by the people who'd changed my life. And when she pointed at the picture and asked who everyone was, I told her simply, *"Ma famille."*

My family.

★ ★ ★ ★ ★

Go back to where it all began…

I SEE LONDON

*Turn the page to sample the enthralling first book
in Chanel Cleeton's International School series!*

1

I couldn't find my underwear.

Knickers, as the British called them.

It should have been easy; there wasn't much to them. They were black, lacy...and shit, I was going to miss my flight home if I kept looking.

"Start by thinking of the last place you had them," my grandmother would always tell me when I lost something. The bed seemed like the best place to start. Or had it been on top of the dresser? Or against the wall by the window?

I'd been a busy girl.

"You leaving?"

I stared down at the boy lying in bed. His voice was heavy with sleep, the sheets tangled around his naked body. The sight of all that skin sent a flash of heat through me.

I wasn't ready to handle the morning after. Screw my underwear.

"Don't worry about it." I leaned down, pressing a swift kiss to his lips, barely resisting the urge to climb back into bed with him. "See you next year," I whispered, grabbing my shoes and heading for the door.

I paused in the doorway, wondering how the hell I'd gone from spending my Friday nights studying to doing the walk of shame sans underwear.

I blamed the Harvard admissions committee.

Ten Months Earlier

I was going to die, and I wasn't even wearing my best underwear.

My Southern grandmother loved to tell me a girl should always look like a lady—even down to her "unmentionables," as she liked to call them.

"But no one's going to see them."

It doesn't matter. You could be in a car accident and then what? Would you want people to see you in those?

I wasn't sure if the underwear rule applied to plane crashes. But if it did? I was about to die in the world's ugliest pair of black cotton underwear.

"Are you okay, dear?"

I loosened my grip on the armrest, turning slightly to face the woman in the seat next to me.

"It's just a little bit of turbulence. Perfectly normal." She looked to be about my grandmother's age; unlike my grandmother's smooth Southern drawl, though, her voice had a clipped British accent. "Is this your first flight?"

I cleared the massive, boulder-sized knot of tension from my throat. "It's been a long time."

"It can be scary at times. But we're only about an hour away."

The plane hit another bump. I gripped the armrests again, my knuckles turning nearly white.

"What takes you to London?"

"I'm starting college."

"How exciting! Where?"

I struggled to focus on her questions rather than the possibility of the plane plummeting from the sky. The irony of my fear of flying wasn't lost on me.

"The International School."

According to the glossy brochure I'd conveniently received the day my dreaded thin-envelope rejection letter from Harvard arrived in our mailbox, the International School boasted a total of one thousand undergraduate students from all over the world.

"Do you know anyone in London?"

I shook my head.

"I'm surprised your parents let you move by yourself. You can't be more than what, eighteen?"

"Nineteen."

My dad hadn't been a big fan of the whole London idea. *He* could travel the world and live overseas. I just couldn't go with him. I'd heard all the reasons before. He couldn't be a fighter pilot and a single parent. It was too difficult for him to predict when he would be sent away on another assignment. If my mom were still around—

It hung between us, the rest of the words unspoken.

I could fill in the blanks. If my mom were still around, we would be a family. But she wasn't. When she left my dad, she took our family with her, my dad's parents assuming the role of my legal guardians. I loved my grandparents, and they loved me.

But it still wasn't the same.

"You must be pretty brave to come to London by yourself. Especially at such a young age."

Brave? I wasn't sure if it had been bravery or desperation spurring my sole act of teenage rebellion. But ever since I'd received that rejection letter in the mail, my thoughts had been less than rational.

It was all I'd ever wanted—Harvard. It was the best. I'd

imagined my dad beaming with pride at my high school graduation, the one he'd ended up missing anyway. Harvard had
been my chance to change everything. It was the reason I didn't
date and skipped parties in favor of doing SAT prep on Friday
nights, the motivation behind me joining every student organization. In the end, none of it was enough.

I wasn't enough.

She nudged me. "We're nearly there."

I turned toward the window, peering through the glass. Fog
filled the sky, the air thick and heavy with it.

"It's hard to see anything."

"Just wait for it. Keep looking."

Lights. Scattered throughout the fog were lights. Hundreds,
thousands of lights. Like a Christmas tree. Beneath us was a
carpet of lights.

"Welcome to London."

I peered out the taxi window, watching as the city passed
me by.

The ride from the airport took a little under an hour. As we
drove, we crossed into more urban areas where the landscape
of little houses disappeared, replaced by large blocks of multi-
story apartment buildings and small shops on street corners.
Little by little the traffic increased, the driver laying on the
horn several times and shouting out the window. BBC Radio
blared through the car speakers.

The sidewalks were filled with people, their strides long and
confident. Everyone looked as if they were in a hurry, as though
wherever they were going was the most important place in the
world. And it was noisy. Even over the radio, I heard the city,
so different from anything I'd ever experienced.

When the cab passed by the infamous Hyde Park and then

Kensington Palace, only to turn onto what the cab driver referred to as Embassy Row, the reality of my new life began to sink in. We passed rows of expensive buildings—mansions, really. Some had guards stationed out front and flew flags of various countries, no doubt how Embassy Row got its name. Others were private residences, each one large and imposing. The taxi pulled through a set of enormous gates, traveling down a long gravel driveway. The driver let out a low whistle.

I stared out the window, barely resisting the urge to panic.

The school was huge. The grounds were perfectly manicured; large trees dotted the landscape. Security buzzed around as students gathered in small groups, greeting each other and joking around. Ridiculously expensive cars, the like of which I had only seen in movies, passed by.

Thank God for my scholarship.

I stepped out of the cab on shaky legs, offering a quick smile for the driver before sliding three crisp twenty-pound notes into his hands. I rolled my two black bags up the drive, ignoring the group of boys lounging in front of the school's wooden doors.

"Samir, check out the new girl."

"Not my type," an accented voice, smooth and rich, called out behind me.

I stiffened, turning to face the speaker.

A boy stared back at me, lounging against the railing leading up to the school steps like he owned the place. He was average height and lean, dressed casually in jeans and a black T-shirt. His hair was an inky black, curling at the ends, his eyes dark brown, his lashes full and thick.

The boy—Samir, I guessed—did a once-over, starting at my long brown hair, drifting down my body, lingering on my boobs—my eyes narrowed—before coming back to rest on my face. There was something appraising in his gaze—a flicker of interest—followed by a smile that had my heartbeat ratcheting up a notch.

He flashed me another cocky smile. That smile was lethal. "Sorry."

He looked anything but.

I wanted to say something clever, wanted to say *something*. But as always, words failed me. I'd never been good with guys—in high school I was prone to what I not so lovingly referred to as deer-in-the-headlights syndrome. If a guy I liked showed any interest in me, I would freeze, standing there awkwardly, all clever thought evaporated. It was a spectacularly effective way to ensure I never had a boyfriend.

Get me out of here, now.

His laughter, warm and smooth, filled the space behind me.

I walked into the school on shaky legs, cursing my rocky start. But as soon as I stepped into the entryway, nerves gave way to awe. The building was incredible, like a work of art.

A woman at the front desk greeted me with a smile. "Welcome to the International School. We're so glad to have you joining our family. Name, please."

"Maggie Carpenter."

"Nice to meet you, Maggie. I'm Mrs. Fox. I'm in charge of Residence Life. My staff and I will be responsible for your dorm room and for getting you settled into your new home here." She thumbed through a stack of blue folders before pulling one out of the pile. "Here you go. You'll find the code to get into your room in this folder along with your schedule. If you need anything at all, don't hesitate to come to my office. It's on the map."

I took the folder from Mrs. Fox's hands, struggling to keep the instructions straight through the haze of jet lag. I headed toward the stairs, moving through the crowd of students. At the end of the hallway, I stared up at the narrow staircase in front of me.

"Need some help?"

A tall blond boy with a British accent smiled at me. He wore a blue polo shirt with the words *Residence Life* stitched on the front.

I hesitated. "No thanks. I can manage on my own."

"Are you sure? Trust me, these steps are intense." He peered over at the sheet of paper in my hand. "And you're on the third floor? That's four floors up."

"Huh?"

"Four floors. Not three. In London the main floor is considered the ground floor and the next floor up is the first floor. It's different from how you do things in America." He grinned. "Your accent sort of gave it away," he offered by way of explanation. He reached out, grabbing the handles of my bags. "Come on. I'll help you get to your room. I'm George."

I followed him up the stairs. "Thanks. I'm Maggie."

"Nice to meet you, Maggie. Where are you from?"

"South Carolina."

His brow wrinkled for a moment. "Is that near New York City? I've been there."

I grinned. "Unfortunately, it's light-years away from New York City. I'm from a small town. There's not exactly a lot to do there."

I followed George up another flight of stairs, struggling to keep up with him. I couldn't stop gawking at my surroundings. I'd seen some pictures of the school online, but I'd figured those were the best shots. I hadn't expected it to live up to the advertising. The place looked like a museum.

"So, who are your roommates?"

I stared down at the piece of paper clutched in my hand. "Noora Bader and Fleur Marceaux."

George turned around, a strange expression on his face. His voice sounded like a strangled laugh. "Did you say Fleur Marceaux?"

I nodded.

This time he did laugh, the sound filling the narrow stairway. "Good luck with that one."

2

George dropped my bags off at the front of a long hallway.

"This is as far as I go."

"Do you turn into a pumpkin past this point or something?"

He laughed. "No. But your roommate is number one on Residence Life's hit list."

"Please tell me she's not that bad."

"Oh, she's worse."

"Worse, how?"

"We call her the Ice Queen."

I groaned. It was hardly an original nickname, but also not particularly encouraging.

"She thinks she's better than everyone else and isn't afraid to let them know it."

"Awesome. What about Noora?"

"I don't know her. She must be a freshman."

"Why don't they put all the sophomores together?"

"Because none of the sophomores would have Fleur as a

roommate. She was supposed to have a single room, but something fell through. She'll probably be even more difficult now."

Fabulous.

"Look, if you want to apply for a roommate change, come by our office. We're on the ground floor."

I smiled weakly. "Thanks."

I walked down the hall, dread filling me as I searched for room 301. I looked down at the room code on the piece of paper, struggling to punch in the numbers on the little metal keypad, my mind muddled by the time difference.

I swung open the door, dragging my first bag over the threshold, stopping short at the sight of the room that was to be my home for the next year. It was small...three small beds, three small wardrobes, three small desks...and two big windows. I walked over, peering out at the view of Hyde Park. The lush green trees, the expanse of grass, the heavy iron gates—the magic of it all—made up for everything else.

I spent the next hour unpacking my suitcases. Thankfully, I was the first one to arrive. I set a few things out—my favorite books, a few mementos from home, pictures with friends.

The sound of the door opening startled me.

"Hi."

A girl stood in the doorway, bags on her shoulders. Her hair was covered by a gorgeous purple silk scarf.

"Please tell me this is the right place," she announced.

"I'm Maggie. Are you Noora?"

She waved with her free hand. "Nice to meet you."

I grinned. "Nice to meet you, too."

She dropped her bags down on the empty bed. "Is this it?"

"Yeah. Hard to believe they mean for three of us to live here, isn't it?"

"Have you met the other girl?"

"I haven't. I heard she's a sophomore, though." I didn't mention the rest. No sense in worrying Noora, too.

"Are you a freshman?" Noora asked.

"Yep."

"Me, too."

"Nice. Where are you from?"

"Oman."

We chatted for a few more minutes, talking about our backgrounds. I liked her immediately. If Fleur was the Ice Queen, Noora was her polar opposite.

As soon as Noora left to go visit with a friend from home, I called my grandmother. It was early morning in the US, but she'd always been an early riser.

"How are you settling in? Have you made any friends?"

A wave of homesickness rushed over me at the sound of her voice.

"The people seem nice so far." I didn't mention Fleur. My grandmother worried enough as it was.

"Have you been getting enough to eat?"

I grinned. "I promise I'm going to eat lunch soon. Although I bet the food won't be anywhere near as good as yours."

I took a deep breath. "Have you heard from Dad?"

"Sorry, honey. I haven't."

I pushed down the familiar hurt that rose in my throat, forcing the words out. "Do you know where he is now?"

"You know how these things are, honey. He can't say where."

"When will he be back?"

"Hopefully, by Christmas. He said he might be able to come home this year. We could spend Christmas together."

I hadn't spent a Christmas with my dad in at least three years, possibly more.

"That sounds great, Grandma."

We talked for a few more minutes before I hung up the call, tears welling up in my eyes.

For a moment I just sat there, homesick.

I'd been traveling for fifteen hours. I needed a shower. I grabbed a towel and my bath stuff, heading for the door.

The bathroom, like my dorm room, was a bit of a disappointment.

I settled into the shower just as the first tears began to fall.

It felt weird walking back to my room in just a towel, but the only places to change in the bathroom were public.

Luckily, the hallway was still empty. This was the first day students could move into the dorms, but school didn't start for a few days. I stopped in front of my door, shifting my bath caddy to the other hand so I could punch in the code. This time I got in on the first try.

Shutting the door behind me, I set down my bath stuff and unwrapped the towel from my body.

It dropped to the floor.

"I was wrong. You're my type."

I whirled around in shock at the sound of that voice, smooth and teasing, the boy from the steps standing before me.

3

I stood there, gaping at him, convinced this was some sort of nightmare I would eventually wake from.

I blinked.

Still there.

Samir lay sprawled on the empty bed—Fleur's bed—his hands behind his head, ankles crossed.

I shrieked.

Lunging to grab the towel from the floor, I wrapped it hastily around my body, as if its mere presence was enough to erase my nakedness from his memory.

"What the hell are you doing here? What is wrong with you? Why the hell are you spying on me?"

"I wasn't spying. I was waiting for someone. The show was just a bonus."

I crossed my arms over my chest.

I wanted to die. More accurately, I wanted him to die.

Samir laughed, the sound sending a flutter through my body. "I'm pretty sure I'm going to be enjoying this little memory for a while." He rose from the bed, his body uncoiling, the move graceful and unhurried.

"What are you doing?"

He stopped inches away from me, close enough that the scent of his cologne teased me. He was taller than I'd originally thought, forcing me to tilt my head up to meet his gaze—

"Samir!"

The voice broke me out of my stupor. I whirled around, staring at the door.

A girl stared back at me through narrowed eyes and a pissed-off expression. She was tall. Dressed in an outfit that looked like it belonged in a magazine. Shiny brown hair and boxy bangs framed a slender face with high cheekbones. One perfectly shaped eyebrow arched at the sight of me. There was only one person it could be—

I'd never seen a French music video, but I could imagine *her* in one.

She brushed past me, her eyes only for Samir. *He* didn't even have the decency to look embarrassed. They hugged in a tangle of limbs, my presence forgotten.

This time I did bolt. I grabbed my clothes, heading for the door. Hell, at this point changing in the middle of the hall was preferable to spending another minute in their presence.

My roommate's boyfriend was the hottest guy I had ever seen.

And he'd just seen me naked.

Fifteen minutes later I was fully dressed but no less flustered. I hovered outside the room, hoping I'd given them enough time to go somewhere else. Anywhere else. I would have stayed out longer, but I was hungry, and my wallet was sitting on top of my desk. I punched in the code, my hand getting ready to turn the knob when the door swung open.

I stared up into Fleur's perfect face.

"Let me guess, you're one of my roommates." Her voice had a heavy French accent; her hand fisted on her hip. The words escaped in a bored drawl, hinting at some irony in us being roommates.

"I'm Maggie. Maggie Carpenter."

She turned her back to me. "American. Of course."

"The rooms suck," Fleur called out, a note of satisfaction in her voice. "The American kids always have a hard time adjusting. Especially if they haven't been to Europe before. They say everything in the US is *bigger*."

A burst of French came from the other side of the room.

"Don't poke the new girl, Fleur." Samir's voice filled the room, speaking English now. He winked at me.

Of course, they were a couple.

It was official.

I had the worst living situation ever.

For a school as expensive as the International School, the dining hall was a bit disappointing. Like the dorm rooms, it was small, but I suppose given the cost of real estate in a city like London that was to be expected.

"Go with the curry. Trust me, it's the only thing remotely edible."

I turned to the girl next to me—a tall Black girl with long black hair. Gorgeous blue beaded earrings hung from her ears, a matching silver-and-blue scarf wrapped around her neck.

"Thanks for the advice."

"No problem. I'm Mya. Are you new?"

"I'm Maggie. I'm a freshman."

"Welcome. American?"

It had to be the accent giving me away.

"Yeah."

Or my outfit. I stared down at my jeans and flip-flops, wishing I'd put something more glamorous on.

"Don't worry. There are lots of Americans here." She gave me a friendly smile, one of the first genuine ones I'd received since I arrived. "This is probably a bit of a culture shock."

"It's different," I hedged. "Where are you from?"

"Nigeria." She shrugged. "We spend most of the year here now. My dad works at the Nigerian embassy." She gestured toward one of the empty tables. "Do you want to sit together?"

"That would be great, thanks."

I followed Mya to one of the tables, sliding into the chair across from hers. "Have most students arrived yet? It seems kind of empty."

"Most probably have, but there are always the ones who push it right up to the last minute. Not everyone lives on campus or eats in the dining hall, either. A lot of students have their own flats and do their own things."

From the other side of the partition, I heard people speaking French. I turned in my seat, a groan escaping my lips. Fleur walked in, Samir trailing behind her.

"Fabulous."

Mya followed my gaze until she settled on Fleur. Her lips quirked. "Ahh, I see you've met the reigning queen."

"She's my roommate."

Mya's eyes widened. "You're going to have your hands full."

I ducked my head, hoping I wasn't turning bright red. "What's the deal with that guy? Samir, right? He was in our room earlier."

"You *have* had a busy morning. That's Samir Khouri. He's Lebanese. His dad is a politician in Lebanon. His mom's French."

"He seems like an asshole."

She laughed. "Yeah, you're not far off the mark with that one."

"Hi, Mya."

My head jerked up at the sound of Fleur's voice.

"Are you going to the party tomorrow night?" Fleur asked, completely ignoring me.

Mya grinned. "I never miss a boat party."

Fleur tossed her light brown hair back over her shoulder. "A bunch of us are going out after if you want to come."

"I might. Thanks."

Fleur nodded, not even bothering to glance my way, her red-soled heels clipping on the wood floor as she walked away.

"Are you friends?"

Mya shrugged, tearing off a piece of bread from her plate. "Not really. I would call us acquaintances that occasionally hang out. We went to boarding school together in Switzerland for a few years.

"So, about that party Fleur mentioned. You're going, right?" Mya asked.

"I don't know. I hadn't thought about it, really."

"You must go. Everyone will be there."

"I don't know. I don't have anything to wear."

"You're coming. I can't allow you to miss your first boat party. Besides, if you need an outfit, you came to the right city. We're going shopping."

She hadn't been kidding about the shopping. Thanks to Mya, I was now the proud owner of a hot-pink dress made of some sort of stretchy fabric. It barely covered my now highly enhanced boobs, courtesy of Mya's padded bra suggestion. The hemline fell just below my butt. High heels completed the look.

A knock sounded at the door.

Mya greeted me on the other side in a gorgeous red dress. She whistled. "Girl, you look hot. My friend Michael's going to give us a ride."

"Sounds good to me."

We walked out to the front of the building, where a guy leaning casually against a black SUV waved to Mya. He walked up to her, pressing a swift kiss on each cheek before turning to me.

"I'm Michael."

"Maggie."

He grinned. "Where are you from, Maggie?"

"South Carolina."

"A Southern girl. Nice. I'm from Connecticut."

He was cute—sandy blond hair and green eyes. He was dressed in a cool-looking T-shirt that looked distressed in a way that wasn't accidental and equally worn jeans that probably cost more than my car payment back home.

"You girls look great tonight."

I fought off the blush. "Thanks."

Mya grabbed my arm before we slid into the back seat of his SUV. "He's gay," she whispered. "I didn't want you to get a crush on him. He's a great guy and I thought you guys would get along. There are a lot of fake people here. Michael's as real as they come. He's an amazing friend."

As we sped off into the city, I couldn't help but feel like Cinderella on my way to the ball.